One For All

Peter Cleverly studied at Camberwell School of Arts and Crafts in London. After working in a variety of jobs, he returned to painting and also began screenwriting with his son Chris. *One For All* is their first novel. He lives in Wiltshire.

Chris Cleverly studied law at Kings College London, became a barrister and youngest Head of Chambers in England. He is co-founder of Made in Africa Inc. and a partner in a number of other pioneering eco-humanitarian enterprises. He lives in London.

www.lulu.com

PETER CLEVERLY
and
CHRIS CLEVERLY

One For All

CALLIDI BOOKS

ISBN 978-1-84799-029-7

Cover design by Peter Cleverly

Website: uk.geocities.com/one.for.all@btinternet.com

To
Dankay
and
Sharon

for countless reasons

CONTENTS

PROLOGUE

Cape Rose, French Haiti, 1780

ONE FOR ALL

Father McGreevy screamed something secular as he hurtled over the edge of the cliff and fell from sight.

It was quiet for a while after that - apart from the splosh of surf against the wave-smoothed boulders at the foot of the cliff two hundred and sixty-three feet below, and the din of hundreds of seabirds surprised from their ledges by Father McGreevy's sudden appearance in mid-air.

Nine-year-old Alexandre Davy de la Pailleterie lay face down, as near to the edge of the cliff as was possible without falling off.

He was not startled when he heard the priest's voice again saying 'Let me go. I'm going to me Maker', though he had seen the priest go over with his own eyes, though he knew that even a saint - which Father McGreevy by no means was - even a saint could not hope to survive a fall of two hundred and sixty-three feet on to solid rock.

He was not startled because he had one arm over the side of the cliff and his hand was locked tightly round Father McGreevy's wrist.

Alexandre supposed Father McGreevy was asking him to let go because the priest might not wish to meet his Maker hand in hand with the innocent child he had just dragged to a premature death.

Alexandre said, 'I won't let you go'.

†

It all started as a prank. Alexandre tried to slip out early that morning. Nanny and his mother barred his way, penning him into his room. The women meant to dress him to their standards, not his. They were expecting Father McGreevy to walk up from Port Jérémie to the Davy de la Pailleterie plantation to say private mass for the family and lunch with them afterwards.

Alexandre did not like wearing a jacket or a shirt - his friends did not, why should he? He did not like having to stay in the house either. Especially he did not like Father McGreevy - who for no reason but viciousness would screw his finger into one of the tight curls over Alexandre's ear, and twist, and twist at it, until tears came.

Alexandre squirmed away from his nanny to the window, to see if his friends were waiting. Down in the yard, his gang - two barefoot Black children, Petit-Jean and Mathilde, wearing the baggy sun-bleached rags he would have preferred for himself – grinned up when they saw his face at the window and gestured urgently to him, 'come down, come down'.

Realizing the quickest way to escape from the house was to let the women do as they would with him, Alexandre stood still long enough for Nanny to drag a comb through his hair and thread his arms into the sleeves of a jacket. To his horror, he saw the jacket exactly matched his breeches. All this primping for Father McGreevy's sake.

Alexandre hated the man. Not because the priest was White - his father was White, so was Nanny, and Alexandre loved them. Admittedly he did not like M'sieu Sully, then nobody liked the slave overseer. Alexandre hated Father McGreevy because the priest made a big show of being fond of children in the company of their parents but tormented them cruelly whenever he caught one alone.

Alexandre kissed his nanny, hugged his mother - she gave him an extra squeeze, she never kissed him now, not since her cough had become so harsh and wet. He promised both women he would keep clean and not leave the house, and they allowed him to escape from the room.

Moments later, he was out of doors, half-hopping half-skipping across the yard, trying to run and peel off his stockings at the same time; he had already rid himself of jacket, shirt, and shoes indoors as he pelted three-a-time down the backstairs. Stripped down at last to his breeches, Alexandre caught up with Mathilde and Petit-Jean, who had started running into the trees the second they saw their leader explode out of the door into the yard. Soon the three children were lost to adult sight in the dense rain forest that covered the mountain behind the plantation house and pressed against its stuccoed walls.

†

The track through the forest from the church in Jérémie to Count Davy de la Pailleterie's plantation was long and steep in places but that did not bother Father McGreevy greatly. The priest was fat but he was young and fit too. His parishioners had offered him a donkey, a strong looking jenny, but he would not get on it. In his estimation, a feller looked a right gobdaw on a donkey - something that always marred Palm Sunday for him.

He only had to undertake the journey over the mountain once a week anyway, to say Mass with the Count's wife, Marie-Cessette, who had consumption and was not strong enough to come to church. Then too, the walk sharpened his appetite and the Count had a talented cook, a fine cellar, and a generous disposition.

The silver coin glinting on the track was an unlooked for joy. There's nothing like a vow of poverty to make you appreciate ready cash. Father McGreevy looked up and down the track. He saw no parishioners, no witnesses, no one at all. The coin at his feet was a penny from Heaven, and the priest did not intend to waste it in the Poor Box. Smiling broadly, he bent to pick the coin up.

In the bushes beside the track, Alexandre hauled the powerful catapult back to his ear.

Mathilde had brought the catapult, which was so big that, slung over her shoulder, the wooden grip bruised her hip as she ran. Petit-Jean carried a dozen round pebbles, handpicked from the beach, bagged up in a twist of calico. Alexandre, the only one with the strength to pull back the triple-banded catapult to arm's length, was the marksman.

THWACK! The pebble punched into the lard of Father McGreevy's left buttock. He bellowed and leapt straight up into the air in agony - his spine arching so he almost kicked himself in the back of the head.

Fearing his assailant might shoot him again, the cleric hobbled, as quickly as the pain radiating from his backside allowed, up the track until he felt he was well out of range.

Then he remembered the silver coin he had left lying on the track.

He limped back, glaring a promise of eternal damnation at the place in the bushes from which the sounds of smothered laughter came - just you dare do that again! The laughing stopped - which Father McGreevy took to mean he had successfully intimidated the perpetrators of the assault. There would be no repetition of this outrage. He bent to pick the coin up.

THWACK! Agony exploded in the other buttock. Losing every bit of interest in the money, Father McGreevy escaped up the track, moving quickly but awkwardly - each leg limping independently of the other.

The children watched the priest from the bushes until he disappeared round a bend in the track, then Alexandre sent Mathilde to retrieve the coin. He had to return it to his father's room - Alexandre had only borrowed it to bait his trap for Father McGreevy. But Mathilde did not get as far as the track, she had to scamper back into hiding - someone else was coming along.

Alexandre peered through the leaves. 'Oh no. Auntie Delphine.'

'How will you stop her picking up the money?' said Mathilde.

'Maybe she won't see it,' said Petit-Jean. The two older children ignored him. Everyone knew Alexandre's auntie did not miss a thing.

'How will you stop her?' Mathilde repeated.

There was only one way that Alexandre could think of. As his auntie stooped to pick up the coin, he drew the sling of the catapult back to his ear once more. He was just thinking, this is the worst thing I've ever done, a sin I can't confess to Father

McGreevy, especially not to Father McGreevy, when Fate intervened. The Y-shaped grip broke in his hand, leaving him clenching a useless stump of wood, whilst the rest of the heavy catapult twanged backwards over his shoulder.

Instantly, there was a roar of pain from the bushes behind. Up sprang Father McGreevy, hot blood spouting from each nostril, the remnants of the three-banded catapult swinging from one ear. In the moment that the children stood, open-mouthed, shocked into immobility by this apparition, Father McGreevy was among them and had grabbed both Alexandre and Mathilde by the hair.

It was Petit-Jean's quick action that saved them – the boy swung the twisted cloth of pebbles once round his head then let it fly up, full into the priest's face. Alexandre and Mathilde broke free and before Father McGreevy could recover his wits, the children scattered in all directions.

Alexandre expected the priest to chase him rather than one of the others - he was the ringleader and, as the Count's son, should be upholding authority not undermining it - but he did not expect the fat cleric to be able to run so fast. Try as he might, racing along the trails left by the wild pigs that crissed and crossed the forest, he could not shake the man off. He tried changing direction at every turn, now going this way, now going that. He even tried turning the same way three times in a row. It was this tactic that was almost the death of them both.

On the third turn, Alexandre burst out onto a new trail and ran slap into Father McGreevy. He dodged back into the undergrowth, tore his way through a thick bush, crashed out onto a patch of open grass, right at the edge of the sea cliff. He threw himself to the ground - saving himself but tripping Father McGreevy who was so close behind, the bellowing priest almost had him by the hair again. Instinctively, Alexandre made a grab as the priest plunged over the cliff edge and reaching out caught the man's wrist.

Alexandre knew he was unusually powerful - things in his vicinity bent or broke off unless he handled them with care. Today he discovered just how strong he was. Father McGreevy was a big man, made even bigger by a lifetime's overindulgence, but Alexandre caught the falling deadweight, checked, and held it.

Father McGreevy did not struggle. He knew he was going to die. His life hung by less than a thread, by the slight arm of a nine-year-old boy. Already he could feel the strength running out of his own arm, out of his hand, out of his fingers. The boy must be in a worse case - he was going to fall. But he did not. Instead, he saw, rather than felt, Alexandre's grip tighten around his numb wrist. 'I won't let you go,' he heard the boy say. Despite all he knew of the world, of what was possible and what was not, Father McGreevy believed him.

Alexandre got one hand and one knee under himself and slowly pushed up off the ground. Once he got his other knee under him as well, everything went more quickly. First the priest's pale face dragged into view, then a desperately clutching hand followed by a scrabbling foot. Steadily Alexandre pulled Father McGreevy back to safety.

They staggered to their feet, relieved to be alive. Father McGreevy crossed himself, prayed briefly, silently, then rested his hands on Alexandre's shoulders and looked down at him with gratitude.

'St Peter was swinging that big old gate open. Opening it wide open for me. If it hadn't been for you...'

Alexandre shuffled his feet, hung his head, embarrassed, but pleased. 'You are welcome Father,' he was starting to say, when Father McGreevy fetched him a tooth-loosening slap round the side of the head.

'If it hadn't been for you - you evil little spalpeen - wouldn't I be up at the big house on my second glass of the Count's good wine? Not dangling one-handed off a thousand-foot cliff pissing in my sandals?'

'Father McGreevy,' Alexandre said, realising as bad as things were now they could get a lot worse in the not too distant future. 'You're telling my father?'

Father McGreevy studied him with what looked to Alexandre like compassion. He began to feel a bit hopeful. Perhaps the priest would weigh things up and decide after all, things had turned out all right, and call it evens.

'If I do tell him,' Father McGreevy said, 'the Count will beat you from here to Tuesday, won't he?'

Alexandre nodded. Father McGreevy nodded back and smiled - but not the sort of smile Alexandre was expecting.

'You're telling him aren't you, Father McGreevy?'

Father McGreevy's grin broadened and broadened until Alexandre was sure the priest's face was going to split in two.

PART ONE

The Countess

ONE FOR ALL

Normandy, 1790

The highflier splashed furiously along the puddled road to its rendezvous at Chateau Davy de la Pailleterie. The shiny gold cockatrices painted on its black side panels the only bright notes under grey skies that brooded from horizon to horizon over the drowned land. In the fields pinch-faced toilers straightened up from their forlorn gleaning amongst the storm-flattened corn to scowl as the phaeton, a sporting conveyance that had no purpose but aristocratic pleasure, clattered past them. A gaunt woman spat towards the flying carriage and her neighbours signalled their approval of her defiance, rattling knife blades against rusty sickles - a threat that one day aristo, one day soon...

Count de Malpas, courtier and bully, drove from a hazardous position standing on the already comically high driving platform, with the reins of the pair of matched black geldings that pulled the racing phaeton laced through the fingers of one hand and a long coach-whip, which he continually cracked over the horses' ears, in the other.

Behind, and far below the driver, Gabriel, the Black page boy, clung on to a narrow perch on the rear-facing bench seat, which was mostly occupied by his master's strapped on travelling bags. The hussar's uniform Gabriel wore - de Malpas was among other things colonel of the King's hussars - was sprayed with mud thrown out by the unshielded wheels spinning either side of him. The boy looked down between his boots at the road rushing by beneath him, feeling miserable, sick, and scared.

Catching sight of a peasant family trudging by the side of the road ahead, de Malpas flicked the reins and cracked the whip to make the horses speed up. The peasants turned at the noise and so had a moment's warning before the carriage veered towards them, bumping up the verge, forcing the entire family to leap for their lives into the waist-deep water of the roadside ditch.

De Malpas giggled excitedly at the mayhem his mischief had caused. His laughter exposed a physical oddity to view - his tongue had a forked tip like a snake's.

As they splashed by the scattered family, Gabriel saw, to his dismay, the distraught mother in the ditch holding her smallest son up out of the swirling flood. He watched as the father scrambled back up the bank, a second boy under his arm, to shake his fist after the highflier and curse the nobleman that drove it.

Gabriel silently cursed his master too. Impulsively, he thrust his hand into the baggage next to him. He had packed it; he knew where everything was. He pulled out the silver-handled clothes brush and tossed it into the road.

The father saw the flash of precious metal in the air, unceremoniously dropped his son back in the mud he had rescued him from, and splashed forward to snatch up the brush. Obviously delighted at such rich recompense, the man grinned and bowed his thanks to Gabriel.

Gabriel grinned back, jerked his thumb over his shoulder, circled his forefinger at his temple to mime - sorry, my master's crazy. The peasant began to laugh then his expression abruptly changed to alarm and the man whisked the silver-handed brush out of sight behind his back. Gabriel realized de Malpas must be looking down at him from the driving seat. Smoothly he slid the circling forefinger from his temple into his ear, and wiggled it around vigorously.

The highflier continued its reckless passage along the road and, after a while, Gabriel began to believe he had fooled his master with his ear-cleaning act. Some instinct - or, perhaps, he heard the faint whine the tip of the lash made as it sliced through the air towards him - made him jerk his arm up over his head. De Malpas' back slash with the whip to punish his page's impertinence caught Gabriel across the raised forearm. Even through the thick woollen cloth of his uniform sleeve, the sting of the blow was so intense he almost fell off the bucking carriage.

Nursing his numb arm, Gabriel resolved to desert his master as soon as he could find a better one, before the cruel nobleman was the death of him.

†

The first sunlight of the day shafted down through leafy, orchid-festooned trees onto dense undergrowth that steamed in the heat. Gaudy parrots flapped and screeched in the canopy. A white-faced capuchin monkey swarmed up a hanging vine. The animal wore a powdered periwig and velvet waistcoat with purple and green stripes. A peeled segment of orange flew through the air towards it. The monkey caught the fruit with a chatter of thanks.

Count Davy de la Pailleterie selected another piece of orange from the silver dish, tossed it to his pet. Although nearly a decade had passed since he had left Haiti after the death of his first wife, his face was still scorched and creased by his many years in the colony.

The Count looked around the little bit of Haiti he had recreated in the huge glasshouse with satisfaction. It had been a colossal expense but worth every sou. It was only in here - not in the rest of the chateau, not in the rest of France - only in here, in the wet heat and lush tropical ambience of the glasshouse, that he felt at home.

†

From the top of the chateau's grand stairway, Nanny looked down, watching the handsome, powerfully built man her young charge had grown into as he paused at the foot of the stairs.

Alexandre listened for a moment to the string quartet rehearsing in the far corner of the hall, in preparation for the soiree that the Countess had arranged for the next day. His stepmother, though indifferent to music herself, knew that her husband loved it and made sure to arrange frequent musical evenings as an easy way of keeping the old man content.

The composition the musicians were playing as Alexandre came down the stairs was by the Chevalier de Saint-George - his father's favourite composer. The quartet's leader had told him that they had performed at Versailles with the virtuoso on several occasions before King Louis and Queen Marie-Antoinette.

Certainly, theirs was a beautiful rendition and Alexandre could not resist dancing a few steps to the music around the life-sized marble of Daphne fleeing Apollo that graced the centre of the hall. Alexandre took Daphne's outstretched fingers, conveniently positioned for dancing, now in his left hand, now in his right, as he danced until the music stopped. Unfortunately, when he made his final bow, he neglected to let go of Daphne's hand - and with a barely audible snick, the Carrera marble arm broke, just above the elbow.

From her vantage point at the top of the stairs, Nanny witnessed this latest example of a long line of similar breakages and shook her head - her little Alex had not changed so much over the years.

†

Two footmen stood at sweat-beaded attention either side of the doorway leading into the glasshouse from the chateau. Maurice and Marc wore wigs and livery humiliatingly similar to those the monkey wore. The other servants were always pretending to mistake Maurice and Marc for the monkey, and the other way round. The footmen spent most of their time together plotting the monkey's assassination.

Maurice and Marc half turned as Alexandre entered, responding to his friendly grin with hurried ones of their own - the Count did not approve of any displays of familiarity by servants.

As Alexandre set off into the undergrowth to search for his father, Maurice pulled out Daphne's marble limb from under his arm - where Alexandre had pushed it as he came in. He held it out for Marc to see - another little job for them to do before the Count noticed the damage.

Alexandre found his father in the clearing at the far end of the glasshouse. The Count greeted Alexandre with a kiss. The old man stepped back from the embrace to inspect his son at arm's length. Vexed at the sight of Alexandre's ineptly folded necktie, he pulled it undone. 'Your stock, sir, your stock. What does your valet do?' The immaculate Count shook his head - behind him, his monkey shook its head in perfect mimicry of its master. 'Make an impression on Count de Malpas. Please. For me. For your mother.'

'Step mother,' Alexandre reminded his father, emphasizing the first word a little more forcefully than he had intended. A memory of loss in distant Haiti that, even years later neither could yet accept, shadowed both men's faces. Alexandre twisted at a ring of plaited gold on his little finger. 'Sorry Papa. I tied my stock myself.'

'Why do your valet's work Alexandre? No work, no bread - your precious servant starves.' The Count quickly raised his palm to forestall Alexandre's indignant protest. The monkey copied its master's gesture faithfully. 'Spare me your revolutionary rants. Remember, de Malpas is the King's man.'

'I'll try not to embarrass your wife's guest,' said Alexandre pushing huge scallop-edged leaves aside to expose the misted glass wall of the conservatory. 'Out there,' he said, wiping the condensation away with his sleeve the better to see, 'where the rich live, and the poor die...' He turned back to his exasperated father and spread his arms wide to encompass the conservatory, the Count's estates, the whole world outside. 'Change comes to France. Soon.'

Alarmed, the monkey scrambled up to his master's breast, and from this safe haven, gibbered aggressively at Alexandre.

'The Human Spirit...' Alexandre, warming to his theme, continued.

'A pox on the human spirit. A pox!' interrupted the Count. 'This would be treason if it made more sense. As I love you, enough Alexandre.'

His son gave a resigned sigh of acceptance.

'Did you know de Malpas was badly scarred?' the Count said, getting back to how he expected his son to treat the guest. He drew a forefinger diagonally across his mouth, mimicking a sword cut. 'A duel.'

Alexandre shrugged - duelling scars were routine hazards in aristocratic life and generally proudly displayed as a badge of manhood. He wondered why his father bothered to mention it.

'Tip of his tongue is cut in two.' The Count saw that Alexandre understood that their guest had received an injury odd enough to provoke spontaneous comment if not warned of in advance. 'Go to your man. Let him dress you this time.'

†

De Malpas brought his phaeton to a racing stop by throwing his body weight back suddenly as he jerked on the reins so that the shocked horses almost sat on their haunches in the drive at the front of the chateau, desperate to get away from the tearing pain of the metal bits in their mouths. The carriage slid to a halt in sprays of gravel.

Satisfied with his spectacular arrival, de Malpas twisted the reins into the holdfast. He stepped out into the air off the high platform, dropped lithely to the ground - scorning to wait for the servants hurrying from the chateau with the ladder a less athletic highflier driver would have needed to dismount. De Malpas left the servants swarming over the carriage and sauntered to the mounting block to watch the lone rider who galloped across the lawns directly towards him.

Gabriel imperiously supervised the unloading of his master's luggage, then dismounting himself, followed the line of burdened servants away into the chateau, as a groom led off the highflier and horses towards the stables.

Countess Davy de la Pailleterie yanked her horse to a rearing halt at the mounting block. She was a woman in her prime - intelligent, sensual, and beautiful. De Malpas took hold of the Countess' booted ankle, encircling it with finger and thumb. He closed his other hand around the rowelled spur. 'How long since we bumped into each other?' he asked.

'Bump?' said the Countess. She kicked her foot free from his importuning hand - the rowel spikes dug across de Malpas' palm leaving a row of little cuts. He smiled as if caressed. 'Bump and back to Paris? What husbands do.' She stared over his head at the sight of the Count and Alexandre, attended by the two footmen, walking into view round the far end of the chateau. 'What more fortunate women's husbands do.'

'I begged you,' said de Malpas.

'Look at all this!' said the Countess.

'I'll kill him.'

'The son and heir too?'

De Malpas shrugged.

'A double murder? How discreet,' said the Countess.

'I love you.'

'So does he.' She shuddered, recalling unwanted intimacies. 'Often.'

'Ugh! With that dried up old thing?'

'That's not amusing.'

As they talked, a groom came from the stables to take the Countess' horse. The nervous stallion shied away from the man, sidestepping into de Malpas and knocking him down into the muddied grass.

Immediately, the Countess raised her riding whip over her head and slashed down at the groom. The Countess made to strike again but did not repeat the blow. She did this several times until the groom, believing his mistress' fit of temper over, stopped flinching - then she slashed down again. De Malpas howled with mirth.

Still some distance away, Alexandre was close enough to see, if not hear, the Countess' deliberate savagery. 'Papa!' he protested. Seeing the familiar vexed expression already forming on his father's face, Alexandre realized that he was alone in his dismay. Before he could rush towards the group at the mounting block, the Count grabbed his arm, held him back.

'Alex! Your stepmother's a French noble. Very noble. Very French. Not like your...' Recollection wetted the old man's eyes.

'Papa. Aristocrat, servant, peasant,' said Alexandre, pointing in turn to himself and the footmen. 'We are the same. All men. Born equal.'

The Count was surprised out of his self-pity into a guffaw at his son's naivety. Alexandre, unable to endure the sight and sound of the continuing beating, shook himself free from his father's grip and ran towards the mounting block. The Count shouted after him, 'Alex my boy! You're an American!'

Alexandre shouldered de Malpas aside, knocking him down into the mud again, and pushed in front of the groom. 'All right Romain!' The formal dismissal gave the groom the permission he needed to stagger away. Alexandre locked gazes with the Countess.

Already angered at her stepson's presumptuous intervention, this additional impertinence was too much. She raised her whip, first glancing sidelong to check how near the Count was, to judge what she might get away with. Seeing her husband so close, she reconsidered the wisdom of disfiguring his beloved son in his presence and hurled the whip at Alexandre's head instead. Reflexively, he snatched it out of the air. She smiled at Alexandre's look of disgust as he discovered for himself how much blood the servant had left on the whip.

The Countess freed her legs from the sidesaddle horns and slid down from her horse, landing lightly on the mounting block. De Malpas stepped forward to hand the Countess down... glowering at Alexandre as he did so.

The Countess moved close to Alexandre, closer than needed to simply take back her whip. She reached out and tugged at the whip handle gently with her fingertips, staring into his eyes and almost imperceptibly arching an eyebrow. Not troubling to disguise his contempt and loathing, Alexandre shoved the whip into her hand.

Hiding her anger at his scorn, the Countess turned as the Count arrived, to welcome him with extravagant innocence. 'Husband. Here's my dear brother come at last.'

The Count and de Malpas exchanged bows. There was a strained moment as it became evident that the Countess did not intend to introduce Alexandre.

The Count took over the social niceties. 'And here is Alexandre,' he said.

De Malpas looked at the Count as if all he had done was offer some trivial pleasantry about the weather that did not call for comment. Brother and sister steadfastly ignored Alexandre's presence.

'My dear son,' the Count added with an emphasis that neither his wife nor brother-in-law could lightly disregard. De Malpas sketched a bow addressed to no one in particular. Alexandre acknowledged it with the slightest of nods.

'You are from Paris. How do matters stand?' the Count asked de Malpas.

'Royal Family, near prisoners. Talk of abdication. A republic.'

'This will end badly,' said the Count. 'Saw this in Haiti. Sold up. Put everything in a Swiss bank. Same smell here now. Bloody Armageddon.'

'Armageddon?' said de Malpas.

'When tyrants are overthrown and the meek inherit the earth,' Alexandre quoted. Everyone turned to stare at this simpleton in their midst.

'The meek are sheep. And sheep must have shepherds,' said the Count, giving Alexandre a stern look - this is exactly what he had asked Alexandre not to do. 'But we bore you Madame. This is men's talk.'

'Philosophy, politics, religion, a sheep, a Swiss bank? Not boring. Not really. We'll go and change our clothes,' she said, taking her brother's arm. 'I for one am feeling filthy.'

†

As brother and sister came into the chateau, de Malpas heard clearly for the first time the music the quartet was playing. He strode across to the seated musicians. 'Who wrote this music?' he shouted at their leader, though he knew even less about music than his sister, he suspected he already knew the answer to his own question.

The leader lifted his bow from his violin. The rest of the quartet fell silent. Clearly believing he was dealing with an irrational individual, but not necessarily one who was dangerous, the leader replied evenly, 'It's by the Chevalier de Saint-George'.

'Play him and you're dead,' de Malpas said.

The leader knew who hired him. He knew who could say what to play and what not to play - and this was not that man. He said more firmly, beating out each word with a little flick of his bow, 'The Count commanded us to play Saint-George'. On later reflection, the leader admitted to the others that it had definitely been a mistake to hold his bow under the irate man's nose.

De Malpas stepped back, drawing his sword. A forward slash chopped the leader's extended bow in half. The returning backslash severed the strings of the cello where it rested against the musician's legs.

Without taking his eyes off what he now knew to be a full blown madman, the leader rocked back his chair to address his colleagues behind him from the corner of his mouth, 'Mozart everyone. Yes?' There was a puzzled silence. Sweat burst across the leader's forehead. 'Play,' he commanded.

'He never wrote anything for a trio,' the fool on the violin said.

'It'll be a duet if you don't start fiddling right now,' said the leader.

De Malpas stood and listened to the musicians for a moment. What they were playing did not sound like any music he had ever heard before but satisfied it was not Saint-George's he sheathed his sword, took his sister's arm, and went up the stairs with her to the chateau's private apartments.

†

The Count had waited until brother and sister had gone into the chateau before speaking to his son. 'Alexandre. These radical ideas. You're so... you puzzle me. Why help that groom?' Alexandre's noncommittal shrug further incensed the Count. 'You will honour my wife and respect her,' he said with increased heat. 'Whatever she does. Whatever, you hear?'

'But she does many things I cannot like.'

'Why do you say that? There's much to admire. Her care for her brother, orphaned so young. Destitute, friendless. She was all to him.' Alexandre half turned away. The Count knew why. 'You're a lost child too, your Mother dead.' The Count reached up with awkward fondness to squeeze his son's shoulder. 'I don't forget you are my son.' Shamefaced, Alexandre embraced his father. 'I'm sure, in time, she will come to love you. As dearly as she loves me,' the Count promised.

†

Frustrated and chastened, Alexandre dragged himself up the grand stairs to the chateau's upper floor. The last sunshine of the day, falling through the glass cupola set high above his head, brought a tinge of ruddy vitality to the ranked portraits of dead White ancestors that lined the walls. He gauged each face as he passed. What a dreary lot. He would end up as dull as they were if he stayed here in his father's house.

Still musing, Alexandre turned into the long top-lit gallery that housed the old armoury. This led to the guests' suites and his private quarters. Nothing exciting, nothing... outrageous, ever happened so far from Paris. Country living was fine for boys, for feeble old men. I am eighteen - a man.

The sudden advent of de Malpas' page jolted him out of this gloomy reverie. He had caught glimpses of a small figure keeping pace with him on the other side of the stands of ancient armour. Now, Gabriel bounced directly into his path. The young African was dressed as a hussar in black uniform with yellow frogging - the colours of his master.

Alexandre waited with patient amusement while the skinny page inspected him from his boots to the top of his head. Alexandre had been subjected to many similar displays of open curiosity from the estate's children - and their elders - ever since he had grown taller, much taller, than the tallest man in the locality. He was accustomed to arriving in villages all around to delighted screams of 'M'sieu Hercule' and to hero-worshipping swarms of children.

The peasants detested his patrician parent - sour disdain characterized Count Davy de la Pailleterie's infrequent dealings with them - but they adored his only son. Alexandre thought he was welcomed, where his father was not, for the novelty of his physical appearance; country dwellers rarely saw men of Mixed Race. Also, for his good-natured willingness to perform the ingenious trials of strength the village children dreamt up; squeezing carthorse shoes together to make a chain, or pulling a haywain with everyone in the village sitting in it. What he was too unassuming to realize was that, in truth, the locals loved and respected him because they recognized a good man, that most rare thing, an aristocrat who could be trusted. They prayed for the day when he would come into his own - if they had to have a lord, let it be Alexandre.

For Gabriel's part, he saw before him the model of the man he himself would wish to be. Any ties of loyalty still owed as servant to Count de Malpas - precious few after the casual brutalities of that strange man - withered and dropped away. Here was the master he wanted to serve.

Without a word, Gabriel sidestepped out of Alexandre's way and snapped a military salute. Alexandre returned the courtesy straight-faced and set off for his apartments again. He was not surprised to hear the boy behind him, doing his best to match him stride-for-stride. The two marched in step past the suits of armour, the breastplates and helmets, the pistols and muskets, lances, swords and tattered flags accumulated by generations of the family's belligerent forebears.

Alexandre stopped to press at a worn spot on the wallpaper - the catch of a concealed door that opened onto the narrow landing of a spiral staircase used by servants. A waft of warm steamy air from below enveloped them, bringing with it the appetizing smells of pork crackling on the spit, of pie crust, hot bread, cakes. 'They're baking in the kitchens' he said as Gabriel pushed by. 'Ask for Jeanne. Tell her I sent you.' Too late. The boy had already clattered down the stairs and disappeared round the first turn.

For some time, Alexandre had been half-aware of puzzling little noises coming from much further along the gallery. As he continued towards his apartments, he became increasingly aware he was hearing the cries and sounds of urgent noisy sex - coming through a part-open door. Had de Malpas dragged one of the chateau's housemaids into his room? Alexandre experienced the briefest of internal struggles as he weighed his father's predictable indifference to the forcing of a servant against his certain anger if Alexandre invaded a guest's privacy. He decided that, since he didn't seem to be able to do anything right as far as his father was concerned anyway, he might as well go straight ahead. He pushed the door wide open.

His stepmother, still fully clothed from her morning gallop, bounced on a man who strained beneath her on the floor, his breeches pulled down over his boots. The Countess was not so engrossed in pleasure she could not hear Alexandre's astounded gasp at the door. Without a pause or a backward glance, she panted, 'One word to that pathetic old man, one word, I'll make you regret it forever'.

Her partner swung his head to stare at Alexandre. De Malpas' forked tongue lolled wetly from the corner of his mouth.

Incongruously Alexandre thought, if ever I meet the man that gave you that wound I'll be his friend.

De Malpas' face tightened in an anticipatory spasm. Alexandre realized that, in some depraved way, the fact of discovery, the presence in the room of the betrayed husband's son, was acting on the lovers' lust, pricking it to new heights of sensation. Sickened, Alexandre backed away from the doorway.

The incestuous adulterers' laughter followed him out into the gallery, hammering in his ears. His poor father. He loved this beautiful woman so. Bad enough she was faithless. But with her brother? How could his father forgive such a crime? Overcome with confusion he ran, stumbling down the servants' stairs, almost falling over Gabriel sitting on the bottom step.

Gabriel got up, the oven-warm apricot pie in his hands forgotten for the moment to watch Alexandre run out across the courtyard to the stables.

Feverishly Alexandre saddled his horse. How can I tell my father? Should I tell my father? He had to get away somewhere quiet where he could try to make sense of questions that skittered like bats trapped in his skull.

†

In the guest's bedchamber, the sated Countess disengaged, stood, and shook down the skirts of her riding habit. It had been stimulating, but it was a pity the boy had discovered them. Now somebody else knew about their little entertainments. Her fertile mind racing, she bent forward to help de Malpas with his breeches as he staggered to his feet. Alexandre, what to do? She picked up her brother's wig from the floor, jammed it on his head.

'Alexandre,' she said aloud, sounding each syllable in the name, no trace of agitation in her calm tones. 'I must do something about him. Something quick. Something... lasting.' There was the money too the old fool mentioned today for the first time. 'The Count must have millions in Switzerland. All those Haitian plantations. All those millions. All for little Alexandre - unless we move fast.'

A plan began to shape itself. She shooed her brother from the room. Still playful, he baulked in mock protest at the door. 'Go greedy boy! Time to murder love.'

Moments later the Countess drew the doors to Alexandre's apartments together behind her. She went to the bell-cord, gave it a sharp tug. When her stepson's valet knocked, she opened one of the doors a crack. The man's jaw fell in surprise to see her in his master's rooms.

'Fetch Aimée,' she said in distressed tones, her eyes cast down in shame. 'I beg you, fetch Aimée. I have sore need of her. Be quick!'

He must have run all the way to the west wing and back, for only minutes later her maid barged into the room. The breathless Aimée gulped with relief when she saw her mistress unharmed. Intrigued, she observed that the Countess shivered with suppressed excitement. She pushed the doors to, denying the openly curious valet a view into the room, and gave her mistress her full attention.

'Raped,' the Countess announced.

Familiar with her mistress's moods and games, the maid asked no questions merely pursed her lips and waited, a mischicvous glint beginning to spark in her eye.

'Brutally,' the Countess added with relish. Aimée raised her eyebrows in exaggerated astonishment. The Countess drew out her hatpin, dragged the hat from her head, punched through its crown, and dropped the torn remnants at her feet. With a perfect understanding of her mistress' intent, the maid ripped open the front of the Countess' riding jacket. 'A wife dishonoured. A husband betrayed,' the Countess proclaimed as she kicked over a small table - sending the vase of flowers standing on it crashing to the floor. 'Run. Bring him here.'

She caught her maid at the door. 'And Aimée, make plenty of noise. People should know. It's not every day the son and heir of a great family rapes his mother.'

†

Not far from the chateau stretched a terrace of small cottages, built for the estate's pensioners. Although Count Davy de la Pailleterie evicted farm labourers from their tied homes when they got too old or infirm to work without compunction, he supported the household menials long after they retired; they knew too many family secrets.

In one of these cottages, Alexandre's former nanny sat in a low chair pulled up close to a fire she had banked high in the cast-iron range, even on this warm late summer's day. Alexandre crouched on a stool next to her, staring into the flames, his hand pressed between the old woman's knuckly hands.

In the chateau, the Countess' maid rushed between the rows of standing armour, along corridors, down stairs. 'Rape,' Aimée shrieked as she went, 'Raped his own mother! His own mother!' Doors crashed open. People stepped out, astonished, alarmed, were caught up in the excitement; began to run along behind her.

†

In the courtyard, Gabriel, his uneaten pie cold and forgotten in his hand, burst into tears.

†

'Can a son talk of such things to a father?' Nanny said to Alexandre. 'He may look at you and wonder how you could bring him such pain and humiliation. He may look at you and wonder - are you even my son? Bitter fruit's often best left on the bough.' She stroked his face as if this man were still her small charge, come to her with a bloodied knee to clean and soothe.

Outside the cottage window, there was a flurry of movement in the gathering dusk. A moment later Maurice burst into the room. 'Master Alexandre. The Count. He's calling for you. He's mad with rage Master.'

†

Night was closing in. Servants ran out with flaming torches to light the darkening courtyard. The Countess at her window on the first floor looked down as the servants milled in the enclosed space below. At her side, but hidden from the view of those below behind the shutters, de Malpas exchanged a look of gleeful anticipation with her as Alexandre rode into the courtyard for his confrontation with the Count.

The Countess' head movement at the upper window caught Alexandre's eye. She's made sure she has a good view. He knew his father's summons must have something to do with the grotesque coupling he had witnessed earlier, but seeing the seething commotion here he felt a premonitory stab of fear - something terrible was about to happen.

In the flicker of torch light, the wild-eyed Count looked even more shrunken and wizened than usual. He waited for his son to dismount and approach him - his frail frame shaking visibly with the vehemence of his fury.

'What is it Papa?'

His father stared at him with an expression part anger, part incomprehension. 'Who are you?' he said.

'What has angered you Papa?'

'You pretend not to know?'

'I do not know. I beg you tell me.'

The Count stepped back. He could hear no guilt in his son's voice nor see any in his face. He looked up at his wife at the window, suddenly doubtful. He spoke again, less assured now. 'I have been informed the Countess was...'

Relieved that he would not have to break the bad news to his father himself, Alexandre cut in, 'You know! I did not know how to tell you.'

'Tell me?'

'About her. Her and her brother.'

The Count's eyes blackened further in his livid face. 'Witnesses saw you run from your sick crime.'

'My crime?'

'Can I bear more? You top shame with more shame. You force your father's wife; then accuse her brother of a fouler sin to save yourself.'

'Forgive me. I should have come straight to you.'

'Forgive? You should be hanged for this! Go! Go! Wallow in filth with your damned peasants. Go!' Broken-hearted the Count twisted away.

Great shuddering sobs rendered Alexandre incoherent. He snatched at his father's thin arm. The Count tore himself free from his son's grasp with maniacal energy. He spat full in Alexandre's face and, with voice and features contorted with hatred, delivered the killing blow, 'You are not my son'.

With a cry of anguish, Alexandre fell to the ground as if clubbed; knelt there, weeping and hammering the cobbles in paroxysms of despair. The Count gestured - a feeble distracted command to the servants to drag his son away. Deaf to Alexandre's piteous pleas the grief-stricken Count made his way back to the chateau.

The servants doused the flambeaux one by one letting the night shadows into the courtyard to shroud the pain and hurt that filled it. Not content to see the consummation of her stratagem accomplished so quickly, the Countess screamed from her vantage point, 'Alexandre! Monster! Lash him husband!'

The Count pulled against the supporting hands of his servants to stare back towards the huddled form of Alexandre. 'Lash him? Yes! Whip that vile wretch off my land.' Under the baleful gaze of their master, the grooms flicked their whips so the plaited hide cracked through the air. In the darkness, the Count jeered at the outcast. 'See how these peasants repay your friendship?' the Count cried with bitter triumph, 'You have paid out my love in the same coin'.

†

A scullery maid led the tear-blinded Alexandre through the blackness of a night made blacker by dark despair. Alexandre's sole comfort came from the small warm hand that kept tight hold of his, guiding him away from the chateau, away from the Count's wrath. As shock ebbed away, cold sweat chilled him. He broke away from his guide to retch at the path's edge. The warm hand found his again to lead him to a stone cattle trough. He slumped down onto its broad edge and cupping his hand, rinsed his soiled mouth, tasting the granite in the cold water.

The moon was rising when he looked up again, first to recognize and then to smile his thanks at the young maid. For long years after he would remember how she had put her arms around his shoulders as he sat there, comforting him, wiping away tears that would not stop, evoking memories of his dead mother's own loving caress.

†

When they reached the lodge, they found his nanny waiting with Maurice by the huge wrought-iron gates that gave visitors wheeled access to the Davy de la Pailleterie estates. The old woman watched as Alexandre came to the gates and, with a great sigh, pressed his forehead against the chill bars - he looked like a man in a cage. Nanny squeezed his shoulder gently, patted him.

'You go Alexandre.'

Maurice handed his master his sword. Alexandre realized, for the first time, that beyond those gates he might have to wear this sword not as a badge of rank but as a real weapon, one that he might have to use to preserve his life. Was he ready to give up all the love, ease, and security that were his birthright?

Alexandre pulled the sword from its scabbard and lofted it over his head, his defiant silhouette black against the blood-red immensity of the rising moon's disk. He took a few irresolute steps back towards the chateau, towards the light shining out of the windows over the dark lawns. But, 'you are not my son' was final. Sagging in acknowledgement of defeat without hope of appeal, he sheathed the sword and retraced his steps to the gates.

Nanny had nursed this motherless child, knew his gifts, his true nobility, of soul not station, knew from the first he had a destiny too large to be confined even within the wide domains of his father. She touched him again, more insistently. In her heart, she knew this unjust exile would help to keep him safe from that evil woman and her vicious brother. 'Best you go, my dear.'

The manservant handed him a greatcoat, 'Here Master'.

'Not master, Maurice.' Alexandre snatched the powdered wig from his head. 'I'm no man's master.' He slammed the intricately curled and beribboned wig down into the dust of the gravelled road. 'I've finished with all this - aristocratic - rubbish. I'll be plain Dumas - my dear mother's name. She would never disown her son.'

His nanny frowned in disapproval at these dramatics. 'You'll never know what it is to be plain,' she admonished him. 'Pray to God you never learn to be poor.' She took the wig from Maurice - who had bent with a servant's ingrained reflex to pick it up - and dusted it off with arthritic fingers. 'Even we, born to it, find it so hard.' She held out the wig to him.

He ignored her gesture, went instead to pull the gates open. They were locked. Frustrated, he shook them until the ponderous ironwork rattled.

'Shall I get the keys from the lodge Master? Errh... Alexandre,' said Maurice correcting himself.

Alexandre shook his head, tossed the greatcoat back to him. Taking deliberate hold of the locked gates again, he paused to summon his full strength. His breathing quietened, his legs relaxed until they seemed planted in the earth, his back straightened, his head came erect. The right feeling came. His feet felt heavy, his body light. He could do anything now.

The two silent onlookers discerned no outward signs of strain, as slowly, quietly, Alexandre raised his arms. As they rose, the gates floated up into the air with them. A harsh grating noise came from the hinge-pins. He brought the dismounted gates down to rest on their ends in the road. It seemed to the astounded watchers the true weight of tons of forged metal only returned to the massive fabrication when Alexandre let go of it. Then the rules of gravity seemed to reassert themselves of a sudden as the gates fell outwards to crash down into the road, setting the ground quaking under their feet.

Half-choking in the cloud of thrown up dust, his eyes rounded in utter disbelief, Maurice handed Alexandre his greatcoat without a word, passed him the leather satchel of provisions Nanny had brought.

Alexandre picked his way across the bars of the fallen gates to take the first step on the moonlit road that led away from home and childhood. Somewhere deep in the barren desolation of his misery, an unexpected emotion began to stir. The new world he yearned for - here it was. The feeling of excitement lifted him out of sorrow, suffused him with pure joy. Life starts now.

†

A fancifully carved high-backed armchair had been dragged into a clearing made in the exuberant undergrowth which pressed up against the glass walls of the conservatory. Count Davy de la Pailleterie, still in velvet dressing gown and cap at noon, sat slumped in the depths of this throne asleep. He seemed ill. He looked senile. With a shriek of alarm, his pet monkey leapt from a shrub onto his chest. The Count woke startled to find the Countess looming over him. She contemplated him.

'Here you are,' she said.

'Here am I.'

The Countess turned away to sniff at a spotted orchid that blossomed next to her head. The monkey pointed at her, pulling at his master's clothes. 'Are you hiding here, or are you dying?' she asked.

'Either. Both.'

The Countess brushed the orchid's stamens lightly with teasing fingertips. The old man's head lifted as the intoxicating scent released by her touch filled the clearing. The Count's apprehension for the rare bloom roused him from apathy. The knotted veins bulged on the back of his bony hands as he gripped the arms of his chair, readying himself to spring to the defence of his precious flower.

'You're the master here. You may do as you please,' said the Countess.

'Leave me I beg you. I am not myself.'

The Countess tested the strength of the orchid's stem. The monkey's jabbers of distress became more urgent. Unable to bear her delicate torment of the flower any longer, the Count pushed himself to his feet. His wife took a firmer grip on the orchid. 'Leave you? Why?' Her voice rose. 'To immerse yourself more deeply in self-pity?' she cried. 'Rehearse again the hurt done to your pride?'

The Count recoiled, driven back by her vehemence. He fluttered his hands behind him, feeling for the chair's arms. 'Enough' he said, collapsing back into the seat. 'I beg you... enough.' Distracted, he rubbed his temple so vigorously with his knuckles he pushed his cap over one ear. It slipped unnoticed from his head and tumbled behind the chair.

'You make over much of an... incident,' the Countess said in more normal tones.

'Enough,' he reiterated wearily, then, as the meaning of what she had just said penetrated, 'What?' The Countess plucked the orchid with one quick twist, breaking the stem with an audible snap. The monkey, silenced by her action, patted the Count's cheek in consolation. The Countess began nipping off the stamens with her fingernails. 'What are you saying?' said the Count.

'I cannot come between father and son. If I can learn in time to forgive him...'

'What a pure soul you are,' the Count broke in, 'a true angel'.

'Then you will find some mercy in your heart?'

The Count did not reply. In the silence, the Countess became aware that she was destroying the orchid. She crumpled the remaining fragments and dropped them behind her to the floor. The flower released the last of its thick cloying musk as it fell. The Count's nostrils dilated as the scent hit him, but lost in reflection, he made no other response. 'I thought I could forgive him anything,' he said finally. 'I can't. I'm making you my sole heir.'

'Dispossess him? Your own son. You must not.'

'He'll never be Count.'

The Countess turned her face away briefly to conceal the look of triumph she could not suppress, and then she moved closer. The monkey screeched in warning as it leapt away to the safety of a vine. The Countess bent to gather the old man's hands between hers; pressing them to her bosom, she lowered herself to her knees before him. 'I see you're determined,' she murmured, conceding defeat.

His wife's sympathy and patent love beguiled the Count. He leaned forward to embrace her but her lips slid away as his approached and she rose quickly to stand over him again.

'Best you act then.' She turned her head and called, 'M'sieu Goton. Come now.' There was an agitated thrashing of leaves in the undergrowth; a diminutive, dishevelled lawyer appeared. 'The notary public,' she explained, as she pulled the Count's disordered dressing gown together, 'I hoped his services wouldn't be needed'. She made a small sound of regret, found his cap where it had fallen and arranged it on his head. She bent over to kiss his forehead - though the full lips did not brush the dry skin. 'I'll go now. Men's talk. I wouldn't understand.'

The Count struggled to his feet, looking from his wife to the lawyer and back again, bewildered at the swift turn of events.

†

Moments later, the Countess stalked grim-faced past the footmen she found at work in the long gallery. Without waiting for a dismissal, Maurice and Marc hurried out, pulling the doors closed behind. As soon as the Countess was sure she was alone, she picked up her skirts and skipped merrily along the gallery - laughing happily at how easily she had manipulated her husband into completing her victory over Alexandre.

Reaching the guest suite occupied by her brother, she entered without knocking. De Malpas turned away from the windows where he had been watching the first snow of winter fall. He flicked a glance towards the open door of the dressing room - a warning to her to be circumspect, that he was not alone.

She embraced him with more decorum than she had planned. Looking into the dressing room, she saw that Gabriel was in there, and that the page was packing clothes into a valise. 'You're not leaving? In this weather?' she said.

De Malpas told Gabriel to finish the packing later. Once the boy had left, he said 'I must'.

'You can't!' The Countess was angry. She had just gained limitless wealth for them, for the rest of their lives, had come to share her triumph with him, and he was leaving.

'A private summons from the King himself?'

'I need you more. I need you here with me.'

'Dearest sister. The King plans to escape. I must take messages to Austria.'

'That's weeks... months,' she wailed. 'You can't. You won't.' She pushed him towards the bed, appalled that she was going to have to do without him for so long.

PART TWO

Marie Labouret

ONE FOR ALL

The blizzard shrieked, hurling ice through the air with a packed intensity that almost turned the winter's day to night. A darker shape advancing from deep within the flurries resolved itself by degrees into the figure of a weary man staggering knee-deep in the drifts. It was Alexandre, his hair long, matted, his greatcoat stained and torn. He faltered, dropped to his knees, to hands and knees, struggled back up, staggered, fell again, to lie unmoving facedown in the snow.

Almost as if the utter defeat of the man marked the finale of some elemental design, the howl of the wind abruptly diminished. The snowfall thinned, gradually reducing to nothing.

†

Time passed. A pale sun emerged to warm a snowflake to melting point on Alexandre's cheek. The small increment in bodily temperature brought by the returning sun began to revive the fallen man's senses. As full consciousness came back, sounds he had first thought random and distant became immediate, intelligible. He realized their source was near – deep-voiced men laughed and shouted.. Horses snorted and stamped ice-clogged hooves. Harness jingled, an axe thumped into wood and a fire roared. Could that smell be roasting meat? Cautiously, Alexandre lifted his head. What he saw over the drift of snow that had almost covered him, made him raise himself higher on stiff elbows to gain a better view.

From a clean blue sky, the strengthened sun bounced into his eyes from the blindingly white surface of the field where he lay. Further off, blackthorn hedgerows gave way to a scatter of leafless trees on the low hills that rimmed the skyline. In the mid-distance, rendered ghost-like, insubstantial in the sun's reflected glare, six Black soldiers stood about a blazing fire they had built in the sheltered lee of an ancient barn - eating, drinking, and socializing animatedly. The deep rumble of Africa in their voices reverberated with a message of comfort, of safety, of family, across the snow towards him.

The troopers wore grey uniforms with black silver-braided jackets draped over their shoulders. An elegant ensemble topped off with the mortar-boarded caps of lancers plumed with green parrot feathers. Each man had a curved cavalry sabre at his side. They had leaned their long pennoned lances together in a freestanding stack before the barn. Holsters on each mount's saddle held a pair of heavy horse pistols.

The soldiers had pulled some stooks of hay from the ramshackle farm building and scattered them in front of the tethered horses.

Alexandre had little time to drink in this extraordinary scene, wearied by cold and hunger he swooned into a waking dream. The sunlight was no longer weak and watery but seemed to scorch him with a tropical intensity: he could feel its heat on his back as bare-chested cotton-trousered plantation workers fed a cane fire in an open-sided sugar-refining shed. Five years old again, Alexandre ran to the men who called out, 'Hey Master Alex,' and 'Where you sprung from child?' A man with a machete chopped a piece of sugarcane as long as Alexandre's forearm and gave it to him.

A horseman approached along the track that curved down from the white colonnaded plantation house. It was his father, the Count, smiling and carefree; the beloved Papa of his infancy, whose joy and happiness went into the grave with Alexandre's mother. The Count shuffled back onto his horse's hindquarters and slapped the empty saddle as a command. 'Alex. Your Mama's waiting. She has a gift for you.'

In the real world, echoed in the dream one, Alexandre felt himself picked up.

The men tossed the laughing boy up into the saddle to ride in front of his father. His sugarcane now a grownup's riding crop, he galloped the horse all the way back to the big house where his mother waited for him on the steps.

He could never recall her appearance when awake. Now with the dream-endowed clarity of a child's eyes, he saw sculpted head on long fine neck, dark glossy skin, darker eyes filled with pride and humour. This was truly She.

He felt once more the comfort of his mother's soft arms and warm breast enfolding him. He could feel actual warmth spreading through chilled limbs. A rational thought intruded. How could I have got so cold in Haiti?

His mother pushed a ring of plaited gold over his thumb. 'This goes on your thumb now,' she said. 'When you're a big man, when only your littlest finger fits this ring, you'll look at it and think of your Mama. One day... one day, this ring will bring you your heart's desire.' His mother's face smiled down at him as she blubbered his bottom lip with her forefinger... smiled down at him... smiled down at him...

†

Alexandre wakened into full consciousness to find himself cradled by a kneeling lancer who pressed the mouth of a rum flask against his lips. The troopers had carried him to their fire and propped him next to it on a horse blanket to revive. The heat of the flames and the potency of the rum united to bring his strength surging back. The anxious troopers watched his rapid recovery with evident relief.

Alexandre looked from face to intent face. 'Who are you?' he asked the Corporal.

'The Free American Legion,' the man replied. Vitality restored, Alexandre climbed to his feet to thank them for his life with proper formality. 'Sir,' the Corporal quickly added. All the lancers snapped to attention - the corporal even saluted. Alexandre was just able to hide the astonishment he felt at this unexpected reaction. After all, he was just another vagabond and many such roamed the countryside in these parlous times.

What he was unaware of was that by surviving hard months of privation and danger since his banishment, his natural confidence had solidified into a formidable self-assurance. An air of quiet authority reinforced an impressive physical presence, eliciting the trained response the men accorded their army superiors and, usually, no others.

'Thanks for... my life. One day I'll repay you.'

'An honour sir,' the corporal responded, grinning with what seemed genuine delight.

During this exchange, a column of Free American lancers had drawn up in the road that ran along the hedgerow at the side of the field behind Alexandre. The snow had muffled the mounted troop's approach so Alexandre was unaware of their arrival until he noticed the corporal's gaze wandering distractedly over his shoulder. He wheeled to see the line of lancers - their horses clouded in billows of steam.

The troopers escorted a modest, though elegant, coach that was stopped in the middle of their column. He was intrigued to see the coach's blinds were pulled up - its occupant travelled incognito. What grandee could command such a formidable escort?

'Sir,' said the corporal, regaining Alexandre's attention. 'Our rendezvous. We must join them. Now, sir.' He sounded apologetic. The men waited. Alexandre realized they waited for his permission to depart. He gave a formal nod of dismissal. The lancers caught up their gear and lances and remounted, leaving Alexandre alone at the fire.

†

The two passengers in the coach sat in warm fur-trimmed luxury. One, a pretty adolescent lady-in-waiting, sat, her hand already on the blind-cord, willing her mistress, the Queen of France, to allow her to let down the wooden blind. On the seat opposite was Marie-Antoinette herself - a woman poised on the threshold of a certain age. Her features were of that slightly ugly cast that, in a strange reversal of the conventional effect, heightens sexual appeal rather than detracts from it.

Implored so charmingly, the Queen gave an indulgent nod of assent to her young lady-in-waiting who released the cord in an instant. The wooden blind rattled down. The girl spied out, smiling in frank appreciation at the sight of a fine strong man warming his hands at a fire in the field. Alexandre smiled back.

'What do you think Highness? Pretty as Saint-George?'

The Queen pushed her own blind to one side to peek out unseen. 'He's big. Young too. Without the dirt... handsome. But could mere man equal Saint-George?'

'Were he here, Saint-George himself would say NO!'

They were still giggling as the coach lurched forward to continue its interrupted journey up the road that wound its way to the top of a hill covered in winter-bared trees.

†

At the hill's crest, the dappled grey stamped its hooves at two boisterous Dalmatians that gambolled around it - too near for the horse's comfort. Their master, standing at the grey's side, slid his brass spyglass shut, wondering about the man his lancers had saved from freezing to death. They looked as small as boys next to the young giant.

Though past the first flush of youth, le Chevalier de Saint-George remained an extravagantly handsome romantic hero. A graceful man of mixed race, in powdered wig, pearly-grey hat, and greatcoat, he had the sensitive face, the long-fingered hands, of the virtuoso musician he was - indeed the neck of a black-lacquered violin case stuck out from his saddle pack. Nothing, except perhaps a trained quality of sinewy suppleness about his movements, gave warning of his greater claim to celebrity as a supreme master of the sword - a celebrity that had spread far beyond the borders of France.

A short distance away, Saint-George's aide, Lieutenant Demoncourt and a trooper, Camille, sat on their horses. Demoncourt called across unnecessarily, 'the Queen's coming, Colonel'.

'So Marie Antoinette still loves me,' Saint-George murmured to his horse. He searched the deeps of the animal's intelligent and empathetic gaze. 'Do I deserve a lover less than royal?' He gave the horse's head a gentle interrogative shake. The animal snorted in apparent dissent. 'No? Of course not! But if she were not royal, Horse, she would be my wife.' He called to Demoncourt, 'Take that young man yonder to the Coin Inn. Ask Citizen Labouret to find him work'.

Saint-George remounted the grey to make his way to the road for his tryst with the Queen. At the last moment before he disappeared into the trees, the chevalier turned in his saddle, raised himself in the stirrups to look back to the oblivious hounds. He gave a piercing whistle. There was a brief attentive pause in their barking, then, with a yelp, the two animals bounded after him.

†

The column of Free Americans drew up and saluted their commandant as Saint-George waited at the roadside. The Queen's young companion dropped her coach-blind. Her eyes shone with excitement as she glanced back and forth between her still hidden mistress and her mistress' lover. Saint-George threw his reins to a trooper and snatched open the coach door. Marie Antoinette's gloved hand half-emerged, was withdrawn for a moment, and then re-emerged bared. Saint-George leant forward to kiss the back of her hand, turned it over to nuzzle the yielding palm. He looked up and said, 'Your beauty silences my poetry'. He said it, and meant it.

Marie Antoinette pulled at his shoulder, urging her lover up into the coach with her. He managed to get a foot on the step, to hang one-handed from the coach's roof-gutter and swing in to give the Queen an ardent smack of a kiss. Inflamed rather than gratified by this, the Queen got her arm all the way around his back and with a lusty jerk hauled him bodily into the coach.

Taking their colonel's dramatic disappearance into the wildly rocking vehicle as their cue, coach and escort set off again. A lancer kneed his mount nearer to close the still flapping door on Saint-George's kicking legs. He got a heavy-lidded look of appraisal and interest from the lady-in-waiting before she pulled her blind up.

†

Alexandre, the collar of his greatcoat pulled up around his ears against the icy wind, turned away from the departing coach back to the fire's warmth. To his delight, he saw the lancers had left a few joints of rabbit spitted on sticks cut from the hedge. He retrieved the skewer and kicked the last of the deadwood gathered by the troopers into the embers. Revelling in the heat of the rekindled fire, he tore at the hot meat eagerly - so eagerly he failed to notice that behind him a second coach was making its tentative way following in the ruts in the snow by the wheels of the first.

The great black vehicle, driven by a coachman bundled up in a yellow and black greatcoat, had door panels emblazoned with yellow cockatrices - the Malpasian arms. De Malpas had trailed Marie Antoinette all the way from the Tuileries, confident that she travelled to a secret assignation with her paramour. He hoped to surprise his old enemy Saint-George made careless by love, to catch him off guard, to kill him.

De Malpas realized he should have anticipated the detachment of Free American lancers that materialized once the Queen's coach left Paris to escort her to the trysting-place. The unexpected arrival of armed guardians, especially a crack force like the Free Americans, had obliged him to hang well back from his quarry. So far back, he was not entirely sure if the churned up ruts he had followed for the last few hours were those left behind by Marie Antoinette's party, or by another party of travellers.

Seeking confirmation the Queen and her escort had passed this way, de Malpas hailed the man at the fire. 'Ho! You there! You fellow!' No response came from the motionless figure; no indication the oaf had even heard his call.

At his master's peremptory gesture, Gabriel hopped down from the coach and unfolded the steps. De Malpas descended into the snow himself, thought better of the indignity of yelling again and, with a lift of his chin, sent Gabriel tramping across the field to question the distant figure.

As the page got nearer the true scale of the man staring into the fire became apparent. Could there be two such persons in France? Gabriel circled the fire to stand on its other side grinning broadly at his old hero through the curtain of leaping flames.

Alexandre looked up. Recognizing the young servant at once, he twirled to locate the master. Alexandre ran towards the road, dragging his sword from its scabbard as he went. He heard the startled de Malpas' exclaim, 'Jesus! It's Alexandre!' as he bounded and slid as fast as he could through the snow towards his enemy - Gabriel close on his heels. This was his chance to assuage much of the pain and misery of the last few months. This lying pervert had helped to shame his father, and to destroy the old man's happiness.

After his initial surprise, de Malpas drew his own weapon with deliberation, not in the slightest degree intimidated by the sight and furious sound of the huge man bearing down on him waving his sword. Giant this boy may be but de Malpas had killed many men in open fights - and murdered as many more privately.

As he watched the younger man's reckless approach, he began to doubt that his enraged opponent had ever been in a fight to the death with anyone, let alone a seasoned swordsman of de Malpas' calibre. A judgement confirmed at once as Alexandre's precipitate haste cost him his footing. He slithered to stop right under de Malpas' sword. Unbalanced, already falling to the ground, the younger man was disarmed with an effortless wrist-flick that demonstrated de Malpas' vastly superior fighting skills.

Alexandre flopped back into snow that had drifted into a deep bank under the hedge. In falling, he brought down Gabriel, who had caught up with him, as well.

The boy wriggled free, rose to his knees, thrust out his bare hand in a vain attempt to protect his hero from de Malpas' menacing sword point. Gabriel's determination wilted under de Malpas' poisonous glare. His master knew too well how to scare his young page. A threatening lunge of the head, a reptilian hiss, a flicker of the forked tongue, and Gabriel's boyish courage utterly failed him - with an anguished sob, he drew himself away from harm.

'A learning opportunity for you Gabriel,' de Malpas said. 'A friend in need is a friend too many.'

Smiling with sadistic anticipation, de Malpas stepped forward between Alexandre's sprawled legs to rest his sword tip just below his fallen opponent's rib cage. De Malpas steadied the hilt in both hands as he tensed to deliver a killing thrust into his victim's unprotected heart and lungs. With grudging admiration, he saw no trace of fear in Alexandre's face. If anything, was that a look of confidence?

He realized it was as a huge shadow fell across the three of them. De Malpas could sense a menacing presence bulked behind him, could feel the blood-heat of a large animal nearby. Something cold and sharp nudged the back of his neck. He swivelled his head slowly round - a mounted lancer looked down the length of a lance at him. Behind the trooper, a Free American lieutenant with hand on hip looked on with amusement.

De Malpas turned full around to face the new threat and consider his predicament. Seeing he was comprehensively outclassed, he sheathed his sword and, snarling, 'Throw yourself on my sword another time,' over his shoulder at the still supine Alexandre, began to edge away towards his coach.

The lancer's horse leaned forward, the tip of the lance followed de Malpas' movement, finding a place to lodge in the pit of de Malpas' throat. The steel tip of the lance was so ice-cold he thought it would freeze to his skin even through the folded linen of his stock. He felt an overwhelming desire to gulp, but he was too dry to swallow.

In his haste to get away from the probing steel, he tumbled backwards over Gabriel, losing his hat. The irresistible threat in the lancer's unrelenting advance eventually drove de Malpas back into the safety of his coach. As he climbed in, he shouted to his coachman, 'Drive on man! Drive on!'

The coachman took a second to query Gabriel's intentions with raised eyebrows. Gabriel shook his head in instant refusal. The coachman shrugged and cracked his whip over the horses.

Alexandre dug under the snow for his sword, scooped it up, and ran into the road. Too late. He crouched there like some frustrated predator staring after escaping prey. Forgetting how near his step-uncle had been to killing him, Alexandre screamed after the coach, 'Fight de Malpas fight bastard coward bastard fight'.

De Malpas leaned out of the window, plainly vexed at being denied the pleasure of so easy, and so profitable, a kill.

De Malpas pulled his head in from the window. What a waste of good luck that turned out. His sister would have been overjoyed to hear he'd finished off her stepson, removing any possibility that a future reconciliation would make the wretched boy heir again. 'Lancers. Poke, poke, poke, poke, poke, poke, poke.' He straightened his wig, gave an exasperated sigh. 'The page? Who cares? But that was my best hat.'

Shaking with sobs of rage and frustration Alexandre noticed de Malpas' hat, lying where it had fallen in the snow. He chopped down on it again, fiercely, as if its owner's head was still in it. Finally, he looked at the sword in his hand - disgusted with it and himself. What good had it been to him? He slung the weapon into the hedge. Exhausted, all fury spent, Alexandre dropped to his hands and knees in the snow.

The two Free American lancers got down from their horses whilst Alexandre composed himself. Unasked, Gabriel dug the discarded sword out of the hedge.

As Alexandre got to his feet, brushing the snow from his clothes, Demoncourt addressed him, 'Lieutenant Demoncourt, at your service. I bring you the Chevalier de Saint-George's compliments'.

'My thanks to you and to the Chevalier,' Alexandre said with real gratitude. He went to Gabriel and rested his hands on his shoulders. 'I nearly got us both killed Gabriel. My thanks to you too.'

Gabriel grinned in delight, shaking Alexandre's hand.

The Free Americans remounted. Alexandre grasped Demoncourt's proffered arm and swung up behind him. Gabriel lifted the abandoned sword up to him, hilt first. After a moment, Alexandre reached down and took it. Once the second lancer pulled Gabriel up behind him, the small party set off through the trees to the top of the hill.

†

The late evening of that eventful day found Alexandre grooming horses in the Coin Inn's stables. A shrill whistle summoned him and the regular stableboy into the lamp lit yard. Yet another newly arrived coach and four stood like wraiths enshrouded in the drifting mist of sweat that lifted off the backs of the hard-driven team. Labouret, the landlord of the Coin Inn, fat, florid, and friendly, welcomed the tired passengers as they climbed down from the stagecoach- their movements slow and awkward from sitting chilled and cramped, for the last hour with cold charcoal warmers and empty brandy flasks.

Labouret beckoned Alexandre over. 'This lot needs to be rubbed down, given a good feed and stabled for the night. But you better do the horses first. Then go to the kitchens, find Marie. For supper.'

It took a while to walk the horses until they had cooled enough for grooming: then take them to their stalls, then leave them with feed and water. As he worked, spicy, savoury smells drifted across the courtyard from the kitchen - the door was wedged open to ventilate the hot, noisy interior. By the time Alexandre finished settling the animals for the night, he was famished.

The kitchen was a large flagstoned room lighted as much by the blazing cooking fire as by rows of oil-lamps hanging from the ceiling beams. Within, all was frantic bustle, a bedlam of perspiring, harassed servants. A young woman of about his own age who seemed to be causing most of the harassment and scurry caught Alexandre's attention. This must be Marie.

The stable-lad had said she was beautiful, though unaccountably he had failed to mention her voice, which astonished Alexandre for its stridency and carrying power. Her speech possessed a degree of severity and candour he had not encountered before. She flung orders, urgings, and curses in all directions like heavy stones shied at crows, allowing the harried menials no safe haven in which to dally or natter. Alexandre fervently hoped that, away from the responsibility of organizing dinner for the inn's guests, there might also be a quieter, more reflective side to her nature - for he felt drawn to her.

Perhaps because, entranced, he alone in that busy crowd was motionless, Marie noticed him. Alexandre realized with a start her tilted sloe-dark eyes were staring straight back into his. He snapped his mouth shut, trying hard to look worth looking at.

'Supper?' she barked. Alexandre could only nod - his tongue for some reason too thick now to answer aloud. She snatched a towel drying on a line near the fire and tossed it at him, 'Wash then!'

Made conscious of the pungent emanation of man and horse that had walked in from the yard with him, Alexandre stripped to the waist, tossing his shirt and waistcoat over the back of a chair. Finding a bar of coarse soap in the bottom of a wooden bucket under the pump, he filled the bucket with water and began to cleanse his face and upper body.

Two older serving-women took advantage of lather in his eyes, and Marie's temporary absence from the room, to bring a gentler touch to Alexandre's rough ablutions.

'Ooh! Isn't he lovely? Let's get these nooks and crannies clean.'

'We need more soap. Lots and lots more soap.'

'This is a nice bit here.'

'Bring more soap. We've such a lot to do. Could be at this all night.'

Alexandre's good-humoured squirming enabled him to maintain a degree of decorum in spite of their attentions. A low whistle that warned of Marie's return saved him from further embarrassment; the mirth-filled women scampered back to their work.

Marie's suspicious glance swept across the chuckling servants as she folded a cloth to lift an iron pot off its hook over the fire to carry it to table. She began to say to Alexandre as she approached him, 'It's country stew for servants...' but her voice tailed off into silence.

She found, though she was tall herself, with each step that brought her nearer to the new stableboy, she had to bend her head back further if she wanted to keep his face in view. When she did look full into his face, the sights, sounds, and smells of the busy kitchen faded away. Marie was as smitten at that moment as Alexandre had been with her a short time before.

An unaccustomed weakness sapped the strength from her arms, the pot banged down onto the scrubbed table, startling her with the sudden noise and snapping her back to the present. 'Sit there. Servants have stew. Fill up on bread'.

She ladled stew into a bowl on the table. He needed a shave and his hair trimmed, she thought.

Hunger compelled prompt obedience. Alexandre swiftly dried, put his clothes back on and sat without further ado.

Seeing the new man made compliant, like any man, by the promise of food, Marie, like any woman, began her interrogation. 'So. Where did you pop up from?' Marie searched in the pot with her ladle; finding a large succulent piece of meat, she plopped it into his bowl.

Alexandre could not trust himself to meet her eyes; instead, he watched her hands as she served. Not a common servant she, her hands were long and white; their touch must be soft. Her voice was soft too, now she had no need to goad the kitchen staff to greater efforts.

'The innkeeper said if I looked after the horses...' he began to say.

'Not local then,' Marie cut in. Living by a main road, she had seen Africans passing and of course, the Chevalier de Saint-George had visited the Sign of the Coin since she was a little girl. But she had not heard of any Black man anywhere near Villers-Cotterêts.

'No. I'm from south of...' Alexandre began, but she interrupted again.

'He's my father.' Seeing Alexandre struggling to work out the significance of this remark, she added, by way of explanation, 'The innkeeper. My father.' She returned to her enquiries. 'Where did you say you're from?'

She fished out a fat dumpling and rolled it off the spoon into Alexandre's bowl. She liked the way the little curls pressed against the backs of his ears.

'Your father? South of here. M'sieu Labouret? He's your...'

'Snow's deep there,' said Marie. 'Yes, the landlord. Were you on foot? And your name is...?'

Alexandre could not keep up with Marie's questions, mostly because he felt that dinner was his main priority. He was so hungry; he could not help but give his full attention to the bowl in front of him. For this reason, he was first to see that there was no room for more in the brimming bowl - and that the ladle with yet another fluffy dumpling in it, was approaching again.

He risked a glance up. Marie looked puzzled; a frown formed a small corrugation between the arched brows, the full lips almost puckered into a moue.

Marie was puzzled - how did this man's bowl get to be so full? She dropped the ladle back in the pot. Fetching a loaf from the basket at the fire, she placed it next to Alexandre's bowl.

He swallowed what he had crammed into his mouth and attempted to give answers to her questions. 'The snow was deep. I was walking. My name's Alexandre Dumas. And you're Marie aren't you?'

'Alexandre the...' Marie interrupted herself, 'I suppose everyone says great.' He nodded. That's better, she thought. Now his mouth is full, he is looking at me properly and seems to like what he sees. This could become enjoyable. 'How do you know?' she asked.

'Uh?'

'My name. You know my name.' She did not have to leave him yet - the guests would be all right for a few minutes more - and for some reason she wanted to make an impression on him - one he would remember. She noticed he hadn't broken his bread up so she picked up the loaf and tore off a hunk for him.

'Marie was my mother's name.' He felt for the gold ring on his little finger. He was getting hot and flustered - things were getting complicated. 'He said. Marie. You. Marie is the most...'

Marie broke into Alexandre's compliment. 'He! He! Who is he? The most what?' Some of the steely tone he had heard earlier was back in Marie's voice. She punctuated each word uttered by ripping a piece of crust from the rapidly shrinking loaf.

'Beautiful,' Alexandre hastened to assure her. 'Marie, the most beautiful. For miles around.' His attempt at flattery was having the opposite effect to that which he intended. In fact, it seemed to be making her cross. Why did he get started on this? Now she was arms akimbo, fists clenched on hips. Luc the stableboy had said nothing about this temper. 'The stable... er... that is, everyone really.'

'The stableboy?' Who cares what the stableboy thinks? This was not what she wanted to hear. She started to ask, 'what do you...?' then stopped herself. No. Now I am throwing myself at you, she thought with angry dismay. 'You're nothing more than a stableboy yourself,' she said aloud, flinging the last crust of the loaf down. As she stormed away she thought, that will keep him guessing for a while.

The sizeable crust she had thrown down splashed into Alexandre's bowl, sending a thick gob of stew over his sleeve, where his arm rested on the table. He watched her flounce away to the dining room. Alexandre knew he had upset Marie because he had... because he... No. He did not know how he had upset her.

As he was trying to find a reason in his behaviour for Marie's change of mood, he felt about for a piece of bread on a tabletop littered with torn up fragments. He picked up, glanced at, and discarded all until he found the perfect crust to wipe the stew from his sleeve.

The kitchen staff had been a discreet but attentive audience throughout the exchange, now consolation floated across the kitchen from the two serving-women, 'Never mind darling, you've still got us'.

Alexandre kept his head down and concentrated on chewing. He was aware that every now and then Marie returned to tidy, once she brought a pie of apples and dates - meant for guests surely. Otherwise, she made a point of ignoring him, and he preferred not to attempt any overture that might turn an utter disaster into something worse.

A red-faced and agitated Labouret ended Alexandre's punishment. 'Marie! Come. Help us serve!' Seeing Alexandre still at table, the harassed innkeeper added, 'You want a place in my hayloft tonight?' When Alexandre nodded eagerly, Labouret jerked a thumb in the direction of the yard and ordered, 'Hop to it.'

†

The whoops and screams of excited children outside woke Marie next morning. From her bedroom window, she saw a snowball fight in the yard was well underway. A dozen small children surrounded Alexandre - some belonging to the inn's people, others, in fur-trimmed coats, were the children of guests. All were united in pelting Alexandre with snowballs..

When she joined them a few moments later, Marie sincerely intended to come to the aid of the almost overwhelmed Alexandre. However, once she had scooped and shaped her first snowball, it seemed to hurtle straight at him of its own volition. Not that Marie's attack on Alexandre made the children automatically treat her as their ally - they pelted the two adults from all sides without discrimination.

A flurry of snowballs left Marie bending over, combing compacted snow out of her long hair with her fingers. By the time she was ready to enter the fray again, new alliances had formed, and new targets found. Girls attacked boys, ignoring the grownups.

Marie saw a small child dragging Alexandre by the hand by towards a snowman the bigger children had made next to the gate that led into Labouret's small field. The girl put her little arms, as far as they would stretch, around the snowman, 'M'sieu Bonhomme de Neige is cold'. Alexandre took off his woollen muffler, handing it to the girl, and then lifted her up so she could wrap it round the snowman's neck.

He grinned when he noticed Marie watching. As he rose up from setting the child down, he brought a double handful of snow with him. He clapped it into a huge ball and sent skimming over the heads of the children towards her.

The huge snowball burst across the back of her head just as she thought she had reached the safety of the inn's kitchen. Laughing hysterically, she fell indoors only to slam straight into her father's arms. She could feel the melting snow sliding down the side of her head as he held her.

Her father gave Alexandre a steady look over his daughter's shoulder. Alexandre had his arm cocked for another throw, but under his employer's relentless stare, he let the snowball slide out of his hand to the ground behind him and, feeling suddenly foolish, sloped off towards the stables.

†

The light from the lamps at the front of the Coin Inn made deep shadows in the face of the ruffian standing in the highway making his brutal features even more menacing. He was leaning in at the open door of a coach, his hat respectfully held to his chest as he listened carefully to what the unseen occupant was saying. The orders issued from within were evidently both simple and direct for he soon bobbed his head in acknowledgement - then once more with unfeigned delight at the heaviness of the purse that clunked into his outstretched palm.

The ruffian pressed the coach's door closed. What's this? Painted on the door. A yellow cockerel with a snake's tail. Got a nasty stinger there too. Vicious. Like the aristo inside. He told himself not to cross that one. Just do what he was told to. The money was good, the work congenial. But he was not used to being scared, and this aristo did scare him.

As the coach pulled away, the ruffian secured the purse inside his shirt and patted the bulge it made with satisfaction before going back into the inn's drinking-room.

Men of every degree packed the low-ceilinged room, though determined drinking would soon reduce them all to the same sorry station. The inn's regulars had been drinking for hours. It was that time of the evening when arguments could veer unexpectedly and a friendly dispute turn to a fight.

Without realizing it, Labouret had come to rely on Marie's fearlessness and ready tongue, which could cut or coax with equal facility, to keep the customers from coming to actual blows. A band of toughs had commandeered the corner by the fire. He warned his daughter to take care near them. They had come into the Coin in twos and threes. By the time he had seen they were all together, there were too many. Too many for him to do much about on his own anyway.

Perhaps he worried without need - they were not boozing. The one with the evil expression who had just come back into the drinking room seemed to be in charge and was not letting the others drink anything but thin beer and not much of that either. Anyway, Labouret reflected, the scattergun he kept loaded was close to hand under the counter. Even better, he could call the new man, Alexandre, in from the stable. One look at the giant's bulk filling the doorway should be sufficient to make troublemakers decide to take their custom elsewhere.

The bravos' leader went to the crowded table next to the fireplace. One of the gang hastened to rise from the coveted fireside position to make room for him. Before sitting down he called over to Marie.

'More drinks girl. Same all round.'

Marie passed the order on to a serving-woman - she wanted to stay near this group herself. They were up to no good, she was sure of it. Unlike her father, she would have been happier if the men had been drinking with less self-control, which would have been normal. It was their unnatural sobriety she found alarming.

At the table, the leader's right-hand man leaned forward with a confidential air. 'Alright?' he queried.

The leader gave him a hostile stare then, relenting, reached inside his shirt and with a smirk pulled out the purse de Malpas had given him - just far enough for the other man to see how it bulged.

Their air of conspiracy intrigued Marie. She went to poke at the fire the better to eavesdrop on their conversation. As she picked up the heavy brass-handled poker, she heard the leader's gleeful reply.

'Alright. We just do the Black man. Tonight.'

†

Alexandre, with greatcoat and sword in his arms, was urged into the small room nestling under the thatch by Marie. With one pink-haloed hand, she shielded the tallow candle that had lighted their way up the narrow backstairs from the kitchens below. His sword hilt rang against the iron bedstead. Marie shushed furiously, 'I would not have my father find us here.'

'Your father? And this is your bedroom? Thanks, now I can sleep easy'.

Marie grinned.

'You're really certain it's me they seek?' Alexandre asked Marie yet again.

'How many Black men here tonight? It's you,' she hissed in scorn.

An alarming thought struck her, 'What have you done? Best not to tell me. Nothing too bad I hope.' Pushing close by him in the cramped space, she set down the candle in its holder on the bedside cabinet. 'Snuff the candle,' she ordered. 'Someone might wonder why a light burns in an empty room.'

She pushed past him again. It was a small room, Alexandre could see that for himself, but it could not be as cramped as Marie seemed to think it was. She paused at the door to promise, 'I'll be back later'.

Confident the rays of the full moon through the window would give sufficient light, Alexandre raised the candle to blow out the flame. Just as he pursed his lips, Marie swept back from the door to snatch at his wrist to pull the candle away. She glared up at him with a stern expression. 'Now listen. You're in my room because...?'

'Is it my dimples?'

'I am going to tell them where you are.'

'You're saving my life.'

Her features softened as his face and voice made the depth of his gratitude clear. 'That's what it is,' she confirmed. 'And that's all that it is.'

Alexandre could feel the strength in the slim fingers clenched about his wrist. Reflections of the candle's flame flickered in the inky blackness of her dilated pupils. She moved her body close to him, and, slipping her other hand to the back of his neck, pulled his head down, and kissed him full on the lips. Her impulse came from some instinct so deep it accomplished its purpose before any rational consideration had time to intervene and prevent it. When she released him, they stood for a moment looking at each other with mutual surprise.

Marie recovered first. 'Now that is strictly forbidden. Strictly. Do that again and I'll scream for Father.' She moistened the tips of her fingers and pinched out the flame of the candle Alexandre still held.

Taking the candleholder from his hand, she left him in the dark - in every sense. He thought he heard a sound, like a stifled chuckle, coming from the corridor outside. He went and pressed his ear against the door panel the better to hear, but there was only silence. She had gone.

He peered out of the small window. A full moon lit the inn yard below. He leaned his sword against the wall under the window. He drew his greatcoat around his shoulders and sat on the edge of the narrow bed in the moonlight. Alexandre half-dozed for some time, waiting for Marie to return as promised. When she did not, he supposed she had doubled-up with one of the maids.

He pulled out the warming pan from between the sheets, undressed and got into the bed. It was truly her room. As the bedding warmed, he recognized the garden herbs he had smelled when she was close, spiked with some musky spice that should have been familiar - he fell asleep trying to recall its name.

†

The brightness of the candle flame held in his face disoriented Alexandre for a moment. When his eyes adjusted to the glare, he could see it was Marie, leaning over him.

She set the candleholder down on the cabinet and shook his shoulder. 'What do you think you are doing? That's my bed.'

'I'm sorry, I thought...'

'I know what you thought. You're to get out. Now.'

Couldn't she see all his clothes hanging over the chair back? She was right next to them. 'But I'm not decent. Put out the candle.'

'No buts. Out now. Quickly, I'm getting cold.'

Alexandre stared at her, tried, and failed to discover any clue in her expression about what she really wanted of him. Well, he couldn't stay where he was. She'd made that plain. He threw back the covers and rose stark naked from the bed.

Covering her eyes with one hand, Marie chivvied him across the room to face the far wall. For someone who was not supposed to be able to see, she managed this manoeuvre with impressive precision - perhaps because once Alexandre had his back to her she felt it foolish and pointless to persist with the pretence she could not see between her fingers. Especially since there was no other witness to deprecate any want of modesty.

Alexandre, thinking he was to spend the night in the chair, made a move to put his clothes on. 'Wait. Stay still.' The whispered request halted him as effectively as a shouted command.

The careful watch she continued to keep on Alexandre as she stripped to her cotton shift was, Marie assured herself, necessary to ensure he did not forget his manners and peep. By the time she had pulled off her stockings, she felt flushed and short of breath; as if her lungs were not working fast enough to keep up with her heart. She huffed - lifting the curls on her glowing forehead - then jumped into the bed squirming in the luxury of the body heat left by Alexandre. Turning to the wall, she whispered, 'Come on then'.

Not daring to believe what was happening was happening, Alexandre lifted the covers to climb in behind Marie. Before he could get so much as a foot in the bed, her arm swept back to snatch the half-raised sheet from his grasp.

'Nooo, no.' she said as she carefully tucked the sheet around her. 'On top of the sheets if you please.'

He felt ashamed of his thoughtless presumption. With a mumbled apology, he slid under the blankets, taking the greatest care to avoid any inadvertent touch or pressure through the sheet that this alarmingly forceful woman might in any way misinterpret as an advance. He need not have bothered for as soon as he pulled the blankets up around his ears Marie wriggled herself around and began hugging and kissing him.

Very soon, Marie knew she had reached the limits of her own self-control and sensed Alexandre had long exceeded his. 'Enough. No more of your kissing and squeezing. Taking advantage. Father will kill you.'

With an air of virtuous finality, she leaned over him to pinch out the candle, and then rested her full weight on him for a last tender kiss in the dark. Marie rolled off him, back onto to her side of the bed, and dragged Alexandre's arm around her. 'It was your dimples,' she confessed, sleepily.

Alexandre lay in the dark with his eyes open for a long time.

†

Marie awoke. It was still night. The unmistakable thrumming of a chamber pot in urgent use vibrated through the air. She remembered - her hand explored the empty dip in the soft feather mattress beside her. It was still warm. The noise went on and on. Trying to keep an unruly snigger out of her voice, Marie said, 'Alexandre? Where are you?', though she could see him well enough, silhouetted as he was against the moon-bright window. 'I hope you are not doing what I know you're doing.'

The noise stopped instantly. With a casualness that almost convinced, Alexandre drawled, 'No. I'm having a bit of a look out of the window.' After a moment, the driddling started again more loudly than ever.

'I've had that pot since I was a small girl.'

Silence. A long silence. Then the floodgates reopened abruptly. Eventually, with a mortified apology, Alexandre lowered the pot to the floor. Snorting with amusement Marie rose from the bed and pushed him away to claim it for herself. 'I'm so glad you didn't fill it right up.'

Alexandre politely looked out of the window, down into the yard. He couldn't understand what he was seeing and thought for a confused moment someone had started a bonfire on the cobbles. Then the random flickers of flame melded into recognizable forms - a gang of bravos, some carrying flares, all holding drawn swords. They faced the inn in a wide half-circle that enclosed the section of wall beneath Marie's window.

'Something funny's going on in the yard,' Alexandre said quietly over his shoulder to Marie, then eased the window open so that he could see what the gang was staring at. He leant out and looked down - onto the head of a man backed against the wall almost directly below him.

Marie squeezed into the window-frame beside Alexandre. 'It's the Chevalier de Saint-George,' she whispered.

Saint-George had already shrugged off his greatcoat. In the same relaxed movement, he must have slid his sword from its scabbard for its deadly length glittered in his hand. The encircling ruffians stepped forward a single menacing pace and halted - their intended victim's composure making them hesitant. No-one wanted to be first to fling themselves into a full-scale assault on the armed man.

From the same scabbard, Saint-George drew a second, shorter, guard-less sword with a narrow springy blade. He exercised both weapons in dazzling circles, shredding the air about him with an intimidating ambidexterity. As one man, the ruffians stepped back. A suspicion wormed its way into the gang's collective brain that, maybe, the wages should have been higher, much higher, for this night's work.

'He is the Black man. Not me,' whispered Alexandre. Here was the man whose lancers had twice saved Alexandre, whose influence had found him shelter and work at this inn. A man known to Marie since childhood, a frequent and honoured guest of her father. But mostly, here was a man who faced certain death at the hands of a score of villains, with insouciance, with style, with courage to marvel at.

Alexandre could feel the chill metal of the sword he had leaned against the wall pressing against his thigh. He reached down with his right hand to wrap his fingers in a firm grip around the sword's hilt. Without conscious volition, Alexandre's bare foot found the sill's edge. As Marie turned to him in surprise, he launched himself out of the window to land, naked as any ancient Greek hoplite, ankle-deep in the snow at Saint-George's side.

As if all he had been waiting for was the distraction of Alexandre's impetuous descent, Saint-George exploded into violent action. All Alexandre could recall later was wondering why the man on his left had decided this was a good moment to spit out a mouthful of red wine. Then he realised it was the ruffian's lifeblood arcing from a punctured carotid as the man pitched forward onto the snowy cobbles. He knew Saint-George must have lunged across from his position at his side to reach his mark, but Alexandre had not seen the movement.

In the stunned silence that followed, Saint-George addressed Alexandre in the nonchalant manner of acquaintances meeting in a Paris salon. 'I hope that you are with us Citizen?'

'Us?'

'This is my honour.' Saint-George lifted one sword. 'And this, my conscience.' He lifted the other. Alexandre noticed blood stained both blades. Made curious, he leaned forward to peer past Saint-George. A short distance beyond, on the other side of the Chevalier, another corpse drummed its heels on the snow-covered stones. Not one man but two had been killed - both dying between one breath and the next.

'Alexandre Dumas. At your command,' Alexandre introduced himself, emulating as best he could in the circumstances, Saint-George's conversational tones.

'Delighted. I see you have two weapons out like me. Pity it's so cold,' Saint-George added - unnecessarily Alexandre thought.

The raised point of the Chevalier's shorter sword described a small tight circle. The torchlight sparkling off the blade left a perfect ring hanging in the frosty air. All the ruffians followed this movement with wide-eyed apprehension.

'Can you use that thing?' Saint-George inquired.

'I handle it well enough. I'm always practising.'

'But never spilt blood with it. No matter.'

The gang stirred back into brutal threat as Saint-George returned his full attention to them. This man, who should have been a bloody heap on the ground minutes ago, now seemed to be in command of events. He raised his voice. 'You face the Chevalier de Saint-George. The finest swordsman in France, and beyond.'

At this announcement, a vainglorious one if not for the evidence of the prone corpses, there was a slithering of many feet as most of the gang shuffled away from the Chevalier to Alexandre's side of the ring. A solitary pimple-faced ruffian, unaware of the judicious relocation of his more imaginative mates, faced the formidable Saint-George all by himself.

Alexandre could feel - could see - a fine tremor developing along the length of his extended sword. Must be the cold, he reassured himself. Copying the Chevalier's even tone, he said, 'Glad to hear that. They are so many, we...'

'So FEW!' Pimpleface interrupted, completing Alexandre's sentence for him with glee. 'Not many of you. Lots of us!' he said, slapping his chest for merry emphasis, Glad to share his wit with his fellows, the ruffian tried to nudge his neighbour's ribs with a knowing elbow. Since his mate had abandoned him moments before, his elbow met no resistance and Pimpleface nearly tossed himself to the ground. He managed to keep his balance by dint of deft footwork only to find, on regaining an upright stance, the tip of Saint-George's nose pressed against the end of his.

There was just time for Pimpleface to utter a puzzled 'Urrhh?' before Saint-George, revealing a familiarity with a repertoire of combat skills not often encountered in the salon des armes, brained his opponent senseless with one brisk hammer blow from his forehead.

Stepping forward over the crumpling humorist, Saint-George, both swords twirling in an impenetrable defence, advanced upon the rest of the gang. The long sword shimmered in the flares, its contours blurring with speed as Saint-George used it to give gentle taps and pats to the men around him. No more than that, it seemed, but each delicate touch maimed or killed.

His second sword he used to parry or to fend off sneaked attacks on his otherwise vulnerable left side. Those trying to outflank the Chevalier in this fashion found their target abruptly gliding in amongst them, working the scalpel-sharp short sword back and forth in their packed bodies as fast as a fishwife gutting her catch for the Friday market.

Alexandre looked on in wonder. Saint-George needed no help from him. It was the gang of bravos that was in trouble. He began to feel chilled and more than a little miffed. The ruffians were much too busy with Saint-George to bother with a boy like him. His sword drooped from the en garde position. He turned to take a quick look up to Marie at her window to see if she had any ideas about what to do next.

He saw the frantic alarm on her face; saw her mouth opening to scream a warning, so he was half-prepared as a desperate ruffian, backing away from the melee, barged into him from behind. Equally surprised, the man reflexively swung a backhanded slash at Alexandre who, all indecision removed at this first physical contact, managed to get his own blade up in time to block the blow. Scowling at the failed stroke, the ruffian broke away to give himself enough room for the one good swing needed to settle the account of this green youth.

Marie had been alarmed from the first at Alexandre's foolhardy action, though thrilled by his courage. Now she was terrified for him - he was such a novice. She had been about to go down to pull him back into the safety of the inn but now he had got caught up in the fighting. Her scream never left her throat. Alexandre batted aside his attacker's sword with irresistible strength, sent it whirling away into the night like a child's wooden toy. Perhaps he was going to be all right after all.

Alexandre took hold of the man's wrist, strode past him, and jerked him from his feet. Two more bravos, hoping for easier meat, stopped in abrupt surprise as they saw the boy they came to kill swing their mate around bodily. Alexandre swung the first ruffian by his wrist in a low arc that skimmed the helplessly kicking body a hand's breadth above the cobbles. On the second turn, he let go. The sliding bravo bowled over the other two assailants as he sped across the icy ground on his way to crashing, unconscious, into the stable doors.

One of the felled men scrambled to his feet and lurched off to Alexandre's right. The other looked up at him; eyes goggled in fear and hate as he reached out to grab his sword where it had fallen in the snow. The ruffian's collar gaped opened to show a brief gleam of sweaty pale skin. Some reflex triggered Alexandre to chop down at the mark in that instant of exposure. The sharp metal sliced deep into the soft corner where neck meets shoulder. The ruffian fell back to the ground.

I've killed him, Alexandre thought, gulping back the acid bile that burned suddenly at the back of his mouth.

Marie's shrieked, 'Alexandre!' brought him out of his nauseated shock. Where was the ruffian who had escaped past him? He wheeled back towards the inn to see the man advancing on him with a dagger. Alexandre got his sword up fast and shook it at the man who quickly stepped back to crouch against the inn's wall.

A peculiar rushing noise in the air above made Alexandre glance up towards Marie's bedroom. She was leaning half out of the window. She had a two-fisted grip on the long handle of the bed-warming pan raised high over her head. Now she swung the pan down with a vicious whoosh.

Seeing Alexandre look up, the man looked up too. Marie's impromptu weapon completed its arc before her intended victim could leap or duck. With a clanging thud that woke everyone still sleeping in the inn, the heavy brass pan hit the bravo's head and bounced it against the stonewall. Alexandre grinned up at Marie's triumphant whoop. Well, their side had made a good start. He would try out someone else.

Saint-George was on the far side of the yard. With the wall of an outbuilding protecting his back, it was not possible for more than a few men to engage him at once. The rest of the gang milled around the middle of the yard, waiting for a turn or more likely waiting for tiredness to take the edge off Saint-George's formidable skills before risking themselves. Alexandre was a little perplexed - they were all looking towards the fighting. He could not attack them from behind without warning; it wouldn't be honourable. He shouted a challenge - but they were all shouting louder. None of them showed any interest in him.

He strode towards them wishing he had his breeches on, though bare soles seemed to give a surer footing on the icy cobbles than leather buskins. He pushed the nearest man's back, a mite harder than he intended. The ruffian rocketed forward bringing down others before ending up sprawled face down in the snow. Now Alexandre had their attention. Everyone's attention.

They turned as one and spread out before him, a hostile half-moon of piercing eyes and sharper steel. He made rapid passes with his sword from left to right at waist height to keep them back whilst he thought what to do. The gang pressed in to the edge of the zone of defence defined by the flickering tip of his weapon as in desperation he wove and rewove a flat figure of eight in the air around his body.

He knew he should attack, but if he attacked one, that would free the others to strike. The ruffians began to inch around on either side of him in what looked like a routine manoeuvre to them. In a second, they would surround him. Now! He had to attack now!

Alexandre completed a swing with his sword to the left. As he swung back to the right, he stamped out in the same direction - catching out his opponents out on that side. However, even as the heavy blade scored a deep path across unguarded throats and faces, from the corner of his eye, he saw a concerted surge of stabbing, slashing weaponry coming at him from his undefended left side. Only primitive reflexes enabled him to duck in time. The swords clashed against each other above his head as he swung to the right beneath the flying sparks. Sheer momentum spun him full-circle on his heels in the freezing slush.

He stood up with four still against him - he had poked his sword up into the guts of the fifth as he rose from his crouch. Facing them, Alexandre knew he had outlived his run of luck. He almost regretted his rash intervention in a fight not of his making. He wanted one last look at Marie - he had found and was about to lose her all on the same day. He dared not look away - he was not going to make killing him any easier for these four villains.

No, not four. It was inexplicable but two were falling, folding backwards at the knees as they dropped out of sight. Running behind Alexandre's attackers, the Chevalier had sliced along the backs of their legs with his short sword severing the hamstrings of two of them. Alexandre caught a glimpse of Saint-George's quick smile of encouragement as his saviour darted back into the main mêlée.

The halving of his adversaries gave no relief, no respite, from frantic activity, as Alexandre fought on, no longer for victory, but for survival.

The remaining two ruffians were fighting him like one man, as if a single mind directed both bodies. They swung and lunged together so two swords jolted against Alexandre's every block, two swords parried aside every thrust. When Alexandre found himself backing towards the inn, he discovered the reason for their uncanny shadowing of each other's moves. Guests had brought lamps to the windows to watch the fight. By their light, Alexandre was able to see the detail of his opponents' features for the first time. They had the same swollen-lidded eyes, the same thin slack mouths. Twins.

Alexandre conjectured the murderous twins timed their blows to fall with doubled heaviness, a technique that on most occasions soon wore down a victim. But if he could make no headway against the brothers, neither could they overcome him. Alexandre was no ordinary man; his strength was more than equal to theirs. Their favoured strategy was futile.

This realization struck the pair at the same time as it occurred to him. Bad luck. Without a word, they split away from one another. One stayed to rain blows at his head, while the other twin dashed to get behind him to slash at vulnerable calves and ankles. Alexandre's longer reach, youthful agility, and sheer terror kept him away from the sharp edged weapons whistling around his head and feet. Turning. Turning. Now rushing one, now pressing the other.

Intent on their own small battle, the combatants strayed from the main fighting towards the dark perimeters of the yard.

Spinning around to confront one brother after a frantic lunge at the other, Alexandre found him gone. Facing him instead was the snowman leaning like a drunk at the edge of the pool of light cast from the windows of the roused inn, with Alexandre's scarf still wrapped round its neck. Two lumps of charcoal made the staring eyes. More lumps marked out coat buttons on its chest. A strip of red flannel had been twisted and curled into a manic grin stretched halfway round the ball of packed snow forming the snowman's oversized head.

Some intuition prompted Alexandre to take a pace back. Had he not already been moving away, he might not have dodged the sword the snowman seemed to jab at him. The second twin emerged from behind the snowman, scowling with disappointment at missing his mark.

The brothers came forward shoulder-to-shoulder forcing Alexandre to take a hurried skip backwards into the moonlit meadow behind the stables. In the middle of the pasture, the three men paused in temporary truce to catch their breaths. Even mortal combat has its rough courtesies, its perverse rules. Bent panting, hands on knees, they glared under furrowed brows at one another, harsh breath plumed from gaping jaws, drifting white on the frosty air.

Alexandre knew he had to break this deadlock. He could not attack one brother all-out for fear of what the other twin might be doing behind him. He had to keep them together in front of him - where he could see what both were doing. Was there a wall or large tree he could back against? No, none near enough anyway. The snowman? Yes, he could still see it from here. It would have to do - if he could reach it before his opponents killed him. Then beyond the brothers, behind the stables, even nearer than the snowman, he noticed the outline of a steep-sided hillock. If he could get partway up that rise, for a few seconds at least his back would be safe.

He charged forward, throwing himself straight at the man on the right, hoping this would give the other pause, afraid to risk a swing at close-quarters that might harm his brother. Alexandre believed he sprang over the intervening fifteen feet in one bound. The deep bloodcurdling roar of some ravenous beast filled his ears. Alexandre almost looked around in alarm, before realising the sound bellowed from his own throat. His target stood petrified, scared rigid at the sudden animal ferocity of Alexandre's desperate frontal attack.

Seeing the man made no attempt to defend himself - his forgotten sword trailed in the snow uselessly - Alexandre changed his intended thrust into a punch between the eyes. His merciful impulse was wasted. The sword hilt gripped tight in his hand meant the blow was given by a reinforced fist as hard as iron. Alexandre's impetus and solid mass of bone and muscle delivered the blow with the force of a battering ram. He heard the sharp crick-crack of the man's neck-bones popping apart as he bounced over him and ran up the snowy slope beyond.

The surviving twin's spontaneous howl of grief at his brother's demise wailed up behind Alexandre. He spun on his heel to face the expected attack. The man was trudging up the incline, crying so hard it was making him half-blind and fatally clumsy. Alexandre took a few more steps backwards up the hillock. He wanted no more killing. Especially he did not want to kill a man who could not see for tears. However, the weeping bravo was determined to avenge his brother and continued to climb towards Alexandre in spite of his impaired vision, swinging a wild sword randomly from side to side hoping a lucky blow would land on his brother's killer.

Alexandre held out his sword at arm's length, intending to let it ring against the other's blade to give the unseeing man at least some warning, a shock that would make him understand that what he was doing was not fighting, it was suicide. In all honour, Alexandre knew he could not kill someone who was blind.

Just as Alexandre stretched his sword out to warn off the disabled man, the ground beneath his feet broke open like a crust. He felt himself sinking rapidly until the ground swallowed him up to the waist. He distantly registered the warm sticky wetness that sucked at his naked skin but his full attention locked onto his assailant who now loomed over him. The ruffian could see all right now. He gazed down at his trapped victim with an enigmatic expression - seemingly in no hurry to finish Alexandre off, now he had him at his mercy.

Alexandre laid down his weapon so he could press down with both hands and push himself up out of this stinking muck. Frantic with fear he tried to extricate himself but the thin crust he had fallen through offered no resistance to his despairing struggles, the surface broke away in lumps. He picked up his sword again, resigned to his fate.

The man standing over him lifted his weapon above his head with tormenting deliberation, clasping the sword two-handed in an executioner's grip. Alexandre held up his own sword crosswise above his head, resting the flat of its blade on the palm of his free hand. He braced himself for the man's downward blow. It never came. The ruffian's weapon slid out of slackened fingers to fall point-first behind him, sticking upright in the snow. His arms came down with painful slowness. He folded them around his belly and stumbled away hunched over, back down the hillock and across the field towards the light and noise of the inn's yard.

Free at last to investigate his predicament, Alexandre dragged up a handful of the soft material that imprisoned him. He had never found the whiff of horse manure unpleasant before that moment, but standing up to his waist in shit was a different matter. He pushed forward, dragging his legs through the clinging muck until he reached the more dried out edges of the dung heap. He noticed a dark stain in the snow where his recent opponent had been standing - must have given him a deep wound with that last thrust after all.

The clash of weapons and men's hoarse shouting in the inn yard still rang out across the dark meadow. Saint-George was still fighting then. Alexandre broke into a weary run towards the lights.

He saw Labouret come from the yard to stand by the snowman. The innkeeper scanned the meadow, his posture radiating anxiety. Labouret straightened to wave with genuine relief when Alexandre emerged from the darkness.

The snowman's grin was as wide and inebriated as ever. The second twin had managed to stagger that far. He must have hung on its neck for a moment - it had lost some buttons but gained a splash of blood for a crimson waistcoat from the dying ruffian. The man's corpse lay sprawled on the ground, arms still clutched about the snowman's foot.

'You're safe then,' the landlord said. 'Marie sent me after you. Said you were in trouble.'

'I am grateful Citizen, I was. Please thank your daughter for her kind attention.'

Labouret grinned as he took in Alexandre's state of filthy undress. 'It must have been some fight. Best you come indoors now.' He showed his gun. 'This will see us safe through the fighting.'

'Thank you Citizen. I cannot withdraw whilst the Chevalier is still engaged.'

'No need for such loyalty, lad. Saint-George is enjoying himself and you look in urgent need of a wash and a hot brandy.'

Alexandre looked down at his legs. A thick layer of brown muck with straws sticking out in all directions covered them. He bent to scrape the drying manure off with his free hand.

A moving shadow on the snow behind Labouret made Alexandre look up. A reflex made him throw the large handful of muck he had gathered in his hand at the ruffian rushing at Labouret's back. The smelly mess caught the bravo full in the face. It stopped him dead. Alexandre and Labouret watched with weapons half-raised. The ruffian just dropped his sword, and walked away from them, shaking his head in disgust.

They continued to watch as the demoralized man, eyes full of manure, stumbled within striking distance of Marie's window. She did not disappoint Alexandre and Labouret who, anticipating what was going to happen next had already begun to laugh. The man was bed-panned with such vigour that Marie cracked the warmer's long wooden handle in two. The ruffian lay unmoving under Marie's window, where Pimpleface found him, having only just recovered after Saint-George knocked him senseless at the onset. Pimpleface knelt, trying to revive his friend.

Seizing this opportunity, Marie disappeared from view for a moment. She returned to balance the brimming chamber pot on the sill. Alexandre and Labouret almost missed the next bit because they were doubled-up with hysterical laughter again. Pimpleface took the thorough drenching well. He did not even look up, which was a pity since, if he had done so, he might have dodged the chamber pot itself that Marie, after a heartfelt sigh of regret, hurled down with all her strength on his head. The downed men recovered from their brief losses of consciousness together and with silent agreement made their escape from the yard on hands and knees.

'Well boys, it's been one of those nights,' Labouret consoled them, the note of deep sympathy in his voice belied by the copious tears of merriment cascading down both fat cheeks.

When Alexandre walked back into the yard with the innkeeper, he saw the fighting had stopped. Bodies lay on bodies strewn all about the yard. Half a dozen survivors, the gang's hardiest fighters, clustered in defeated silence in the middle of their fallen mates.

Saint-George stood facing them in the pose adopted by lion-tamers and matadors as they outface a beaten but still dangerous animal, bearing down on it with the power of their will. The posture seems relaxed but, with the feet placed at right angles, the body balanced lightly over them, the arms hanging away from the torso, it is just the opposite. The Chevalier looked to be at rest, but his every sense and fibre was poised for sudden action.

The lull in the fighting emboldened the inn's staff and guests to file out in their nightclothes, picking a careful path between the bloodstains and bodies in the snow to find vantage points at the edges of the yard.

Saint-George caught Alexandre's eye - signalling he needed no assistance. Labouret took the young man's arm but Alexandre declined his hospitality with a smile. He did not want the inn's comforts just yet. He wanted to see the end of all this. He looked up to Marie and found she was already gazing down at him. He was surprised when her head snapped away, wondered why she had not returned his smile. Then out of the extreme corner of his eye, he saw her father's round face examining his with a dawning suspicion. Alexandre let his gaze wander away from Marie, in a natural sort of way, to inspect other windows, idly, as if none of the several people leaning out, the landlord's daughter for instance, was of more interest to him than any other.

Pretending to be unaware of her father's continuing narrow-eyed scrutiny, Alexandre swung his sword up to rest on his shoulder and with a blithe step joined the ring of spectators. He murmured a polite greeting to the matrons on his left, but they were too engrossed in events to notice him. The man on his right responded with a cursory nod, unwilling to miss one closing moment of the drama he had left a cosy bed to watch.

The woman on Alexandre's left gasped at the sudden strong stench of manure that assailed her. Following her nose, she found a handsome Black youth standing close beside her. Close and utterly naked. Had she been content with this first glimpse of the young Hercules all might have been well. The second, more painstaking, physical inspection proved unwise. Only the alertness and quick reflexes of the woman's companion saved her fainting friend from injury as the woman buckled at the knees and dropped like a sack of coals to the ground.

The instant she glimpsed Alexandre for herself, the second woman was equally entranced. She let her friend lie disregarded in the snow - whilst she herself finished the thorough survey her more susceptible friend had only managed to begin.

Saint-George addressed the remnants of the gang. 'You are paid assassins,' he said. 'But you at least have had the courage to face me. Even at odds of twenty to one you show more honour in this than your paymaster'. His lip curled with contempt, 'I can guess who he must be. You have afforded me some refreshing exercise this evening, and, since I am not a bloodthirsty man, if such is your wish, you may depart without further hurt'.

The ruffians lowered the points of their swords thankfully. The survivors made a shuffling half-turn towards the gates - moves that ceased immediately when the ruffian at the back leaned forward. 'I wouldn't advise any of you to try leaving,' he growled. Labouret and Marie recognized him as the gang's evil-looking leader.

'So be it,' said Saint-George. 'Now I... We...' He sketched a gracious wave that included Alexandre. 'We wish you goodnight and adieu.'

Death's own scythe could not have dispatched the men with more efficiency than Saint-George. He strode through the ruffians, each time he said adieu, a man died. The spectators started to clap each individual victory but Saint-George's quickness obliged them instead to maintain a continuous rolling applause. Seeing his men cut down before him, their leader cursed and fled.

From her vantage point at the first floor window, Marie saw the scoundrel drop his sword the better to scramble over the ivy-covered wall separating the Coin's yard from the highway. For the first time she noticed a coach standing in the road, its lamps unlighted, apparently waiting on the outcome of the fight.

The ruffian hung at the coach's open window for a moment. Whatever it was he reported, it was not pleasing to the unseen listener inside. Marie saw a metallic flash from the hidden interior of the coach as a long blade jabbed out at the villain. It took him under the chin with such force it stuck out a foot beyond the back of his neck. The sword jerked back, powerfully, several times, each jerk banging the rag-limp body against the coach's door until the blade slipped free.

A loud cheer drew the horrified Marie's attention back to the yard. Saint-George acknowledged the crowd's applause with graceful flourishes to left and right. He gave a little shrug of irritation as he noticed what a butcher's apron the fighting had made of his clothes. Then, remembering his manners, he tucked the wet blades under one arm and went to shake Alexandre's hand. 'Thank you Dumas. Thank you... Alexandre I should say. You've done well by a stranger.'

'We have just met, but you are no stranger,' said Alexandre sincerely.

'We shall always be friends. At need, call me. I make no light promise, Alexandre. God...' he raised his voice so all might hear, 'And these good people be my witness. Only call, I shall hasten to your side. Even if that be through the shadow of the Valley of Death, I shall come to you'.

Somewhat embarrassed at the extravagant language Saint-George was using to express his gratitude - surely, this is excessive; I was not that much help - Alexandre tried to hide his pleasure at the honour done him.

'First, please dear new friend, I beg you...' with a player's exaggerated gestures, Saint-George pinched his nostrils with his fingers, '... the dung?'

Saint-George took his swords from under his arm and, using the pommel of one, smashed the ice on the rainwater butt that stood outside the kitchen door. He smiled a challenge. Alexandre, who had been growing colder and colder since he stopped fighting, and was now perishing, nevertheless accepted the dare and passing his sword to Labouret, stepped up onto an overturned bucket and jumped into the barrel. As Alexandre's head re-emerged from the freezing water, the black coach in the road clattered past the yard's entrance. Seeing the yellow cockatrice on its door, with one voice Alexandre and Saint-George exclaimed, 'De Malpas!' They looked at one another with astonishment - they had a mutual enemy.

Marie called down to Alexandre, 'Hey! Stableboy! Catch!' and threw down a blanket.

As Alexandre climbed from the butt, he noticed Labouret aiming a speculative look up at his daughter. When the landlord directed the same increasing suspicious stare at Alexandre, he felt it prudent to leave at once. 'I'll be getting to the hayloft.' Labouret gave him a hard stare as Alexandre took back his sword.

'You have nowhere warmer?' asked Saint-George. 'More inviting?'

Marie's involuntary titter from above moderated seamlessly into a fit of coughing when it attracted her father's peeved attention. She pulled her head in and banged her window shut.

'No need,' said Alexandre, wrapping the blanket about him more closely and backing away, 'I shall be happy in the hay. Back in the hay I should say.' He strode off rapidly to prevent further discussion.

Saint-George called after him, ''Til the morrow then.'

†

The local militia were not able to return to their homes until much later that night. They had come running, once the fighting was over, and taken their time clearing the dead from the yard, mainly because Labouret broached a keg for them and they would not leave until they had emptied it. Now the inn and its immediate surroundings were quiet again. Still Alexandre lay awake. In spite of the blanket, the heaped up hay, and the animal warmth rising from the stalled coach horses below, he could not stop shivering.

When a soft glow lighted up the undersides of the roof beams, he lifted his head curiously. He heard the horses shifting about in their stalls at the disturbance. Someone had come into the stables. A point of light moved below, gleaming up from gap to gap between the rough-hewn planks of the hayloft's floor. The open trap door from the stable lit up as he heard the ladder rungs creaking. He sat up, his heart pounding, his mouth dry. A long pale hand hoisted a shuttered lantern through the trap door and pushed it into position to one side of the trap. Marie's head emerged far enough for Alexandre to see her eyes. She paused on the ladder, subjecting him to a solemn regard. Neither of them spoke. She stepped up another rung - a small mischievous smile that tightened the corners of her mouth came into view.

'Papa's on watch. Knows you are dangerous.' Marie came all the way up the ladder and stepped into the hayloft. She had thrown a thick black blanket round her against the cold night air. It trapped the ends of her dark hair. Made her look like a nun. 'I have your things.' She dropped a bundle at her feet - his empty scabbard and his buskins rolled out as it unfolded. Marie bent to pick up the lantern then hooked it above her head on a nail in the roof timber. Alexandre noticed her legs were bare. He made no comment. No doubt, she would reveal everything in good time.

'And something to warm you.'

'Brandy?' he gave a hopeful croak.

'No. Not brandy. You'd rather have brandy?'

'No. I want the... er... the warm something.'

Marie's smile promised nothing, everything. 'The warm something? You don't want to know what the something is?'

'I already know.'

'You do?'

'I can see it clearly from here.'

'You can?' squeaked Marie, dragging the ends of the blanket more tightly together.

'It looks soft and warm.'

She narrowed her eyes - he was grinning, just a little bit too widely. 'You're talking about the blanket.'

'What did you think I was talking about?' Alexandre laughed.

'This,' Marie said as, still gripping the ends of the blanket, she stretched her arms out wide. The lamp-illumined cruciform of her bare body a heraldry of gold against the sable wool. The sight of her stopped his laughter dead. She watched the change in his expression with growing satisfaction as initial stupefaction gave way to - worship? Laughing with astonished delight at the discovery that Alexandre adored her, Marie, a tease to the last, leant forward slightly, teetered for a long moment, and then let herself topple full length on Alexandre. The flutter of the blanket billowing behind her extinguished the lamp.

†

The lamp was alight again. Alexandre lay on his back; Marie lay on him, in his arms.

'You might have been killed,' Marie muttered into his chest, concluding aloud the silent argument with Alexandre she had been pursuing, and winning easily, in her head. No response. Her lover's chest continued to rise and fall with the same even rhythm. 'Alex?' She lifted her head, saw he was dozing. Being asleep doesn't stop him losing the argument she decided - and she needs to tell him he lost it.

She rose and straddled him. His breathing changed immediately, becoming faster, shallower. He seemed to be having trouble opening his eyes though she could see them working under the delicate lids. She gripped his ears and banged his head, not stopping until his eyes popped wide open.

'You could have been dead now too,' she began again. 'Lying out there. In the snow. With the other dead people. Instead of being alive. Here. With me.' A new argument occurred to her. 'We would never have...'

'I am here,' he interrupted sleepily. 'We have. And shall again, you keep on squirming like that.'

'Be serious. You aren't ordinary. You're the sort of man who carries a sword.' She pulled the scabbarded sword from the hay. 'Your own sword. It really belongs to you.'

Marie half drew the blade. The lamp light reflecting from it went skittering across their bodies as she examined the blade. 'Why did you fight? Why risk your life for him?'

'He was surrounded by his enemies. My enemies have taken everything from me. My whole world. Except my life.' He took the sword from her hands, 'and this sword,' slid the blade into its scabbard, laid it back on the hay. 'When the fighting was all over,' he continued, 'I felt Saint-George and I had become true brothers'.

'Run round naked with swords and you're brothers?'

'It was only me without any clothes.'

'You know, I think that worried everyone.' She returned to her theme. 'Brotherhood, Liberty? Equality too? You're one of these Jacobins aren't you?'

He felt it more dignified to address the sense rather than respond to the running sarcasm in her words. 'I hold those things dear. I would die for them.' Alexandre groaned inwardly. Why did he say that? Rhetoric would get short shrift from Marie in this frame of mind.

'Die for them? That makes you a real man.'

Oh. That's more like it. Rhetoric seems the right approach after all. 'You mean brave?' he fished. He had been brave after all.

Marie nodded - could be.

'Courageous even?'

Marie nodded a little harder - getting closer. That just left...

'Heroic,' said Alexandre, not trying to hide how proud he felt.

'Stupid,' she agreed, as if that was another way of saying the same thing. She shook her head in despair. 'To risk everything!'

'Wealth? Gone. Position? Gone. Family? Gone. What's left? I've nothing more to lose. Have I?'

She took hold of his ears again and pounded his head even harder this time. He seemed resigned to letting her murder him. 'Fool! Fool! Fool!' She stopped. He was looking up at her wonderingly.

'You care.'

Marie leaned forward to kiss him, softly, slowly. She looked down into his eyes for a moment, her long hair brushing against his face. 'I've no idea why.' She rapped her knuckles on his forehead. 'Boing! Boing! Nothing going on up here.' Marie settled back on her haunches. Wriggled her bottom. Cracked an anticipatory grin. 'Plenty everywhere else I'm pleased to say.'

†

From the roof of a low outbuilding, a cockerel crowed the sun up. In the stable loft, Alexandre slumbered on undisturbed in the hay. Down below among the snorting curious horses, Marie rescued her creased clothes from the feed-box where she had stuffed them the night before. She rushed to dress – Luc the the stableboy would be arriving soon to harness the teams of horses so the overnight guests could start the next stages of their journeys.

Marie pushed open the wicket in the stable doors and peered out into the yard. Melting snow dripped onto her head from the eaves above. Spring was coming. She was in love. Her eyes ranged across the yard. Good. All clear. Marie was about to dash across to the kitchen door when, with a startled gasp, she realized the motionless figure of a man stood where the snow had been scraped from the paving at the rear of the inn.

It was Saint-George, his posture still and relaxed yet full of imminent potency. Without any observable transitional movement, he initiated and completed a forward lunge onto his right foot, a drawn blade appearing from nowhere in his outstretched hand. Marie watched as he began to execute a sequence of exercises of increasing complexity without apparent effort.

The cock's second harsh call broke Marie's entrancement. Hoping to scamper unseen across the yard she froze mid-step when Saint-George whirled to face her. His quick smile of recognition warmed into a frank grin as his eyes flicked from hers to the stable from which it was plain she had just emerged, and from which Alexandre's snores rasped against the morning air. He saluted her with an eloquent flourish of his sword as, cheeks shining with embarrassment, she stalked to the longed-for sanctuary of the kitchen.

†

Alexandre woke sensing Marie had gone. His searching hand explored the empty place where she had lain. He sat up and gathered a double handful of girl-warm hay, pressed it to his face, inhaled the lingering odours of her body. He twisted the hay into a fragrant pillow, wedged it under his head and smiling slept again.

†

During the days following the foiled assassination attempt, Saint-George busied himself in discussing Alexandre's plans for the future. The more the Chevalier discovered about the young man the better he liked him and the more determined he became to offer a helping hand.

As commandant of one of the few cavalry regiments left in the new Republic, Saint-George was always on the lookout for officers of quality. Troopers he could raise easily. Plenty of freed Africans on the island of Santa Domingo - Haiti they were calling it now - volunteered for the military to earn house and plot as rewards for faithful service. On his recruitment expeditions to the colony, he enrolled officers for preference from the long-limbed former nomads of western Africa, the Fulani, the Temne, and the Mandinka. Even among these descendants of generations of fierce warriors, he had found no one able to take his place. Now in Alexandre he saw the military potential he had been seeking, the intelligence, the courage, the commanding physical presence.

Nor did Saint-George overlook Gabriel's future. The boy's spirited attempt to defend Alexandre made an impression on Lieutenant Demoncourt on their first meeting - his recommendation was enough to get Gabriel inducted into the Legion. Gabriel stayed in the Coin Inn so that he could attend Saint-George - though he seemed to devote more time to Marie whom he adored from the first. Each day he went to the Free American field headquarters that had been set up in farm buildings at the other end of Villers-Cotterêts. Here, he had weapons training and music lessons, to prepare him for his new position as the Legion's bugler.

Alexandre and Saint-George, with Gabriel trailing behind, rode in the idle silence of old acquaintances beside the blue-cold stream burbling in its rock-filled course next to the road. The spring sunshine glinted from the water where the brook rushed between stones or rippled in pools, fell on lush new pasture and greening copses and on the three companions - though not fully upon Saint-George. To the Chevalier's growing irritation each time he surrendered himself to the agreeable torpor induced by the sun's heat on his back, Alexandre's great height in the saddle cut off the warming rays.

'Alexandre. Must you spread your great shadow so widely? Rein back, I beg you, surely God has made sun enough for three?'

The Chevalier's peevish complaint roused Alexandre from his reflections. He slowed and cut in behind Saint-George to ride on his other side. He had been thinking about de Malpas. Saint-George had coaxed most of the details of Alexandre's short and disastrous association with his step-uncle, but had told him little of the part de Malpas played in his own history.

'Stop me if I pry,' Alexandre ventured, 'de Malpas. How do..?'

'In my company you may see much of him,' Saint-George cut in. 'we are in opposing camps. He feels he has unfinished business with me. For all his skill, he dare not face me in combat. Hence, these continual attempts at assassination.'

Alexandre was unable to disguise his curiosity. Saint-George sighed in reluctant acceptance of the young man's interest. 'Let us say,' he went on, 'The man exercised his sour wit on a lady. One whom...' He paused, how best to describe the oddities and complexities of his relationship with the Queen of France. 'This lady... I love.'

'You duelled.'

Saint-George lifted his shoulders in an eloquently dismissive shrug. 'Hardly. One blow, one wound.'

'Honour was satisfied. That was the end.'

'It would've been, but for how I ended it.' Saint-George pulled his horse to a stop and with another sigh, dropped his chin on his chest, making Alexandre strain to hear the next words. 'His tongue caused the offence.'

Alexandre saw again de Malpas leaning over him in the snow, felt the paralysing pressure of the sword on his belly. He remembered his step-uncle hissing at Gabriel, the rigid forked tongue quivering in the gaping mouth. 'You cut his tongue,' he said.

'His tongue caused the offence,' whispered Saint-George. With an effort, the Chevalier recovered his usual erect bearing. 'I wish I had not scarred him so, that was wrong.' Evidently deciding he had revealed enough, Saint-George looked about him, keen to change the subject. 'Since we are stopped let's rest the horses.' He pointed across the brook. 'Beneath those trees.'

They left the road and splashed across a fordable shallow. The horses slowed to snatch a drink. After a moment, the small party rode up the far bank into the shady wood and dismounted.

Saint-George examined Gabriel in his newly sewn lancer's uniform, his silver bugle sling over his shoulder. 'It's good to see you out of that man's livery, Gabriel.' He tossed his reins to the Legion's newest recruit. 'Don't permit the horses too much water.' Beckoning Alexandre to follow, the Chevalier strolled off along a narrow trail into the woods. A short distance on from the stream the track widened out into a quiet verdant glade dappled in pale cool light filtering through the freshly leaved treetops overhead.

Saint-George stopped before a tall ash that stood in the middle of the clearing. 'I had to promise your Marie you would come back from the Legion alive - with all her favourite bits and pieces still attached and in reasonable working order.

'Are you going to teach me sword fighting?' asked Alexandre.

'Teach? No. More unlearn. I will teach you Nothing.'

'Oh!' was all that Alexandre could think to say. He had been hoping for so much more.

'You fight well, but you use your blade like a peasant scything grass. Strength is not all. Big as you are, some other galumphing Goliath will come along and you'll be the one harvested. So. I will help you find a way to use that great sabre with delicacy. With finesse.'

The Chevalier held out his forearm and hand, the wrist locked stiff to make a blade. He pretended to slash across the trunk of the ash merely brushing the smooth bark with the tips of his fingers. 'You must learn to stroke your opponent's breast as gently as your lover's. Remember. Though the battle may end there,' he pressed his straightened fingers into the tree, 'your blade in his heart, it is always won, or lost,' he stabbed his finger into Alexandre's chest, over his heart, 'Here. In your own'.

'If I could fight like you.' No. Alexandre stopped the rushed words. He was presuming too much - Saint-George was a matchless genius. 'That is, more like you.' Still too presumptuous - Alexandre decided to cut his losses. Drawing himself up, he addressed the older man with extreme formality. 'Saint-George. I would be most honoured to become your pupil.'

Smiling, Saint-George nodded his acceptance. Eager to begin, Alexandre started to draw his sword. Saint-George folded his hand around Alexandre's fist and pushed the blade back into its scabbard.

'You won't need that. You haven't managed to cut your own feet or head off in practice so you must have had a fair fencing teacher. 'Everything you desire comes from Nothing. From stillness - inhuman speed of movement. From rest - inhuman strength and energy. The hand that holds the sword must be empty.'

With this aphorism, Saint-George fell silent. The wood, that had been so tranquil before, now seemed full of calls and stirrings, plashes and swirls, creaks and squeaks. Alexandre stood breathing quietly. At first his awareness sharpened, his perceptions deepened. Then by degrees his sense of self, of surroundings slipped away. The wood's sounds melded into a single frozen thread of birdsong - the mesmeric carrier wave almost drew Alexandre's soul from his body. A doe glided from a thicket, eyed the still men with calm liquidity, with one step more was lost to view.

†

Whenever Alexandre was in Saint-George's company, Labouret treated him as an honoured guest, indeed showed a real liking for him and more than ordinary respect. However, when Alexandre was doing his chores, Labouret made him work harder than the servants. The only concession the innkeeper made to his employee's dual status was to bring him in from the stables to lodge in a narrow roof chamber snuggled between two of the inn's huge rafters. Labouret had also taken the young man to a storeroom stacked with luggage left behind by careless or defaulting guests. A few garments fitted well enough to allow Alexandre to dress for dinner with Saint-George each evening. Marie and Gabriel served on these occasions, and Labouret sat with them when he could.

Saint-George was delighted to discover how comprehensive Alexandre's military education had been - the Count had made sure his only son was well prepared to follow in the family tradition of army service. 'Your tutor was Ferrer? A clever man. I served with him in the Netherlands. He did not suffer fools.'

'Indeed he did not,' Alexandre replied with feeling. 'But he was a good teacher. We took opposing sides and refought all the great battles of history.'

'Could you win against him?'

'Whenever I took the role of Claudius or Hannibal. He never understood elephants. You know he died in Haiti?'

'So I heard.'

They lifted their glasses in a silent toast to the old soldier.

†

Alexandre and Saint-George stood a dozen paces apart in a wood of slender young birch. The thin mist floating between the trees, softening the outlines of the silver-black trunks, was backlit and shot through here and there with golden beams as the sun's rim lifted over the unseen horizon. Both men stood, stripped to the waist, hip deep in a sea of leafy ferns with dew-heavy fronds that drooped over into the spongy ground litter. They made slow graceful passes with their swords - now with the right hand, now with the left. From time to time, the blades cartwheeled through the air from one man to the other without warning, yet in perfect synchrony.

†

Alexandre began to feel that Saint-George and Labouret were conspiring to keep him and Marie apart. No sooner had he finished with one man than the other appeared with something else that needed doing. At mealtimes, he was able to exchange a few words with Marie, and countless longing looks. Sometimes she would lean against his back as she served, or knot a finger in the hair at the nape of his neck as she stretched across him to refill a glass. Alexandre was relieved that Labouret failed to notice Marie's surreptitious caresses - he did not want the innkeeper's paternal suspicions reawakened.

In that quiet hour after lunch when guests retired to slumber in their rooms and Labouret dozed behind the closed door of his counting room, Marie would summon Alexandre to her side with a covert glance. There was a chamber at the back of the common room's great hearth, a storage space for the inn's linen stacked on slatted shelves. Here in the dim lavender warmth he could hold her and they could share whispered thoughts and kisses. As well they dared no greater intimacy for, inevitably, one day Labouret woke early from his postprandial snooze and, looking for Marie, discovered their trysting place.

Alexandre was first to become aware that the innkeeper was standing at the opened door. He tried to disengage from Marie but she, unwilling to part from him for so much as one of these stolen moments, pressed all the closer. Only when Alexandre gently pulled her arms from his neck did she realize they were no longer alone.

'As I suspected,' Labouret said in severe tones. 'You,' pointing at Alexandre, 'follow me.'

Marie caught at Alexandre's sleeve as he went to obey the innkeeper's command. She seemed about to utter something, had second thoughts, gave Alexandre a little push towards the door instead. He went after her father.

Labouret was already sitting in his leather-padded chair, burly arms folded magisterially across his chest, when Alexandre entered the counting room. The innkeeper unfurled an arm to point Alexandre to a seat in the corner. Alexandre felt eight years old again perched on the low stool waiting for the storm of parental anger to burst over him.

'As Marie's father and your employer, I believe I am owed an explanation,' Labouret began, in the same heavy tones he had used in the linen room.

'Sir. I love your daughter. I love Marie,' Alexandre blurted out.

Labouret frowned at him for a long moment, his lips paling as he clenched his jaws, fighting back some powerful emotion. Alexandre was astonished when tears started from the man's eyes. 'Thank goodness for that,' the innkeeper cried, slapping his palms on his thighs, 'It's plain my poor child loves you.' Labouret pulled Alexandre up from his stool embraced him and kissed his cheeks.

'It was never my intent to deceive,' Alexandre tried to explain between Labouret's delighted hugs. 'Without money of my own, I could not...' He never completed his sentence. The door swung wide open. Marie stood trembling with anger on the threshold.

'I will not wait outside being talked about,' she thundered. Astonishment washed the outrage from her face as she realized that Alexandre and her father far from being in dispute had their arms about each other. Then her eyes narrowed in suspicion. 'What are you two getting so cosy about?' She observed Alexandre's fond smile. 'Alexandre?' She noted her father's wet cheeks. 'Papa?'

'I want...' Alexandre began.

'He wants...' Labouret chimed in eagerly.

'To marry you,' they both roared in chorus.

Marie stared at them in round-eyed disbelief. 'You surprise me. Consent has not been sought.'

Alexandre looked to Labouret for guidance. Something was wrong. The older man should step in now, sort the misunderstanding out, use the greater wisdom he must have gained after years of dealing with women in general, and Marie in particular, to put things right. Labouret just gazed back at him with an expression that simply mirrored Alexandre's own perplexity.

If the innkeeper was not going to be of any help, then Alexandre would have to trust his own instinct. In addition, instinct told him that this was the moment to play his ace so he took her hand, looked into her eyes with eyes that were full of his deep and passionate love and said, 'Will you marry me, Marie?' Even as he spoke the words, he realized although this was the right thing to say, it was exactly, precisely and completely, the wrong time to say it.

'What can I say? No!' Marie spun on her heel and stamped away down the corridor.

Labouret ventured outside to watch her go. He looked back into the counting room at the mortified Alexandre. 'Perhaps you ought to..?' the landlord began to suggest, then fell silent, his shoulders slumped, and he came back into the room. He threw himself into his chair, buried his face in his hands, 'Then, what do I know?'

†

Marie would not speak to either man for the rest of that day and all the next. Nor for the day after that, even though she must have known that Saint-George was preparing to return to Paris, and that Alexandre would be going with him.

She did appear in the yard as the small party leaving for the capital got ready to mount their horses. Ignoring Alexandre, she kissed Gabriel goodbye. She kissed Saint-George goodbye. Then Marie broke her silence.

'I beg, Chevalier, that you teach this young man better manners.' Alexandre sighed inwardly; would Marie ever forgive the insensitive way he had proposed marriage? She glanced at him - his sigh of misery must have been audible after all. Her voice trembling, she quietly added, 'And pray you, keep him safe.'

With a relieved smile, Alexandre stepped forward to take her in his arms. At last, his punishment was over. Marie stepped back out of his reach. 'You presume Alexandre. Again, you presume. I will not be taken for granted. Not by you,' a look at her father,' not by others... who at their age should know better.'

Alexandre caught Labouret's heartfelt murmur in his ear, 'I know who that came from, and blessed be her memory'.

'Marie I beg your pardon most humbly. Won't you please forgive me?'

Marie seemed to relent. 'Do you mean to return?'

'Here?'

'Of course here.'

'Yes. Yes, I do.'

Marie smiled sweetly. 'Ask me then.' She whirled around and ran lightly back into the inn leaving the older men grinning and

Alexandre and Gabriel wondering what words, if any, in the short interchange made sense.

†

Two days later, with only another day's ride left to Paris, Saint-George sat on a boulder gazing across a wide lake at the setting sun. He tucked his violin under his chin, lifted his bow, and began to play a slow and plaintive air.

Gabriel had made a rod from a straight hazel pole cut from the hedge. When he had curried Saint-George's horse earlier, he had plucked enough hairs from its tail to make a line - a grey horse so the line would be well nigh invisible in the water. The hook was fashioned from a pin left by mistake in his new lancer's jacket by the seamstress, and discovered by him the painful way. A marsh tit's feather made a fine lure. He floated the knotted line over the backs of the trout darting in the deeper pools of a fast-running stream that tumbled down into the lake. Skill or luck had already won him two small fish from the torrent, which lay side by side in wet dock leaves by his foot: a third would give them all a tasty supper.

Alexandre exercised with his sword, alone at the lake's edge. His silhouette was dark against the soft pink and grey lights sent shimmering across the lapping waves by the crimson disc of the sun as it dipped beyond the far shore. The music caught Alexandre up, and lost him to the world. Under its influence, the exercise shifted into a dance of extraordinary grace. When the piece ended, he stood motionless for a few moments to let body, mind, and spirit reunite. When he looked up, a beatific smile shone from his face.

Saint-George lowered his violin. 'Yes that's right Alexandre. A good start. Dance. The best of us dance... only dance.'

PART THREE

Chevalier de Saint-George

ONE FOR ALL

Restless crowds of ragged, dirty, diseased, and underfed citizens prowled the narrow cobblestoned streets and tiny squares of Paris by day and night. Traders shouted at the thronging citizens with little expectation of making a sale. Street musicians struck up a tune, singing more for their own consolation than with any hope of reward.

According to their nature, pigs, dogs, and people, rooted, pawed, or picked in the mess of rotting filth clogging the narrow lanes around the Palais-Royale. Snarls and raised voices signalled the discovery in the stinking heaps of something worth fighting over. The victorious human scavengers dragged out the purple-faced corpse of a priest choked to death with his own rosary, and after stripping it of everything of any value, left the remains for the waiting beasts

Along the front of the Palais-Royale, a row of long pikes lofted the severed heads of men and women who gazed with empty sockets down at the milling townsfolk - some with looks of fresh surprise as if they had been sure and certain of their reprieve right up to the death stroke. The last thoughts written on the beak-drilled features of others never to be known, obliterated by the busy attentions of hordes of town sparrows that rose, resettled, and rose again over the grisly buffet.

A soldier of the Garde Nationale stood on duty at the door of a baker's shop in the square. The menace of the soldier's fixed bayonet subdued for the moment the surly queue elbowing its way towards open violence. The smell of loaves raked from hot ovens could tantalize hunger's grip beyond sullen endurance into sudden ungovernable rage.

In the entry to a nearby alley, a noisy and partisan crowd bet on a man and a woman, earlier customers at the bakery, as they brawled over possession of a loaf too small to share. No matter how severe the privation, people can always find a few coins for sport and pleasure.

A coach clattered at great speed across the square: black paint slapdashed on the door panels to hide once flaunted coats of arms; blinds pulled up to conceal from covetous eyes the fat cheeks and swaying dewlaps of the noble passengers.

A slowly moving pedestrian, undernourished muscles too wasted to spring to safety out of the coach's heedless path, was knocked down. The coach bounced to one side on leather springs as front and back bumped in turn over the victim's body, leaving it pulped by hooves and wheels. The air over the fleeing coach was of a sudden storm-dark with cobbles flung from every corner of the square by the crowd. The flying stones crashed down with a thunderous rat-a-tat-tat upon the coach's roof and panels.

'Dirty aristo.'

'We know you.'

'We'll be coming for you.'

The clop and scrape of iron-shod hooves on cobblestone intruded into the almost tangible silence of undischarged tension that followed the coach's escape from the crowd's retribution. Riders meant aristocrats. The crowd turned as one maddened beast to view this alternative prey.

Saint-George and Alexandre rode into the square on their way to meet Philippe-Égalité in the Palais-Royale to find the face of every citizen there turned towards them. At the sight of Saint-George's finery, the mob's seething wrath found a new vent, reignited, and flared to new heights. A hostile buzz whirred across the packed square. People stooped to pry up fresh missiles from the cobbled street. As the two riders slowed to a stop in the middle of the square, a killing ground opened up all around them.

A freckle-faced man strode into the cleared space. He looked around to gather everyone's attention then lifted one foot high and stamped it down - the sabot's boxwood sole slammed onto the cobbles, a musket-loud crack echoed off the buildings, bringing people out onto the narrow balconies overlooking the square. A man wearing sabots was an armed man - his kick could break bone, maim, or kill. As the freckled man stamped his other foot, all over the square others joined in. Within seconds, the square shook to the rhythmic din of scores of sabots hammering together on the stones, faster and faster. With each ear-splitting crash, the enclosing ring of vengeful citizens tightened perceptibly.

Unhurriedly, as if it had been his intention all along, Alexandre dismounted from his horse, and stepped into the thick of the crowd. The unexpectedness and breathtaking bravado of this act might have delayed, perhaps diverted, the imminent attack.

What defused the explosive situation entirely was the excited curiosity the sight of a giant suddenly on foot in their midst provoked in the slum dwellers of Paris. Smiles replaced scowls, clenched stones dropped to the ground, and the rhythmic stamping disintegrated into a noisy scramble to get close to the man who towered massively above the pale, stunted denizens of the urban alleyways. The infamous 'frogs' at whose merest croak even the most powerful in the land shuddered, flocked about Alexandre with the same childish delight as the simple peasants on his father's estates.

Saint-George sat on his horse for a moment longer, forgotten by the eager crowd that flocked about his young friend. A novel experience for him; not to be the centre of attraction. Given time, everything passes. When the new generation is ready to spread its wings, make room on the perch, or get shoved off. With a wry smile, the Chevalier dismounted too, and led his horse after Alexandre as the young man eased his way through the press of bodies.

Alexandre's admirers dropped away as they approached the Palais-Royale itself, to be replaced by the professional beggars and prostitutes gathered to accost the better-off patrons of the cafés and restaurants that occupied its lower floors. A middle-aged woman pushed her two pubescent daughters in their way. Misreading the men's refusals, she turned with a knowing leer to drag out the girls' even younger brother.

Ignoring these importunities, Alexandre and Saint-George left their horses with a stableman and went to climb the stairs up past the galleries of brothels and gaming places. Leading republicans patronized these, like the eating establishments below. The level above this contained the apartments of Philippe-Égalité, patron of the Free American Legion and the Palais-Royale's owner.

†

On a raised area at the far end of the audience chamber, Philippe-Égalité lounged in an ornate gilded chair, one foot resting on a brocaded footstool. A secretary hovered at his elbow. As they walked towards the dais, Alexandre glanced out of the tall windows that looked down on the square and across to the Tuileries Palace and the River Seine. No sound from the teeming streets they had just come through penetrated the silence of the room.

'Citizen Dumas,' the seated man began without preamble, 'your family is known to me. Your father, Count Davy de la Pailleterie. You do not use your patronym?'

Alexandre let the question, if question it was, hang in the air. He had told Saint-George everything of his recent history, but he did not wish to expose anything so intimate, so hurtful, to this supercilious man. Philippe-Égalité was not that interested after all, for he did not pursue the matter.

'The Countess,' he went on, 'Your stepmother I suppose? Mother. Not a word I ever thought to hear applied to her.' Philippe-Égalité must have known the Countess well. 'You do not share their royalist..?' Alexandre shook his head emphatically. 'No indeed. Why should you? Why should any of us? I myself prefer to be plain, unadorned, Philippe-Égalité. Citizen Égalité. A common man amongst common men.'

Philippe-Égalité gazed up at the ceiling for a moment, revelling in his ordinariness. 'The days of kings are numbered,' he said, returning to his theme, 'My brother will find this out for himself.' He leaned forward conspiratorially, 'Soon'.

Philippe-Égalité leaned back, crossing one leg over the other. 'You've read Paine? The Rights of Man?' He stretched a languid hand behind him, signalling his secretary with the merest flutter of fat white fingers. His man, anticipating this command, was already hastening to fetch the book from its shelf. Alexandre was astounded to see the elderly secretary kneel to make a lectern of his arms and chest for Philippe-Égalité to rest the book upon. The secretary had also found the page from which his master intended to read. Not the first time this little scene had been enacted.

'Lay then the axe to the root and teach governments humanity,' Philippe-Égalité quoted. 'Can you, Dumas, swing an axe at the roots of power and privilege in France? Will you join us citizen?'

A dismissive flick sent the secretary scuttling away to return the book to its place on the shelf.

'Saint-George,' said Philippe-Égalité, glancing at Saint-George, acknowledging his presence in the room for the first time. 'Saint-George detects some genius for the military in you, young man. He recommends a commission in my Free American Legion. Is this agreeable?'

'Yes,' Alexandre blurted in reply. He had been dreading the arrival of this moment since he had set out for Paris from the Coin Inn. Now it was past and he had what he wanted. He hoped Marie would be pleased for him - if she was talking to him. He started to express his gratitude with more formality, but Philippe-Égalité rode over his thanks.

'We have intelligence about de Malpas. A plot for the Royal Family to escape from France. I would let them be gone and good riddance but...' Philippe-Égalité uncrossed his legs and leaned forward again, resting his hands on his knees. 'Louis alone in exile? Hardly a threat. With Marie Antoinette?' His eyes slid across Saint-George's face. 'Few would miss her I imagine.' The Chevalier's expression did not betray his attachment. 'Would the Austrian Emperor invade? To help a fellow monarch? Probably. For his sister, our Queen's sake? Definitely!'

Philippe-Égalité rose to his feet and stepped to the edge of the dais. A deliberate ploy designed to let him loom over and dominate his audience. This time something felt out of place. 'Oh no,' he pressed on, his increasingly puzzled manner at odds with his forceful words. 'For France and Liberty. We cannot allow it.' Something was certainly wrong, but what? Philippe-Égalité tried to carry on. 'Whilst Marie Antoinette is here with us, France is safe.' He was so distracted, he was not really attending to what he was saying anymore, and his voice slowly trailed away.

Philippe-Égalité realized all at once what the problem was. Even though he had the advantage of standing on a platform, he still had to look up at Alexandre - he preferred, very much preferred, to look down on people. He reseated himself. With his sense of superiority restored by the authority conferred by the high-backed chair, he picked up where he had left off. 'Citizen Dumas. Is de Malpas still close to his sister?'

Alexandre hid his surprise at the question; or rather, the way Philippe-Égalité asked it, with a slight additional weight on the word 'close'. If he knew about the incestuous relationship of the siblings, he must know the Countess well indeed.

'I could not say citizen,' Alexandre replied as neutrally as he could. 'It's a year since I saw my home. I have never been on good terms with my stepmother. As for my father...' Alexandre could not think of any way to avoid talking of his private circumstances. 'My father disinherited me, and...'

Philippe-Égalité flapped a hand at him impatiently - evidently he did not want to hear any more. This did not interest him, or, perhaps he had all these personal details from his spies already.

'Would the Countess know anything of an escape plot?' Philippe-Égalité asked Alexandre directly.

'I know nothing Citizen.'

'I see,' Philippe-Égalité said, cutting Alexandre short. 'No help at all.' He threw himself back in the chair, and resting his chin on steepled fingertips, closed his eyes.

After a minute or more of silence, Alexandre risked a glance at Saint-George. What was going on? Saint-George just winked. The secretary approached them making little shooing gestures, indicating without words that the audience was over and they should leave.

†

Long after his visitors had gone, Philippe-Égalité remained slumped in the chair, brooding. Count Davy de la Pailleterie's son was suitable he supposed. At least Saint-George thought so. He resented having to look up at the fellow all the time. Perhaps he should have the dais raised, have another step put on the top.

He went to stand by the windows, to get a view of how much taller the extra layer might make him.

Philippe-Égalité looked out of the window, his attention caught by the sight of the Tuileries palace, where the King, Queen, and Dauphin were imprisoned. Well not exactly imprisoned, more involuntarily entertained. Should he turn a blind eye, let his elder brother escape? Leaving the throne vacant. An appealing idea, a secret desire. With a strong new sovereign on the throne, might not republicanism wither and die? Philippe VII. A potent name. King Philippe of France. Just a dream. Where would he find the political support to put him on the throne? The royalist faction regarded him as a traitor already, and his Jacobin allies would instantly become enemies if he abandoned his egalitarian stance. No, he decided. Regrettable. But no.

'Have the Countess Davy de la Pailleterie arrested,' he called to the secretary. 'I should like to renew our acquaintance...' I had rather be an old fool's wife than a young fool's mistress she had jeered at him, then married that desiccated lizard Count Davy to prove her point. We are going to deal on my terms this time, he promised himself. Scare her a little, he thought, and who knows, she might well reconsider his offer.

Philippe-Égalité called after the secretary. 'The Count too. Why leave him at home worrying about what I'm doing with his pretty wife? Let's see if either of them knows of de Malpas' whereabouts or what mischief he plots.'

†

De Malpas strolled along the Quai des Tuileries beside the Seine's cold dark waters. A little way ahead, a young boy tugged and twisted at his mother's hand. He tugged until his squirming hand slipped from hers. He was off immediately, with his matronly mother in heavy-footed pursuit. The playful child halted, let the woman nearly catch him, and then scrambled up out of reach onto the broad top of the riverside parapet. The mother's exasperated cries turned to shrieks of apprehension as her son teased her by skipping along the broad top of the embankment wall.

Turning his head to laugh to his mother, he tripped over his own feet, lost his balance, and tumbled backwards out of sight. A frightened yell from the other side of the parapet, a small, distant splash, all too certain confirmations of his fate.

The frantic mother tried - failed - to see over the just too high wall. Despairing, she turned that way, she turned this. She saw de Malpas, beckoned him to her with an urgent gesture, and threw herself again with reckless determination at the parapet, scratching frenziedly at the ground polish of its dressed stone to gain a finger hold on the far edge. At last, she was able to drag her ample bulk up onto the flat upper surface.

As de Malpas strolled nearer, she had one knee up. By the time he reached her, she had managed to get both knees up and crouching on parapet's top could see at last her darling boy struggling in the current as the swift waters carried him away.

Without breaking step, de Malpas brought his forearm up sharply under her protruding toes, upending her, head-over-heels, into the murky flow below. One second she was there, the next she was gone from sight - too surprised to so much as scream. Well, the grinning man thought as he sauntered across the road to the Tuileries, anything to help, a boy needs his mother.

In the gardens of the Tuileries palace, de Malpas soon found the personage he had been summoned to meet - Louis XVI. The portly King of France stood by an ornamental pond. Around his slippered feet, exotically feathered waterfowl squabbled, greedy for scraps. Possibly the last poultry in the starving city, their unlikely survival depended on continual patrols by the King's Swiss Guard and a daily ration of fresh bread from the King's own hand.

Two elderly advisors escorted Louis. All three were in fine clothes that rivalled the beauty and delicacy of the pallid lilies floating on the untroubled waters of the pond. Nearby the ladies and gentlemen of his, much reduced, court flirted and gossiped, greedy eyes as alert as any duck's for titbits from the King's hand.

The King nodded absently at de Malpas' deep courtier's bow, his main attention reserved for a party of more soberly dressed republicans that approached along the lakeside path. They were led at a brisk pace by a round fleshy man - at first glance much like Louis himself in appearance - except that the eyes of Philippe-Égalité glittered with an intelligence that Louis had always found frightening, not possessing much of that attribute himself. Louis also thought that his younger brother's eyes revealed covetousness, envy and ambition - three more attributes that he was grateful he also lacked.

Philippe-Égalité delayed his progress towards the Royal party to say a word of warning to Saint-George - who walked at his side attended by Alexandre. 'I see de Malpas with the King,' he said with a meaning look. He knew a long-standing enmity lay between Saint-George and Louis' spy, and he knew why.

'Your Highness,' said Philippe-Égalité as he came up to King Louis. He had renounced his own title of Duke of Orléans but could not bring himself to address his older brother as Citizen. 'Do I find you well today?'

'What is well brother? You're not too poorly yourself?'

'Painful backache. Perhaps I should hunt more? Shake up the liver.'

'How I wish I could still hunt,' said Louis with regret. 'Of all things, I enjoy hunting the most. But your Assembly forbids me even so small a pleasure.'

'We think that finding yourself on the back of a fast horse might prove too...' Philippe-Égalité smiled with fraternal malice, '...too tempting'.

'I might leave you mean? Here? I love living here... in this rattrap. Dear Philippe, don't encourage me to such fantasies.'

During the brothers' exchange, de Malpas had begun to seethe under the coolly contemptuous gazes of Saint-George and Alexandre. Finally, he could take no more. 'Forgive my interruption Highness, but I see some familiar faces in Citizen Égalité's entourage.' De Malpas stepped forward - he would enjoy ruffling Saint-George's feathers. 'Saint-George? Up? Before noon? And such busy nights.'

This unsubtle reference to the Chevalier's intimate relations with the Queen mortified de Malpas' royal master much more than his intended victim. Louis, the Queen's husband, stirred uncomfortably. Philippe-Égalité, the Queen's brother-in-law, raised a handkerchief to his mouth to mask a small spiteful smirk. Similar covert twitches flitted across the features of the King's followers - at least those not in his direct sight.

'I get up early to punish insults.' The Chevalier's tone of voice was mild, but de Malpas jerked back as if something carnivorous had bitten him. Saint-George's smile belied the menace in his steady gaze. Realizing that his ill-judged jibe had nearly provoked a fatal challenge, de Malpas searched desperately for a way out. His eye fell on Alexandre - a much less perilous target for his raillery. 'The People's Champion,' he mocked, 'Not dead yet then?'

'Not yet. I have a small score to settle first.'

Bored at de Malpas' pettish attempts at provocation, Philippe-Égalité turned his shoulder on him and addressed Louis. 'Highness, I must protest. This animal of yours fouls the path.' Without waiting to see how Louis would respond, Philippe-Égalité set off across the lawns. Alexandre and Saint-George bowed to the King and followed their employer.

They caught up when he paused at a large fountain carved like a mountain torrent.

'I admire your taste in enemies, young man.' Philippe-Égalité did not look directly at Alexandre as he addressed him, indeed he ignored the naked nymphs and satyrs frolicking in the pool too, his eyes roamed the Tuileries gardens instead as he spoke. 'You seem to have offended the most dangerous person in France.'

'The most vicious perhaps,' Saint-George corrected, 'Alexandre has had the good sense to make a friend of the most dangerous.' The Chevalier tried to execute the modest bow that usually excuses such blatant boasting - but failed, having little innate talent, and no practice at all, in the art of self-effacement.

'You have the truth of it,' Philippe-Égalité agreed vacantly, still surveying the lawns. His head swept from side to side as he searched for something or someone among the trees and shrubs. Alexandre was about to ask what or whom he sought with such diligence when, with a rustle of leaves, a young boy appeared from behind the fountain and with a murmured apology in Philippe-Égalité's direction, set off half-running back along the path they had come.

Philippe-Égalité's intent posture relaxed immediately. He turned to Alexandre and Saint-George with a look of relief and satisfaction though he did not volunteer any explanation for what had just happened. Without a word of farewell to either man, Philippe-Égalité strode away in the direction of his apartments in the Palais-Royale.

†

Meanwhile the King's party had continued round the lake and come to an arched gateway which gave entry into a high-walled secret garden in the shelter of which frost-tender fruits from the south could be cultivated. The King pushed open the gate and went through with his advisors. De Malpas followed them into the enclosed garden. The hot unmoving air was heavy with the drone of bees, the zip of sapphired dragonflies, and the arid pungencies of Provence.

As soon as de Malpas got through the gate, he spun on his heel in the path to confront the courtiers that crowded after him. The chattering nobles about to come through the narrow gateway froze at the hatred in the scowl he directed at them. He had heard their stifled sniggers at his humiliation by Saint-

George. Laugh at him would they? He went on glaring, his look becoming madder by the moment. They began to mill about uncertainly, backing away out of the garden, unwilling to defy this notorious duellist who additionally seemed half-insane.

Only one of their number refused to be cowed - an austere marquess of ancient blood ready and willing to protest at such unmannerly treatment. Grinning fiercely, de Malpas slammed the heavy iron gate full in her face, leaving her to stagger back speechless with fear and outrage into the arms of her peers.

Louis sighed; he had watched the clash from the corner of one eye as he pretended to be lost in admiration at the crop of juicy cordon peaches ripening against the old red bricks. He had to ignore much now that he would not have tolerated, or even been exposed to, earlier in his reign. If only de Malpas were not so central to the plan for the Royal Family's escape. The man was nothing but trouble these days, his obsession with Saint-George had all but deranged him - but who else was there?

He saw a good peach but he was unwilling to soil his brocaded slippers in the thick mulch of damp leaf mould piled beneath the wall. He was thinking to send an advisor to find a gardener for the task when, fortuitously, a young boy with a trug let himself in at the gate.

Louis beckoned and the lad ran to bow in front of him. The King thought he looked more an apprentice than a proper gardener, not that it mattered - the boy who did not know how to pick a peach had not been born. Louis pointed at the fruit he wanted. After a few false tries - not that one, that one - the boy's fingers circled the chosen peach, and twisted it deftly from the bough.

Louis spat out the first bite - the flesh was not as ripe as it appeared at a distance. Vexed, he hurled the peach with all his force at the gardener. The boy swayed a little to one side, enough to let the peach go by him, but not enough to seem disrespectful. Louis sent him to climb on the lower branches to reach another peach that looked perfect. Louis sank his teeth in it. It was perfect. He strolled back to where the advisors and de Malpas waited for him.

'About our escape,' began Louis. 'We have decided...' He got no further in his exposition than that.

'Not now Highness!' cried the advisors in agitated unison. 'No no no no no,' they begged, 'Not now.'

'What not! What not! We're out here on our own.'

'But we are not private, Your Highness.'

Louis was getting tired of these continual challenges to his authority. Why couldn't they just do what he wanted without putting real or, in this case, imagined difficulties in the way all the time? With sarcastic theatricality, he peered into all four corners of the garden. It was empty, as he knew it to be. 'It's plain is it not, there's no-one here but we four?'

The advisors jerked their heads, and pointed their hands, over the King's shoulder. Louis turned as they indicated. The youthful gardener stood with his back to them by the peach tree, tying up a branch that had dropped under the weight of fruit. Surely they could not mean..? Since when where menials thought of as people?

'That is a gardener. A stupid brute.' the King drawled, by way of, surely needless, explanation. His audience gave emphatic nods - it was the boy they meant.

The King threw back his head and stared up at the sky, breathing heavily. Servants? People? Servants! What did it matter what menials saw or heard? Next, these opinionated advisors would stop him peeing in the hedge if a horse or dog were watching. With all his heart, he wanted these endless days of impotence and anxiety to be over. His deepest wish now was to become a retired gentleman, living a quiet life with his family in the country. Some other country... obviously.

'Go away,' he bellowed at the gardener, who leapt from the tree and scampered out of the garden. The King gestured with a limp-wristed hand at the advisors. 'Tell de Malpas about this escape. Give him the orders for General Choiseul. I'll just...'

Exhausted, Louis wandered over to a bench and slumped down on the hard slats - then with a slow smile that lit up his usually melancholic features, remembered the peach, forgotten in his hand. As the advisors closed in about de Malpas, the King slurped the peach's soft flesh. Its copious syrups dripped from his chin soaking, unregretted, into the elaborately knotted and starched linen folded around his throat.

†

It was the dark of the moon, and the night hid a large part of the great press of peasants milling about the steps and terraces at the front of Chateau Davy de la Pailleterie. They encircled and pushed against a disciplined, but woefully insufficient, detachment of Garde Nationale which had brought out the Count and Countess through the tall entrance doors. The officer in charge and his militiamen struggled to protect the recklessly defiant Count from injury though not insult. Slowly, they pushed their way through the densely packed mob toward the coach that waited to carry the prisoners off for interrogation by Philippe-Égalité.

Buffeted in the surging crowds, the Countess' maid Aimée could only look on apprehensively, powerless to help except by keeping safe the jewels her mistress had entrusted to her at the militia's arrival.

There was a blaze of light as the heavy main doors of the chateau were pushed open again, and swung back to crash against their stops. A frantic group of would-be looters filled the doorway, escaping from inside. The ragged figures leapt from the threshold, launching themselves bodily onto the hastily backstepping crowd.

The cause of their panicked flight was a huge white-hot fireball that roiled behind them across the instantly vaporized carpets of the great hall. Hundreds of candles melting in the elaborate chandeliers that hung over the conflagration let down long runnels of wax up which rushed eager flickers of coruscating fire, shattering the multifaceted crystals above and setting fire to the upper floors. On each side of the great hall, gilt-framed paintings and ancient tapestries blistered and burst into ruin as the intense heat curled them from the walls.

The out-rushing ball of flame slowed at the entrance then stopped, as if to catch its breath. Its direction reversed, back it went into the interior of the chateau, as the fire inhaled a great draught of fresh oxygen through the newly opened doorway. The inrushing whoosh of air sucked the terrified and enthralled spectators' hats and bonnets through the entrance into the conflagration - only the automatic grabbing of their mothers saving several of the smallest children from tumbling after.

The heart of the fire now boomed up the virtual chimney made for it by the grand staircase to glow like a trapped sun in the glass cupola high above on the black slated roof. For one moment, the stairhead roof-light shone out brightly as a mariners' beacon over the surrounding countryside - then the fury of the fire trapped within blew out its fragile panes. A red-gold fountain of scintillating glass fragments floated down in a razor-edged drizzle on the upturned faces in the gardens below, scarring the unwary many, blinding the unlucky few.

Taking advantage of this distracting spectacle, an improvised commando of peasant matrons buttocked their way through the militiamen's line to drag the Count and Countess out of custody and into the surging mass of people. The burly women pulled at his arms, stretching the skinny Count between them tight as a clothesline. They ran their powerless victim with gathering speed back towards the open furnace of the great hall, letting go at the last second, leaving him to race on alone, helplessly, into the roaring inferno. The Count surely died instantly, but for a second or two the slight figure waved its arms, swimming in the sea of blue and green flame, flesh crackling and popping into cinders as the corpse sank out of sight.

No such clean death by instant immolation for his wife. The detested Countess was getting the first taste of what promised to be a lethal succession of limb-wrenching bone-breaking bumps. They tossed her high up into the air. 'ONE!' they yelled. Even the children kicked and tore at her when she fell back to the ground. 'TWO!' the mob howled as up she sailed again, twisting bloody and tattered high above their heads.

With the crowd absorbed in the joys of retribution, the Garde Nationale's detachment was able to regroup and regain the initiative. Bayonets levelled in a wedge formation, they pressed determinedly back into the mêlée in the direction of where she was last seen to fall, driving the Countess' tormenters before them. Self-possessed in spite of cruel abuse and torn clothing, the fallen Countess lifted her head, quickly appraising the new situation as the militiamen formed a defensive wall around her. She got up on her knees, the better to project the full force of her predatory appeal at the middle-aged officer who came to bend solicitously over her. The Countess threw her arms about his hips and gazed up to beseech him, 'Citizen! Save me!'

She appeared not to notice her passionate entreaties repeatedly swung the weight of a naked breast against his thigh - though the man himself could think of little else. With a grace not entirely buried beneath wattled cheeks and swaying belly, the officer gallantly shed his greatcoat and drew it around her naked shoulders. He readied his men; they brought their muskets up to their shoulders. 'Take aim!' he commanded. 'Back!' he warned the surly crowd, 'Back all of you or my men will fire!'

Faced with the threat of the militia's levelled guns the mob quickly lost its interest in blood sports, dispersing instead to loot the parts of the chateau not already reduced to ashes. The officer, satisfied that his prisoner was safe from harm from the crowd for the moment, turned his attention again to the Countess. She drew his arm around her, leaning her whole body length against his, as he helped her to the coach. Feeling the pressure of the bolstered hip, the slide of the supple thigh moving against his, the captivated officer's hopes of more intimate acquaintance soared to certainty. He tightened his embrace proprietarily.

A slack-jawed Garde handed the woman up into the coach, ogling the pale softnesses that briefly shone in the folds of the flapping greatcoat. He got ready to pull himself up into the coach after the woman. Amused at the effrontery of the young man's crude gawking, the sergeant slapped the Garde's eager foot off the step.

'No Lapin. The officer will escort the prisoner on this occasion. You can mount... his horse.'

Under his breath the Garde muttered, 'Equality? That'll be nice when it comes'.

With a smirk that mingled contempt at the randy private's futile pretension with anticipation of his own imminent enjoyment of the lady, the officer carefully set his own boot on the step.

The Countess leaned forward in her seat so that she could address him face to face through the open door. 'You are a hero Citizen. There's no doubt in my mind a fitting reward for your bravery awaits you...' Her mouth curved slowly into a sensuous promise. He could not look away from her cushioned lips, hardly heard the hope-pulverizing words they next shaped. '...But not here, maybe in Heaven.' The laughing woman jerked the door closed with a vigorous finality that might have cost him a kneecap had he not snatched his leg away.

Aching with humiliation and slapped-down arousal, the officer gave a deep bow as the coach pulled away, holding the pose overlong in an attempt to conceal his mortification from the uncouth attention of his subordinates. He was surprised and touched at the respect, the delicacy of understanding demonstrated by the sergeant and the private in this difficult moment. They abstained from jocular comment or, what would have been worse, rough masculine sympathy. They simply executed a smart about-turn and marched away.

As he looked after them, his gratitude slowly shifted to suspicion then to anger. Their shoulders, their shoulders were shaking up and down. A few pained snorts of their ineffectively suppressed mirth carried back to him through the night air. Still in plain sight, the two men fell to their knees, poleaxed by glee, brought low by merriment, pounding the earth with their fists as ungovernable laughter finally overwhelmed them.

†

It was some days before Alexandre learned from Saint-George that his father had died resisting arrest. He always thought the Count would send for him eventually, that there would be reconciliation, and that this would expose his stepmother's lies. Now that familial healing could never be.

Alexandre arrived early in the morning at the gates of his late father's estate, his stepmother's now he supposed. Behind him trailed a small detachment of Free American lancers - Gabriel and Demoncourt had insisted on riding with him too. He was not sure of his own reasons for coming. The Garde Nationale found no trace of his father's remains the day after the incident, when they returned in force to make sure the mob had dispersed.

The countryside outside the estate walls had been silent as their company approached, deserted except for occasional far off figures, half-crouched as if ready to turn and flee, watching as they passed. The gatehouse gave ample evidence of violence done by many hands. Its lower windows had been broken open.

The front door hung out into the road, swinging from one twisted hinge. Alexandre leant down from his saddle to peer in awkwardly through the ground floor window. The room inside was bare. The rioters had thoroughly ransacked the property.

There was a clatter of sabots on the bare wooden steps of stairs inside the house. Alexandre shouted, 'Who's there?' An unseen door slammed. He threw himself from his horse and sped round to the back of the gatehouse, just in time to see the groom and his wife running away into the orchard with stolen clothing and blankets in their arms. 'Pierre! Cécile! Come back!' The pair looked back in astonishment and terror at the sight of him. 'I only want to talk,' he promised. The couple exchanged a deciding glance then dropped their booty and ran off into the trees.

Alexandre returned to the front gates puzzled and hurt at his reception by such old friends. Perhaps they had been involved in his father's death? Perhaps they believed the Count's son meant to revenge himself on them?

He realized he was gripping the bars of the gates as he had gripped them once before all those momentous months ago. This time, the gates swung open at his push with a muted squeal of reluctant welcome.

Once inside the grounds he directed his horse off the gravelled main avenue to approach the kitchen quarters at the back of the chateau along a green ride that led through stands of old gnarled fruit trees. The lancers followed behind, without speaking, respecting the sombre introspection of their commander.

The troop's almost noiseless arrival in the orchard surprised the ragged men and women stripping unripe apples from the trees. The peasants fled in all directions at the sight of the soldiers, abandoning their overturned baskets of unripe fruit in fright. Alexandre kneed his horse a little way into the thick of the orchard after them, hoping one soul braver than the rest might stay to talk to him.

He got down from his horse to present a less intimidating figure. As he went in under the trees, a dozen dirty children dropped from the branches all around him to run shrieking through the long grass after their parents. Sadly, he recalled how often these same children must have run to greet him in better days when he was just M'sieu Hercule. Now all they saw was the uniform and the mounted soldiers. Alexandre gave up any further attempts to communicate.

The roofless walls and blackened windows glimpsed above the trees, as they approached, helped prepare him for the first sight of the destruction visited on his old home. Who had fought the flames? Clearly no one. Indeed, it looked as if the mob fed the fires with anything burnable that they did not want or could not carry off. The fire must have raged for days, gutting most of the chateau. Some trick of the architecture or the prevailing wind had preserved his father's conservatory intact. In all that great ruin, it alone remained habitable. Indeed as they dismounted, sounds of music and laughter drifted from that direction towards them.

'Wait here please,' ordered Alexandre.

'Citizen-Captain,' said Demoncourt, 'They could be inside. What if they recognize you - the Count's son?'

'As you wish,' Alexandre conceded the wisdom of his lieutenant's words.

The lancers followed their captain towards the conservatory, leaving the Corporal and Camille to mind the horses. The corporal looked at Camille and shook his head in wonder at the roundabout workings of Fate.

'He's got brains. He's strong as an ox. Women? Women love him. But God has looked down and said, Captain Alexandre Dumas. You've got more than your share. I'm taking back the chateau,' said the Corporal.

Camille considered this. 'I'd have said, take the brains God. I will need the chateau to keep all these women in.'

†

Alexandre entered the conservatory unnoticed at first by its occupants. Most he recognized - they were the chateau's former servants, known to him since childhood. Some wore items rescued from the wardrobes of their late master and mistress, pulled haphazardly and without consideration of appropriate gender over their own clothes. Most had crude headdresses and necklaces fashioned from orchids and parrot feathers. The former chamberlain, the only man to prefer a tall beribboned court wig - an essential accessory for the Countess' silk ball-gown he wore hanging off one bare shoulder. In the wreckage of once-lush jungle undergrowth, a half-comatose maid clumsily obliged a wine-impaired footman on a litter of giant fern leaves.

The mob had smashed up the Count's desk in their search for anything that burnt. A small cooking fire fuelled with fine veneers and inlays smouldered eye-wateringly on the paving stones. Heat and smoke from previous meals had already browned and shrivelled the leaves of the nearer plants. A monkey's carcase - spitted on a sword balanced between upended desk drawers - sizzled deliciously over hot ashes. Wicker baskets of wine salvaged intact from the deepest cellar were stacked amongst the torn and battered greenery. The floor was a hazard of rolling empties through which the befuddled servants kicked and stumbled as they danced to the arrhythmic sawing of the gardener's fiddle.

These various pleasures slowed to a halting stop as the lancers crowded in behind Alexandre. Once Alexandre was recognized, drunken bonhomie replaced the initial anxiety of the revellers at the sight of armed men.

'It's Al everyone,' announced Maurice after a swaying scrutiny of Alexandre.

'Al? Al who?' asked Marc.

'Big Al. Used to live here.'

'Oh that Al,' said Marc. 'Never seen him before in my life.'

'Respect Marc. He's a count.'

'He is a count Maurice. And I reckon his mate's another.'

Alexandre turned to Demoncourt, 'Is anyone sober here?'

'You'll have no sense from them. Any of them.' Demoncourt lifted a bottle from an open case to read the label. 'The pick of your late father's wine cellar. He kicked at the fire. The lieutenant picked up the sword spit. 'This is a fine blade.' He scraped the greasy monkey carcase off using the side of his boot and held the weapon out for Alexandre.

Alexandre was looking at the remains of the monkey on the floor. He knew this must have been his father's pet. It had always done exactly what its master had done. It had copied him right up to the last - burnt to cinders, just like its master.

Alexandre finally took the sword from Demoncourt, but did not even glance at the long blade. For a moment, he stared away into the mid-distance, making the little testing movements of the hand that reveal a weapon's quality and mettle. His father's armoury had contained many swords but this had a familiar weight and balance that made it instantly identifiable to the man who held it. Alexandre sighed. 'It belonged to a fine man - in many ways. It's my father's sword.'

'We can duck a few of these in the lake,' offered Demoncourt. 'Then we will find out who's responsible.'

'Who's responsible? Who are the culprits? Who the victims? I know how the people were mistreated. I will not be their judge and jury now, even for his sake. We'll go. There's nothing here for me. My farewells were, I now find, said long ago.' He lifted the sword and gave a wry smile, 'My inheritance.'

†

Night skulked in early beneath the thunderclouds that had rumbled since dawn along the Belgian frontier as the enemy allies gathered their armies. With the coming of dark, the storm's promise paid out in full measure with awesome crashes, flashes, and driving rain that doused the sleepless exiles' camp, thrumming the fabric of their tents and puddling the hoofmarks of hundreds of miserable horses that shook and shivered in long lines across the encampment.

When the French aristocrats became exiles, abandoning their ancestral lands to escape death or ruin at the hands of the revolutionaries who now ruled the country, the national army lost nearly all its mounted regiments. The aristocracy was the cavalry. The fleeing officers had galloped their strings of horses to swell with their thousands the already overwhelming numbers of the combined Austrian and Prussian armies of invasion that loomed here at the border.

The tent of General Choiseul, the French exiles' commander, was so brightly lanterned against the night and the storm that his staff moving about inside projected stark misshapen silhouettes of themselves upon the bleached canvas of the tent walls. The King's clandestine messenger stood, scowling with impatience under the meagre shelter of the awning over the entrance, one hand holding back the entrance flap.

As soon as de Malpas heard the General's voice speak his name, he thrust his way in, barging past the startled officer coming to admit him. Choiseul glared up from his desk, anger flaring at de Malpas' brusque entry. He relented when he saw the exhaustion that drew his visitor's handsome features into a rigid mask.

'Wet. Miserable. Hope it's important,' he said, pushing a bell-shaped bottle across the desk. The weary man half-shook his head as he drew a leather wallet from the inside pocket of his sodden greatcoat. The General leaned forward with interest.

'I come straight from King Louis,' said de Malpas, passing a heavily sealed letter from the wallet to the General.

Choiseul read rapidly from greeting to signature then again more carefully. Finally he slid a small wooden chest that sat on his desk towards him and unlocked it. Looking at de Malpas over the open lid as he dropped the orders on top of other confidential papers, he said, 'No more spying. Rejoin your regiment. When the time comes, take your hussars to France.

Rendezvous with King Louis at Sainte-Menehould. You will rescue the Royal Family.'

†

Alexandre had spoken little during the ride back from the burnt out chateau. The escort had left Alexandre and Gabriel at the Coin Inn before going on to the Free Americans' field quarters. Outwardly, Alexandre seemed unaffected by his visit to the scene of his father's death, but he had fallen into a self-absorbed reverie so intense that his companions were unwilling to disturb him.

All his thoughts had been of his father. When Alexandre was a boy, their relationship had been simpler, stronger, the mutual love unqualified. In the misery of his expulsion and exile he had forgotten those years, that love, the essence of that man.

His introspective mood persisted after he arrived at the inn, even though he had the joy of seeing Marie again. She understood at once the nature of the burden he carried, saw too, with amazement, that he was unaware that grief was the source of his melancholy.

'Sit here in the shade and rest from your journey my love,' Marie said, settling him at a table outside. She laid her hand on the nape of his neck, gently rolling the small curls at the back of his head with the ball of her thumb. 'Shall you want drink? Are you hungry?'

'Can we just walk Marie?'

She took his hand and they started up the overgrown track behind the inn together. The sun was so warm on their backs that, almost immediately, his hand became hot in hers. Marie pulled them to a stop to push at the backs of each of her shoes in turn with the other foot, to lever them off. Then she stretched up to ease the strap of Alexandre's lance-cap from under his chin. He bent his head to accommodate her, obedient as a child home from school, smiling his gratitude as he let her ease the confining helmet from his head.

Marie left her shoes at the side of the path to be retrieved on their way back. Alexandre yoked his arm across her shoulders, more like a friend than a lover, as they resumed walking. Marie hooked her arm round his waist and swung the lance-cap by its chinstrap from her free hand, knocking the heads from oxeye daisies and wild marigolds with the edge of its mortarboard.

Before long, they were able to turn and look down on the mossy, red-clay roof tiles of the Sign of the Coin. Marie waved to Gabriel who had taken Alexandre's place at the table in the garden below them and was visibly enjoying the food and drink Alexandre had declined. Gabriel interrupted his meal to stand and bow politely in response.

Where the path led into the trees they found a wayside shrine so neglected that a dense tangle of ivy and briars and nets of twisting woodbine had almost taken it over. Half hidden in a recess in the rotting brickwork, a chipped and glaze-crackled Madonna gazed meditatively at the sun-withered posy of meadow weeds laid at her feet long ago by some passing Romany child. Judging this to be the moment to begin helping Alexandre come to terms with his unacknowledged bereavement, Marie, not wishing to push Alexandre into confronting too soon how he felt about his father, instead asked more peripherally, 'Of what is the Countess accused?'

Alexandre shrugged his shoulders. Marie was jolted from her carefully composed expression of neutrality at this normally considerate man's lack of interest in his stepmother's fate. Alexandre's eyes shifted away from hers under her puzzled scrutiny. He took a step up the path as if to cut off further questions.

She caught at his arm. 'Be careful here Alex. There's an old well somewhere hereabouts.' Holding him tightly as much for her own safety as his, she stretched her bare foot out before her, exploring under the cool damp mat of grass with her toes. Parted, the long grass revealed the rim of the thick round slab of weathered sandstone that capped the well - it rocked slightly at her probing, making a hollow grating sound. 'We must take care. It's deep.'

Marie pushed Alexandre back to a safe distance and put her arms around his neck, leaning back to look up into his face. She studied him minutely. 'Your stepmother's fate. You seem unconcerned.'

'We tolerate each other for father.' Alexandre looked uncomfortable now; his face animated at last by some deep emotion, though one she could not readily interpret. Not embarrassment, not guilt. Perhaps something of these - and something darker? She waited, letting the silence draw out. He snatched a downward glance at her, looked away. 'And for his memory's sake, I shall endeavour to see she's not treated ill.'

Encouraged at least, that the resolution to take some positive action had perhaps let some small element of reality break into his morbid self-absorption, she led him out of the shading trees to a quiet sun-filled pasture she knew. There she pulled him down into the sweet-smelling grass. Marie reached up to frame his face in her hands, lifted her lips to kiss each eye tenderly. Her gesture unlocked some hidden door within him. As she hugged him to her, she felt the first great sob shake itself free from the core of his being as Alexandre at last began to weep for his lost Papa. Their lovemaking after was gentle, healing.

†

Later Marie knelt in the grass at Alexandre's side. He lay on his back watching the shifting cloud-sculptures in the sky. She watched his face. There was much she did not know about this man.

'Alex, must you be the new Count?'

'No! No. No fear of that. I was disowned.'

'I still don't understand how that happened.'

'She did it. I cannot say why myself.'

'You mean... the Countess? Is she evil then? Alex, I love you. You can't make me stop. Is there something bad you're not telling me?'

Alexandre shook his head, and then returned to watching the clouds again, avoiding eye contact. 'All that unhappiness is over now, Marie. My father's dead. And she's in gaol. Worst part of my life... over. History. The past cannot harm me ever again. I have you Marie.'

'We have each other.'

He pulled his mother's ring from his little finger. 'Will you wear this for me?'

'On which hand?'

'This.'

'On which finger?'

'This.'

'Yes Alexandre.'

He slipped the narrow gold band on her ring finger. 'This was my mother's. She said this ring would bring my heart's desire.'

Marie bent over him and they kissed.

'I lost my mother too when I was young. I shall wear it as long as I love you.'

'Is that forever?'

For answer, Marie kissed him again. She lifted the locket she wore on a silver chain about her neck. She snapped open its lid with her fingernail. A small silver coin fell out from inside. 'My mother gave me this... because we lived at the Sign of the Coin.' Alexandre scooped the coin from her lap and held the shiny keepsake above his face, squinting up at it against the sky's glare. 'It comes from pagan Carthage our priest said. You keep it. For luck. When you...'

'You are more precious by far than me,' Alexandre interrupted, pressing the coin back into her hand.

Half-vexed half-pleased Marie examined the coin again, turning it slowly over in her fingers as if seeing it for the first time. 'Oh! This Carthagenian king is you.' She stretched out next to him holding the coin up to his face to compare profiles. 'You would be the more handsome, if only you knew how to smile.' At this, he did smile. He folded her fingers around the coin. Their next kiss became another embrace.

The cooling shadows of the trees had lengthened across the meadow, though the sere summer grasses hung on to the solid heat of the late afternoon sun. Alexandre and Marie dozed in each other's arms. Marie awoke to wriggle herself more tightly against Alexandre. She opened the fingers of her hand where it rested on his chest, just in front of her face. The little silver keepsake sparkled in her palm.

Why hadn't he accepted it? She so wanted him to carry something of hers. She had a happy thought. His lance-cap lay at arm's distance, upturned where she had dropped it in the grass beside them. Without disturbing the slumbering Alexandre, she reached out to hide the coin where he could not discover it, tucked out of sight inside the brim of the lance-cap. She smiled with satisfaction to herself and fell asleep again.

†

Leaving Gabriel watching the enemy gun position in the valley below, Alexandre crawled back down from the brow of the hill until he could sit up without his head breaking the skyline. He saw that Saint-George was already scrambling up the steep slope to join him. Below the labouring figure, the troop of sixty lancers hidden in the col, took the opportunity to stretch their legs and ease themselves whilst the officers conferred.

'No sign of them yet Colonel,' said Alexandre as Saint-George flopped down beside him.

Saint-George just grunted at Alexandre's information, his chest still heaving from the strenuous climb. After a moment, he gestured to Alexandre to lead the way to the top of the hill.

'Well Gabriel you've made yourself comfortable here,' Saint-George said as the boy shunted himself to one side to let the Chevalier crawl into position next to him.

Gabriel thought of attempting to salute, thought better of it since he was lying down, and grinned instead. He had uprooted a few gorse shrubs from lower down the slope as he waited and slowly pushed them out to cover the front of their position. The brush screen was sparse enough to see through but thick enough to stop the Austrian gunners in the valley bottom immediately below them from catching sight of heads moving against the sky.

Gabriel had also used a broken off branch as a brush to sweep their observation post clean of the soft black sheep pellets piled in the spaces between the tufts of thin dry upland pasture. His housekeeping would save their uniforms, but nothing could obviate the smell of greasy mutton that clung to every blade of grass.

As Alexandre slid into the gorse hide, Gabriel saw what they had been waiting for. He pointed to the head of the valley. Coded flashes of sunlight reflecting from a heliograph winked towards them.

Late the previous night, Lieutenant Demoncourt had taken a half squadron of lancers in a wide circle behind enemy lines to outflank the Austrian battery so that the enemy now lay between them. Gabriel readied his own heliograph and looked to Saint-George for orders.

The Chevalier lowered his spyglass. 'They look to be ready. Send the command Gabriel.'

Gabriel peered through the little hole bored in the back of the heliograph's mirror held in his right hand. He stretched his left in front of him until the pin he gripped between finger and thumb pulled against the thread that joined it to the mirror. Sighting along the hole and pinhead, he lined the heliograph up with Demoncourt's position. He worked the mirror up and down to send the return flashes that let the lieutenant know the main troop was ready, and that he should proceed with the decoy movement. Gabriel had to be careful not to depress the plane of the mirror so much that his signals flashed downwards for the enemy in the valley to spot. Alexandre's strategy depended on the Austrians who manned the battery remaining unaware that Free Americans occupied the heights above them - until it was too late.

Saint-George kept watch on the top of the valley through his spyglass, 'Here they come.'

Demoncourt's men began entering the valley. For some moments their progress over the soft peaty earth was almost soundless and went unnoticed by the battery - the Austrians stationed here kept a watch down the valley towards France, not behind them towards Belgium. They were not expecting a force of French lancers to appear at their backs from a supposedly friendly direction.

Eventually a nonchalant gunner strolling back from the latrine trench spotted the black and silver uniforms of the approaching lancers. His startled shriek sounded loud even to the three watchers above.

The Austrians burst into a frenzy of activity, hauling the heavy guns around to face the new threat. Though they worked quickly, the gunners were not yet alarmed. The advancing cavalry were still some way off. Even at full gallop on a downward slope the French could not reach the battery before the Austrians readied their guns and fired. From the Austrians' point of view, the Free Americans' attack looked like military suicide.

Saint-George chuckled and lowered the little brass spyglass. 'Just as you predicted Alexandre. I'm going to let you lead the charge. I'll observe from here.'

Alexandre and Gabriel half-ran half-slid down the steep slope. Except for the sergeant holding Saint-George's mount, the troop was already moving off as they clambered into their saddles.

When Alexandre's column of lancers debouched at the gallop from the narrow tributary valley and spread out in line of attack only seconds from their position, and the Austrians realized how comprehensively the French had tricked them, they panicked. Their artillery was loaded and ready to fire but was all aimed in the wrong direction. This new threat was too close, too sudden.

The gunners had time to fix bayonets - no time for more than that before the Free American Legion was on them. Bayonets wielded by foot soldiers are of little use when matched against the long reach of lances couched in the arms of mounted men. Those gunners that escaped the lance points died anyway - knocked down and trampled by horses as two ranks of cavalry ran over them.

Without thinking, Alexandre steered his horse at the only mounted Austrian, the battery commander. The officer was kicking his horse to get it moving towards him. Alexandre had meant to use his lance but a chivalrous impulse made him drop the weapon and draw his own sabre to meet the plucky Austrian on equal terms.

The man's bravery was greater than his skill though, he swung his sabre wildly like a Hungarian in the hopes of delivering an edge-cut, whereas Alexandre held his blade out straight and rigid - he could hear Saint-George's voice telling him that in the charge, you use your sabre like a spear. The tip of Alexandre's sword caught the Austrian under the jawbone, tumbling him, dead or dying, arsy-versy out of the saddle and back over the horse's croup to the ground.

Finding himself in the open again and unopposed, Alexandre wheeled his horse round to look for new targets. He was not surprised to see Gabriel replicating the same manoeuvre at his side - the Legion's youngest recruit was fearless and stuck by Alexandre even in the bloodiest fighting. Alexandre had given up trying to look after the boy during engagements - anyway Gabriel seemed to think that it was actually his duty to shield Alexandre from harm.

The rest of the troop began to reform into a line behind Alexandre and Gabriel, but seeing there was no need for a second charge, Alexandre told the sergeant to stand the men down.

At this moment, Demoncourt's half-squadron arrived, too late to do anything but abort their charge, pulling up as they reached the enemy gun position and saw there was nothing left for them to do. No Austrian had survived Alexandre’s first rush. Demoncourt's men walked their horses through the fallen bodies with their lances up.

Saint-George had said he did not want them to carry off the artillery pieces - it would reduce the Legion's mobility - so the lancers dismounted to search the gunners' tool chests for spikes to hammer into the cannons' touchholes.

A sergeant fetched the officer's satchel. Alexandre stuffed the dead commander's orders in his own saddlebag for Saint-George to study later. He gave the satchel back to the sergeant - Austrian officers often had Bohemian-forged razors much prized by the men. Before they left, the lancers would strip the bodies and the enemy encampment of anything of value. Military goods would go into the Quartermaster's stores; personal items auctioned among the men or sold off, and the receipts shared out amongst the Legion's widows and orphans. Saint-George was full of praise when he arrived, well pleased with his protégé's success. 'And what is most marvellous,' he said, 'I see no scratch on man nor beast.'

The sergeant lifted his lance into the air, 'Lancers!' he shouted. Free Americans hurried from their various duties at his summons, bringing their lances with them to gather in front of the officers. Wondering what was happening, Alexandre looked to Saint-George for clues. The Chevalier gazed back enigmatically, volunteering no information, and all Demoncourt would say was, 'This doesn't happen often'. The sergeant, who had come to stand by Alexandre's horse, raised his lance again. Again, he called, 'Lancers'.

Everyone was looking at Alexandre. As one, the men lofted their lances. Saint-George and Demoncourt drew their sabres too. Then the Free American Legion gave out a deep-chested roar of acclamation – a sound so far down in the vocal register the rolling boom seemed to shake and pull at the surrounding hillsides. Twice more the deafening bass ovation rumbled out, over the dead enemy and the wrecked guns, across the grassy bottom pastures and up into the far corners of the valley as the Legion paid the bewildered and embarrassed Alexandre its highest compliment.

†

The enormous and slow-moving berline, painted a sickly chocolate and yellow, overburdened with a monstrous cargo of trunks and boxed supplies strapped and roped to its exterior, groaned to a halt in the road outside a quiet country inn. According to papers carried by the three occupants, the coach conveyed the Baroness de Korff, a Russian lady, her young son and their valet.

A portly man, wearing the drab grey suiting and the small wig that betoken a servant, let himself down with wheezy caution from the coach. Once on firm ground he flapped his arms a bit then, keeping them spread wide, strode around, stopping at times to gingerly bend his knees a few degrees. The lady also left the coach though not to exercise her travel-stiffened joints. Plainly annoyed at the servant's public display, she hastened over to the man and angrily caught him by his arm.

'Be more circumspect Louis,' Marie-Antoinette hissed, 'you're supposed to be a lowly valet.'

'Enough! I am wearing these dull rags and this dog's arse on my head. Can I do more?' The King shook her restraining hand from his arm. 'Where are General Choiseul's hussars?' he demanded of her, as if the blame for their non-appearance was all hers. 'I've had enough of this mummery.'

'Patience Louis. Our rescuers will come. Orders went to Choiseul long ago.' She tried to keep annoyance at his petulance, and fear at their predicament, out of her voice. 'Our best strategy is to travel on. Keep going so we meet them on the road.'

This proposal got short shrift from the King, not because he thought it was not sensible - he had never ever heard the Queen say anything foolish - but because for the first time in his life he was out among the people and that terrified him. He had no courtiers or servants with him, and, crucially he had no royal bodyguard - the Paris mob had wiped out his Swiss Guards.

The King was alone, and among his people, among the peasants, which meant the taxpayers - for only the peasants paid taxes in Royal France. The taxes funded the lavish pensions with which the King bought the loyalty of his aristocrats.

At some level he knew the unfairness of taking money from the poor, who had little, and giving it to the rich, who had plenty, is what finally brought his kingdom crashing down. He knew it but he did not want to think about it - it made him feel bad. He wanted to feel good. He wanted to eat. He did not want to spend any more time worrying about hussars.

'Dinner's overdue. They must come to me,' he decided. Before Marie-Antoinette could protest this edict, he strode off towards the entrance to the inn.

The landlord was standing at his inn's main doors taking mail from the postman. He had been keeping half an eye on the magnificent coach that had stopped in the road wondering if it would pull into his yard.

'Landlord! Landlord! To me fellow,' bellowed Louis as he lumbered towards the startled men. 'Run! I'm starving!' The landlord rushed out into the yard to him.

The postman frowned as he watched his friend fawn and bow as the fat servant quizzed him imperiously, and in detail on the contents of the inn's larder and cellar. The fellow dresses like a lackey but acts like a prince, thought the postman. Or, maybe, a king!

He moved back into the concealing shadow of the doorway and dropped his leather postal pouch onto the flags. He had heard the rumours of the King's escape from Paris. Could this greedy blowhard be Louis himself? He pulled an assignat from his pocket. Carefully he smoothed the crumpled banknote on the wall with his fingers. The profile on the assignat looked like this loudmouthed valet.

The landlord and his new guest brushed the postman aside as they pushed past. The close contact removed all doubt from the postman's mind. Rising strongly above the familiar rankness of human sweat was some fragrance so rare he could not guess the perfume's name. This must be the King. What a reward there would be. He would never carry letters again. Dropping the postal pouch on the floor, he ran out to unhitch his horse. Once out of the yard, he turned towards Varennes and whipped his animal into a gallop.

†

It had been light when Louis sat down to eat. Now it was dark and he was still at table. The Dauphin lay asleep on the cushions of a settee. The Queen fretted backwards and forwards across the room. Now at the window, now at the door, then back to the window - fearful of betrayal, discovery, and arrest. She parted the curtains again just widely enough to peer down into the yard. A horseman had clattered into the yard a short time ago - her heart still thumped. She imagined government agents everywhere.

The Queen dropped the curtain and after a moment went back to the door to listen for footsteps in the corridor. Someone, likely the lone horseman, had gone along the corridor and not returned. His footsteps had faltered outside her door as if the stranger was tempted to knock but thought better of it.

Strange. Was that music? She eased open the door a fraction and listened at the crack. The faint scrape of bow on string strayed down the hallway. As she stepped out of the room to hear better, an air she knew well began on the violin. She knew the composer of that sweet melody, knew the hand that drew that bow.

The Queen hurried towards the music and flung open the door to reveal a smiling Saint-George. He hardly had time to set down his instrument before she threw herself into his welcoming arms. The Queen knew she could not enjoy the protection of Saint-George's unexpected presence for long but, surely, no one could begrudge her a few fleeting moments of comfort now? For the first time since their coach had left Paris, she felt safe.

'Has Philippe-Égalité sent you here?' she enquired, 'Is this arrest?'

'Never fear me. I shall ever be true.' He kissed her and she knew he did not lie.

'Can a crowned queen, trust a republican?'

'You must. Not just for the sake of our love. For your life, trust me. You must leave this place. The countryside hums with news of your flight. I found you so easily.' He held her shoulders, squeezing as if seriously contemplated trying to shake some sense into her. 'Why tarry?'

'We are in Champagne. Fine food and finer wines. The King of France must sample all of them.'

'Leave him to gorge and die.' He pulled her close again. 'Bring your son here. We'll be across the border by moonrise.'

'You would do that for me, Chevalier?'

'I'd sooner betray France than you my love.'

'I share your devotion.' Now it was her turn to push him to arms' length. She stared at him earnestly. 'Not your courage,' she went on. 'I cannot put feelings first. Duty rules.'

The Queen turned away from Saint-George. She drew her nail across the strings of the violin, an ugly discordant sound. Her head dropped as weakness and despair overcame her. The Queen lifted her head to look into his eyes. 'I am more slave than Queen, my brave Black Knight. Go. Don't let me be the cause of your death.' She caught up his hands in hers, pressed them to her breast, lifted them to her lips, and kissed the fine-boned fingers. Reluctantly she let go, pushed herself away from him. Unable to speak, knowing she would not change her mind, Saint-George picked up the violin and bow, and laid them back in the open case.

'Wait.' She stopped him closing the lid of the instrument case. 'But no,' she said sadly, lowering the lid herself. 'It's best to abandon hope. I'm sorry for the pain, my love. I feel it too.' Salt tears mingled on their lips as they kissed for the last time. 'I shall not look upon your dear face again. Farewell.'

†

The Queen stood again at the window looking down into the yard. Saint-George, straight-backed, disciplined, exercising iron control, waved once then rode off into the night. With her lover's departure, she turned on her husband, her anger suddenly boiling over.

'And what would you sacrifice for love, or any other thing? Nothing edible for sure. Your gluttony threatens all our futures. Is just one more bite of that pie more important than your child? France? Your own life? Or mine?'

Her bitter accusations woke the Dauphin. She went to help the boy rise from the settee. The Queen hugged the small figure reassuringly against her skirts as she spoke over his head to Louis. 'I can at least save the next king.' She gave Louis a last contemptuous look, and then hastened from the room with her son.

Louis sat stunned at the cold finality in the Queen's voice - he was too drunk and bloated to understand what she had meant by her accusations. After a moment, he realized that she had called him a fool, what's more a selfish fool, and abandoned him to his fate. Stung into shambling activity, he pushed himself up from the table to his feet.

Halfway to the door he paused. Returning to the table he inexpertly wrapped the half-eaten carcase of a poached chicken in a napkin and thrust it into the pocket of his tails. Then, snaffling two bottles of wine by their necks, he hurried after his wife and son.

†

Saint-George, Alexandre, Demoncourt, Gabriel, and four Free American lancers were sitting on their horses a little way down the road as the Royal Family's luggage-festooned berline lurched out of the inn yard and trundled up the rutted road in the direction of Varennes.

Saint-George leaned towards Alexandre and confided in him with quiet insistence. 'Whatever she says, I must follow her.' He swallowed, for a second he could not continue. 'I must be with her. You understand that?'

'I do,' said Alexandre. He pulled his horse's head around towards Varennes.

Saint-George caught the younger man's bridle and wheeled their horses back to face the other direction. 'Alexandre no. You go to Paris.'

'The escort can go back. I'll come with you.'

'Good friend. You strain your principles to breaking to help. I know it. I love you for it.' Saint-George saw Alexandre was still determined to accompany him. 'That New France that you want. Liberty. Equality. Fraternity. It's not my France. It bores me. I'm happier with Old France, the one that's going into exile with that ridiculous man in that coach up there. There's nothing here for me. No poetry. Dear friend, don't look at me so. Understand. Luxury, Pleasure, Idleness. And Love. The true Rights of Man... of a man like me.'

Saint-George's horse took a few impatient paces towards Varennes as if it sensed its master's desire to be off before the coach was lost to sight. The Chevalier took off his hat and shook his head in the air. 'Did you feel the wind change then?'

'I did Saint-George.'

'It blows away from France,' said the Chevalier. 'Lead my men for me.'

Alexandre made one last plea though now he knew it would be in vain. 'You're certain you won't let me come with you?'

'My last order is you return to Paris.'

Alexandre nodded in resigned acceptance. Saint-George flicked his reins, smiled, and with an exuberant wave of his hat set off after the coach. The six men he left behind sat silently in the moonlit road until first the coach and then the Chevalier trailing it at a distance disappeared from their view.

Camille blurted out, 'Is the Citizen-Colonel a traitor?'

'Silence!' commanded Demoncourt.

'Have you never loved anyone Camille? Alexandre enquired quietly.

The lancer reflected, gave a rueful shrug. 'The Revolution can wait, I suppose.'

†

The royal berline swayed through the wheel-churned mud of the road as the moon rose higher in the clear star-glutted sky. The moon was full and so bright it made wayside herbs and flowers easily identifiable in the untidy late-summer verges. Though undeniably beautiful, in the absence of any colour, the stark moonlight-bleached fields beyond the velvety black hedgerows seemed like the hinterland of some otherworldly land of nightmare.

A large, white-faced owl, hunting beneath the roadside oaks, flew up in front of the lead horses, its sudden hoot alarming them into a rearing halt. The Dauphin put his head out of the window and was first to see the six armed horsemen who blocked the road ahead. 'It's the hussars! Mama! Papa! Hussars!'

Louis clapped his hands to his chest in undisguised relief. 'Thank you God! Thank you. We are safe at last.'

One of the horsemen up ahead shouted words that were so different from those the occupants of the coach expected to hear that, for an instant, they could not make sense of them. 'Stop!' the reedy voice unused to command cried, 'In the name of the Nation!'

The Queen clasped her hands in prayer. 'No, not safe Louis. We must be brave now husband. The Garde Nationale have us. We are no longer in God's hands but the Revolutionary Government's.'

There was a flash of rapid movement at the coach's window - a mounted man riding by with a drawn sword. The Dauphin craned out his head out of the window again and saw the man reining to a halt to confront the six militiamen. 'The Chevalier de Saint-George, Mama!'

At these words, the Queen pulled her son from the window and, without waiting for the footmen, threw open the door and jumped to the ground.

'I am in command.' Saint-George's tone compelled obedience. 'Stand back. Let us pass.'

The militiamen hesitated before Saint-George's supreme confidence. They began to move to the sides of the road. Then they saw the detested Marie-Antoinette approaching and their resolve hardened. The Chevalier saw the change, knew he would have to fight. He was already drawing his horse pistol when the Queen grabbed at his leg.

'Desist I beg you! No blood on my head!' she begged.

He lifted her hand where it rested on his thigh and leaning down pressed her fingers to his lips.

A large number of new militia appeared and quickly surrounded the royal party on all sides. The moment in which

Saint-George could have done something to save them all passed. The possibility of saving his beloved from the terrible fate that threw its foul coils around her had become impossibility.

Emboldened at the heavy reinforcement of militia, the postman who had raised the alarm, intent on securing beyond any doubt the life of luxury and ease that was almost his, began working his way past Saint-George's position. Two of his cronies in the Garde Nationale trailed after him. Unnoticed by the main protagonists, the three raised the heavy muskets they were too cowardly to aim when they faced the single lone horseman.

Heedless of the presence of a woman in the line of fire, unmoved that the Chevalier had let his horse pistol drop back into its holster, uncaring that the couple were tenderly intent on each other, the three men fired a ragged but lethal salvo.

The volley of heavy shot at close range in the small of his back snatched Saint-George from the saddle and threw him forward onto his horse's neck. He pushed himself back, fighting to sit straight in the saddle, then, overcome with pain and shock, slumped forward over his horse's withers and, half-supported by the appalled Queen, slid senseless to the road.

†

Alexandre and his men, trailing the coach but keeping back out of sight, reined in at the sound of distant gunfire. 'Muskets!'

'Two at least...' Demoncourt began to say when Gabriel interrupted.

'I can hear something else. Over there.'

Alexandre stood up in his stirrups straining his senses across the fields in the direction Gabriel pointed - there was a drumming, so low but so heavy he could feel as well as hear it. He could see nothing. Then a company of cavalry came into view all at once as it jumped a distant hedgerow on a broad front. The mounted soldiers surged in an all out charge across the moonlit meadows towards the point where the gunfire had sounded.

Several lancers shouted as they recognized the shadowed contours of old rivals, Hussars! Then Alexandre knew that if his friend had not been in danger before, he certainly was now. 'Saint-George!' he cried, 'Forward!' and the lancers spurred their mounts furiously up the road in the direction of Varennes.

†

Though the Garde Nationale who had captured the coach greatly outnumbered the hussars who came to rescue the Royal Family, they were hemmed in between the roadside hedges - a poor position for any mounted force, especially one made up exclusively of inexperienced militia. They were wholly unprepared for how quickly the attacking force fell upon them. It seemed no sooner had the charging horses been heard in the distance than a solid wall of yelling cavalry rocketed over the hedgerow onto the heads of the half-ready militia. The hussars crashed down amongst them to cut and slash. Most struck a single blow then immediately jumped the opposite hedge away into the field beyond, leaving shocked survivors and empty saddles behind them.

A few of the attacking hussars finding themselves amongst raw recruits poorly led, gleefully set out to butcher as many of the terrified militiamen as their sabres could reach instead of leaving with their comrades. One discovered the postman trying to bury himself in the hedge and with one stupendous chop down with a heavy cavalry sabre, split him in two from shoulder to hip.

Racing along the road, Alexandre and the lancers arrived just in time to engage this murderous rump of hussars. The chaotic jam of friend and foe forbade any battlefield manoeuvre with lances. The Free Americans resorted to picking their way gingerly into the fight - impeded rather than helped by the militiamen whose recklessly swinging swords threatened the friend at their side as much the foe in front of them.

Looking about for a sight of Saint-George, Alexandre caught a flash in the moonlight of the white plume worn by a hussar officer. He decided discovering what had happened to the Chevalier would have to wait. He guided his mount forwards, easing aside a Garde on foot to get nearer the enemy officer. Incredibly, the Garde was attempting to use his musket in the violently confused press. Fearful he might bring down one of his lancers, Alexandre grabbed the long barrel, plucked the weapon up out the man's hands and threw it down in the mud of the road. He directed a hard look at the man who stared up at him, slack-jawed with astonishment.

When Alexandre got close enough to see the enemy officer's face in the moonlight, he was somehow unsurprised to recognize his old enemy, de Malpas. He had come to believe that they were destined to meet again and again until they settled what lay between them. He smiled grimly. De Malpas would find him different from the boy he had so easily disarmed at their last encounter. Alexandre had learned much from constant practice with Saint-George, the greatest swordsman of the age. Moreover, this time he had the ancestral sword of his family in his hand - the family de Malpas and his sister had destroyed. This confrontation would be their last.

The unexpected discharge of a musket by his stirrup made his horse shy from the loud report, but the frightened animal could not get away from the source of its fear in the packed road. Alexandre was still close enough to grab the perpetrator by his collar and lift him up into the air. He dangled the wretch at face level; the man's legs kicked ineffectually, his eyes rounded with alarmed disbelief at being handled like a baby. Alexandre recognised the same dangerous fool he disarmed only seconds before. With a disgusted backwards throw, Alexandre tossed him into the hedge, where the man hung struggling upside-down, hooked fast by his coat in the blackthorn and briars.

When Alexandre turned back, the fray was over. No hussars - no living hussars - remained in the muddy highway except de Malpas, who stood hands half raised in surrender next to his dead horse. So that's where blind chance sent the fool's musket ball.

The Garde Nationale commander was evidently in shock, wringing his hands, peering around distractedly. Alexandre estimated the unfortunate officer had lost a third of his men in this opening encounter. He kneed his horse towards him. The man was pathetically glad to see a regular army officer and gratefully ceded command to him.

'Citizen-Captain. Dismount your men. Position them along the hedgerow.' Alexandre beckoned urgently to Demoncourt.

'Chase the loose horses into the field. We may perchance spoil the hussars' next charge.'

†

In the field beyond the hedgerow, the hussars regrouped. Their uncertainty was almost tangible. They could not know if their commander de Malpas was dead or captured, or whether at any moment he might appear to reassume command. The few moments of indecision in the attackers' ranks were sufficient for some of the militiamen to find gaps in the hedge to shove the barrels of their muskets through. Alexandre directed others to round up the riderless horses in the lane and herd them towards the gate that led to the meadow.

The sound of a bugle from the meadow signalled the beginning of the hussar's second charge. As the attacking force spurred towards the hedge behind which the militia crouched, the loose horses in the field were whipped into flight. The impact of a dozen startled animals plunging headlong into the disciplined attack formation wrecked the charge's speed and momentum forcing many of the hussars to slow or swerve away.

The disrupted charge made the milling knot of attackers into easy targets that begged for bullets from the waiting Garde Nationale, but Alexandre did not want the hussars to retreat and reform while their numbers were so great. Since they were not advancing at full gallop, he wanted them to get closer, where the massed fire from the novice militiamen would do some real damage. Even as he called a precautionary, 'Wait,' a man, unable to resist the temptation of an almost stationary hussar in his sights, discharged his weapon. 'Hold I say,' Alexandre roared.

Another damned fool who should be thrown into the thorny hedge.

In the meadow, the hussars had reorganised and were coming forward again, though nothing like as tidily and rapidly as before. When Alexandre finally gave the order to fire, the line of militia released a devastating volley of musketry through the hedge that cut the hussars from their horses like a boy beheading flowers with a switch. With no officer to rally them, the surviving hussars wheeled and fled, sped on their way by the triumphant jeers of the hugely relieved militia.

Alexandre quickly dismounted when he saw that the Garde Nationale officer was about to accept the formal surrender of de Malpas and take his parole not to escape. He snatched de Malpas' proffered sword before the Garde Nationale officer's outstretched hand could close about the hilt.

'Citizen-Captain, forgive this intrusion, but this man's parole is worthless. I know him to be unworthy of your trust.'

'Jacques! Er. Citizen-Sergeant that is. Tie this prisoner's hands,' the officer said, readily accepting Alexandre's advice. 'See he's well guarded.' The militia commander took Alexandre's hand and shook it gratefully. 'Thank you for your timely help, Citizen-Captain. We have never faced the enemy before.'

'In that event you and your men have done well. The Revolution is safe in your hands. Release half of your force to my lieutenant and he'll chase those hussars back to Belgium.'

Gabriel's distressed treble pierced cleanly through the clamour of the jubilant militiamen. 'Citizen-Captain Dumas! It's the Chevalier.'

Alexandre looked across to see that Gabriel was at the berline. All need for secrecy gone with the Royal Family's apprehension by the Garde Nationale; the driver had relit the coach's lanterns. A warm yellow glow illuminated the young lancer on his horse. Even at this distance, Alexandre could plainly see Gabriel's shocked expression as the boy gazed with horror in at the open door. Alexandre ran to the berline and peered in at the tragic scene inside the coach.

King Louis and the Dauphin sat close together on one bench; father and son in almost identical postures, hands tightly clenching knees, leaning slightly forward, their appalled attention fixed on the still figure of Saint-George stretched on the opposite seat. The Queen knelt on the floor between the benches pressing a wad of embroidered linen - table napkins? - against Saint-George's belly to staunch a steady flow of blood that had already darkened the unconscious man's shirt and breeches.

Alexandre had never been presented to Marie-Antoinette but she said, 'Thank God you've come,' when she saw him as if at the arrival of an old friend - perhaps the sight of the uniform of the Free American Legion inspired that instant familiarity and trust. 'He must have a surgeon's care,' she told him. 'Soon, if he is to live.'

Alexandre tried to push the anguish he felt to one side, he had to think. Saint-George undoubtedly faced execution as a traitor for his actions this night. Somehow, Alexandre must get the Chevalier away from the Garde Nationale before they put him in a prison cell beyond any possibility of rescue. Yet his injuries were severe and medical treatment urgent. Alexandre could see no way at present to achieve both aims. There were reasons to hope though. Saint-George had not been in uniform when he confronted the militiamen so there was no obvious connection between him and the lancers, and the militiamen were grateful for the lancers' intervention.

When Alexandre stepped back from the coach's door, he found the officer had followed him and now stood at his side. Alexandre said in as disinterested a tone as he could manage, 'This prisoner seems badly injured. He may be important.'

'I'll make sure a doctor sees to his wounds in Varennes. The hussar prisoner and these others must be taken there too.' The Garde Nationale officer looked from face to face as he spoke, realization dawning that here indeed was the King, the Queen, and the Dauphin of France, and he was hero of the hour.

†

For all his republican ideals, the Garde Nationale officer had not for one moment considered keeping the Royal Family in Varennes' cramped and dirty town lockup - though they pitched the King's coachman and footman into the noisome hole without a second's thought. Instead, he had commandeered Varennes' small theatre as a place to keep these exulted captives together surrounded by his most reliable men.

The remainder of the Garde Nationale patrolled the square outside the building with a newly militant gait that soon blossomed into a full-blown swagger as news of their exploits roused the townsfolk from their beds and a crowd of gawping admirers gathered.

Inside the theatre, lamps lighted the boarded stage as if for a show, throwing the auditorium into semi-darkness. The Royal Family sat silently in the misery of defeat in the dark of a box set to one side of the stage. Off-duty militiamen gathered in murmuring groups here and there smoking their pipes.

Saint-George lay on a chaise longue, centre stage. He swam back to painful consciousness after suffering the ministrations of a provincial surgeon more accustomed to pulling teeth than dealing with gunshot wounds. The man, recognizing his own limitations, had wisely not attempted probing for the musket ball. He poured diluted sulphuric acid into the shot-holes to arrest the internal haemorrhaging, covered the wounds with carbolic-soaked pads - tightly bandaged to hold them in place.

Saint-George found the surgeon had pulled up his stained breeches and re-buttoned them over his bandages - the tails of his shirt hung loose, starched to stiffness by drying blood. Saint-George pulled at the grey coat lying over the back of the chaise-longue. He looked thoughtful when he found two ragged holes in the back, just above the split of the coat tails.

†

The militiamen made an enthusiastic, but inexpert and consequently fruitless, attempt to question de Malpas in the dressing room behind the stage. The aristo had been knocked about somewhat, as much in anger at his patrician arrogance as in hopes of eliciting information. Eventually they pushed him out from the wings to join the other prisoners, shoving him so roughly that he fell full-length on the boards in front of Saint-George's chaise-longue. De Malpas raised himself nonchalantly on one elbow and addressed the Chevalier, 'Fancy meeting here. What a pleasant surprise'.

Saint-George sighed, 'I was just thinking... things could be much worse.'

De Malpas inspected his archenemy leisurely from the floor, noting with insincere murmurs of concern the signs of pain and injury that the events of the night had visited upon the normally impeccable and invulnerable Saint-George. 'Looking very cheerful... for a dying man.'

'It's knowing you will be hanged next to me.'

The Queen acidly cut across the verbal fencing. 'We find you in good humour de Malpas.'

Disconcerted at the discovery that the Royal Family was present, de Malpas got to his feet and bowed towards the dark interior of the box. 'Your Highness...' he began a smooth apology.

Louis broke in, spluttering almost incoherently with anger. 'Ten hours, ten hours late for our rendezvous. You are incompetent. Your men? Cowards.'

'Yet here you are,' the Queen said, taking over the attack. 'Smiling. Joking. Regrets? You have none it seems. Neither have you shame.'

'Your Highness,' de Malpas began again - without even a show of remorse in his voice now. He was not to be humiliated in front of Saint-George even by the King, and most especially not by the woman he regarded as Saint-George's whore.

'That man...' the Queen overrode his interruption, '...you mock is noble of spirit.' The Queen's voice broke, 'Great-hearted. He is...'

'...is a man of parts,' completed de Malpas venomously. 'Yes. And you know full well the quality of his parts my Queen.'

Incensed at this crude affront, Saint-George tried to force his shattered body up from the chaise-longue. 'I'll tear that tongue out.'

'Do what?' challenged de Malpas, knocking the struggling man back into his seat with a negligent slap. The Chevalier looked up at de Malpas, his contempt a felt blow that rocked de Malpas momentarily back on his heels. Recovering, de Malpas leant forward, putting all his weight on the clenched fist he bored down and buried in the wounded man's stomach. 'What?' he demanded, grinding his knuckles into the bloody bandages, relishing the helpless agony he was causing in the man he hated above all other men. 'Cripple!' he taunted, but Saint-George had fainted beyond the reach of further pain or insult.

†

In the theatre's green room, Alexandre and Gabriel, pretending indifference to the captives' condition or fate, were toasting the night's success in champagne with the Garde Nationale commander. Somewhere between the second and fourth bottles, the officer had agreed that, since Alexandre was returning to Paris anyway, why not take the civilian traitor with him – the authorities there could interrogate the man properly?

The commotion on stage brought them running from the dressing room. Alexandre managed to stop Gabriel hurrying to the Chevalier's side - any overt sign of concern or familiarity might spoil the arrangements they had been making to get the Chevalier away from Varennes, to somewhere he could be hidden whilst he recovered from his wounds.

'Silence!' commanded the Garde Nationale officer as he took control of the situation on the stage. 'Prisoners will not talk.' He gestured to a militiaman, 'Put that man over there'. The militiaman pulled de Malpas' chair to the side of the stage and, although he did not bind him, he stood at his back.

The officer briefly examined Saint-George. He looked towards Alexandre, 'He's badly injured, Citizen-Major. How shall you bring him to Paris alive?'

'Throw him on a cart,' Alexandre replied with a convincing show of heartlessness. 'If he dies, he dies.'

The lancers took a leg each of the chaise-longue and stretchered Saint-George down the narrow steps into the auditorium, followed by Alexandre and the Garde Nationale officer. As the procession reached the top of the aisle, the officer took hold of Alexandre's arm. 'What of the other one?' he enquired.

Alexandre stopped, and both men turned back to the stage, to see de Malpas' empty chair lying on its side. No decision about the disposition of this prisoner would be necessary after all. There was no sign of him nor of the armed man who had been guarding him. When all eyes had been on the lancers manoeuvring Saint-George from the stage on his chaise-longue, de Malpas had silently overpowered his guard and escaped.

†

After leaving Varennes, Alexandre and his men travelled that night and most of the next day, moving slowly for the sake of Saint-George's injury along quiet country lanes away from the busy highways and curious eyes. The Garde Nationale officer had commandeered a tinker's wagon for them - the tinker was in the town lockup, three of the crimes he was there for carried the death penalty so there was no need to return the wagon. Alexandre blessed the officer's choice of vehicle for the wagon had a canvas cover that could be closed. Once away from Varennes no one would know a wounded man lay inside.

They filled the wagon with bales of hay and rested the chaise longue on top to cushion the Chevalier from the worst effects of an unsprung vehicle lurching along deeply rutted tracks. Gabriel sat at Saint-George's side all the way. Whenever the Chevalier regained consciousness, they stopped the wagon to give the injured man water.

They halted when they got within an hour of the Sign of the Coin and waited for nightfall in a quiet wood whilst Gabriel rode on alone to alert Marie and Labouret.

†

The wagon rolled into the inn's yard after midnight, once the last regular had been pushed out to stagger home. Alexandre and the lancers gently lifted Saint-George's chaise-longue from the back of the cart and carried him inside. Marie ran ahead to open the concealed door to her father's private cellar. Saint-George bore up well only fainting with pain when they had to pick him up from the chaise-longue to put him into a chair, so he could be manoeuvred down the narrow stairway to Labouret's deepest cellar.

Several candles stuck on top of a barrel in the far corner of the vaulted chamber lit up a mattress tucked in amongst the stacked casks and racked bottles. Marie had rushed to get a hiding place ready in the cellar when Gabriel brought the news of Saint-George's misfortunes and imminent arrival.

Once laid on his pallet, Saint-George began to recover his senses. Alexandre and Marie knelt at his side whilst Labouret hovered anxiously behind them.

'You'll be safe enough here I think,' the innkeeper said to Saint-George. 'This cellar's our secret. I don't pay taxes on anything here.'

'My thanks Labouret,' said Saint-George. He grasped Alexandre's hand; his grip seemed strong. By an act of will, he managed to throw off his weakness and for a few minutes become his usual commanding self. 'Alexandre. You must get back to Paris. Be first with your version of the news of my disappearance. With the Royal Family's capture, no one'll be interested in details. Tell Philippe-Égalité I've gone to Belgium - joined the emigres.' His amused laugh was lost in a coughing fit that threw him sweating back onto his pillow. He fought back to normality again, half-raising himself, pulling at Alexandre's hand. 'Go Alexandre! Marie will soothe my brow. Go! Take care of my Legion. All for one and one for all!'

Marie intervened, insisting the Chevalier lay back on his pillow. Seeing an ally in her, he sought her support. 'Marie, tell him not to worry about me. I'll soon heal. Never wounded before. Seem to have got my life's ration all at once.' He smiled philosophically. Marie looked at Alexandre and nodded. It was obvious to her that what Saint-George wanted would be the wisest course for everyone. Acknowledging acceptance of the Chevalier's reasoning, Alexandre held Saint-George's hand for a moment longer in unspoken farewell, then, followed by Labouret, climbed the narrow stairs up from the cellar.

Once the two men had gone, Marie took Saint-George's hand in hers, 'You don't fool me'.

'Thank God. This really hurts child.'

Now that Alexandre was gone, he allowed himself an agonized grimace. Marie poured a measure of liquid from a small bottle into a glass. Supporting his head, she helped him swallow the draught. 'Wine of opium. It will dull the pain.' She gave him a motherly kiss on the forehead, pinched out all but one of the candles. 'I'll stay with you 'til sleep comes.'

Marie sat on a low stool at the foot of the pallet, watching the flame of the remaining candle as it fluttered against the dark of the cellar. She gave a guilty start when she realized the morbid direction in which her thoughts were drifting. Marie looked across at Saint-George to find his eyes already on her. When he smiled, she could see he knew well what she had been thinking. She lit a new candle from the old, attempted a confident smile back, one that denied any problems - it did not convince her, nor did it convince the dying man on the mattress.

Outside the already mounted lancers waited in the yard. Gabriel held the reins of Alexandre's horse whilst his commander finished speaking to Labouret.

'He talks bravely Alexandre.' The landlord sighed, 'He won't be fighting or even playing the fiddle. The small of his back... it's shattered. He's finished.'

'Does he know I wonder?'

'He's a soldier. He knows.'

'Of all men why him? To die at a coward's hands.'

Labouret shrugged - he had no answer to that. 'Saint-George won't want you to feel sorry for him. He took his wounds honourably. That's all that matters. I know he is something of a father to you, as well as a friend. Do as he asks.'

'I'll be back as soon as I can. Depends on how my report to Philippe-Égalité goes. And any orders he has for the Legion.'

'Marie means to marry you. She's used to getting what she wants. So. Come back safely. Come back soon.'

†

In Philippe-Égalité's apartment in the Palais-Royale, closed and barred shutters let in a few slots of bright sunlight to cut across the fuggy murk of the interior. The overhead chandeliers were unlit, but dozens of candles revealed the extent of the room's filth and disorder. The person setting out the candles had deliberately ignored the numerous candelabra, preferring to press the flame-softened ends of the tall church candles onto any flat surface - a glacier of cooled white wax even inched out across the green furred baize of a card table. The corners of the main table bore clusters of candles set on mounds of old wax which held in place a huge crumpled map of France that covered much of the polished surface, except for an end that curled over the table's edge to the floor - the map itself half-hidden under a litter of wine bottles and dirty glasses.

A scruffy sansculotte slouched on guard in a chair by the door - a clay pipe stained brown from constant use clenched in his teeth, a naked cutlass resting across his thighs. Other sansculottes, in the red Phrygian caps the men from Marseilles affected, dozed untidily in the gilt and velvet luxury of Philippe-Égalité's salon.

Alexandre and Philippe-Égalité sat at the table, sitting upright in the high-backed dining chairs, trying not to let the sight and smell of these offensive manifestations of France's continuing plunge into war and social anarchy to intrude on their conversation. After weeks of forced intimacy with the lower classes, Philippe-Égalité abandoned his usual hauteur and attempted to be cordial. The man was pleased, Alexandre realized, to have someone with a social status nearer his own to talk to for a change.

'Saint-George was always loyal to me personally,' the man started, 'but politically? No. Temperamentally he was a traditionalist. A royalist even. And with Marie Antoinette and he...' Philippe-Égalité was silent for a moment. 'I'm rather relieved he's gone. Had the Chevalier remained, I might have had to...' He leaned forward, clutching with a veined hand at Alexandre's knee. Eyes rolling to indicate the sansculottes, he confided hoarsely, 'They're from Marseilles. The Sans-Culottes Battalion. Great patriots. Fierce.' His voice dropped so low he just mouthed, 'Too fierce'.

Philippe-Égalité sat back. The public face reasserted control over the private emotions. A bland conceit smoothed the fretted forehead, temporarily stilling the tic that had jumped under his left eye. 'The Assembly is flushing out and executing royalist traitors wherever we find them in the Republic. We will cleanse the whole of France of these parasites.'

The inner turmoil was too severe to let him keep a grip for long on his professional politician's mask. The air of smug arrogance fractured as involuntary starts and nervous twitches broke out, his body movements betraying his state of mind more eloquently than any words.

He leaned forward again, cupping a hand to the side of his mouth to whisper confidentially. 'They..,' he began. Flashes of white showed round his enlarged pupils as he frantically swivelled his eyeballs to let Alexandre understand that 'they' were these sansculottes, in this room. 'They dragged the nobles from the prisons. Butchered them in the streets. Men, women, children. Chop! Chop! Chop!'

Overcome at the recollection of these horrors, the man rubbed his face with his hands, tearing at his forehead and temples with his nails, as if trying to scrape the dread from his features. Then Philippe-Égalité shook himself free of guilt and fear, stood, struck a declamatory pose.

'The guillotine bites and swallows our enemies. Soon the King himself will be...' His voice faltered, he looked down in confusion at the seated Alexandre then found a new thread, 'Robespierre, Danton, Marat, these are our men, your men...' His voice cracked and wavered to a halt again.

Philippe-Égalité dropped back abruptly into his chair as if some unseen puppeteer had just then snipped his strings. He sat silently, lost in anxious introspection. When at last he roused himself he seemed by some great effort to have regained a more normal composure.

'Well! These are matters of high policy,' he said in a businesslike way. 'Your concerns are more mundane than mine. Saint-George thought highly of you. You are young - no harm in that I suppose. You have the right background. Anyway, how many cavalry officers left in France? Every one is an aristocrat. All ran off to Belgium and the Austrians long ago. So Citizen-Colonel Dumas. Will you take command of the Free American Legion for me?'

'I will. I'm...'

'Yes. Yes. Honoured. Good!'

Philippe-Égalité waved a hand in summons. He looked around impatiently, and then remembered, with irritation, that he no longer had a secretary to anticipate his needs, to fetch and carry what he wanted. The sansculotte at the door, woken by the sound of Philippe-Égalité's voice, stared at this aristo pretending to be a man of the people with sullen hatred. Unable to bear the man's contempt, Philippe-Égalité rose from his chair, went to the escritoire himself, and fetched a sealed letter. Alexandre stood to receive it.

'Saint-George's orders. Yours now. France is taking the war to the enemy. To push back the Austrians and royalists from her borders.'

With his customary discourtesy to inferiors, Philippe-Égalité turned on his heel and walked away to a side door without a word of farewell. Then he astonished Alexandre by pausing before leaving the room to impart news of a more personal nature.

'The Countess was released. She...' His lips pursed with remembered vexation. 'Your stepmother claimed she knew nothing of the escape plot. I put her to the question myself but...' he cleared his throat, '... nothing. Nevertheless, she has been sent into exile'.

Philippe-Égalité turned to leave, then again paused. 'About your late father's possessions. I know you had no expectations but you might wish to know that the Government ordered the confiscation of all his French possessions. Your stepmother is destitute.'

†

The Countess sipped the hot chocolate, her eyes fixed on the bundle of papers the Swiss banker had left on top of the large desk in front of her - the confidential financial records of Count Davy de la Pailleterie. There was little she regretted about the death of her husband; a pity it had not happened earlier. As she looked at the sheaves of documents tied in pink tape and heavy with seals, she almost felt gratitude towards the deceased for his foresight in placing the bulk of his wealth beyond the reach of the revolutionaries in Paris. Not that she had immediate need of funds. Aimée brought away a box of her mistress' valuables from the burning chateau - a fortune in itself sufficient to attract a new husband or maintain a comfortable widow's station for life.

During her mistress' confinement by Philippe-Égalité, the maid kept the jewels safe. After her release and exile, the Countess asked her servant one morning if she were not tempted to abandon her, to stay in France with the box. Aimée had wept with rage at the suggestion that she might have betrayed the only person she had ever loved. How could her mistress doubt her?

The Countess was amused at the vehement declarations of devotion with which her maid sought to reassure her, and at Aimée's redoubled attentiveness when, as was often the case, the physical intimacies of the daily toilette provoked sensations that called for the maid's talented ministrations.

Recollecting herself, she realized her late husband's banker had not responded yet to her opening question. Instead, the man stood at the long casement windows with his back to her, gazing up at the snow-peaked splendour of the Bernese Oberland. She had expected things to be unrushed, to be conducted at a civilized pace - business was always good in Switzerland when Europe was at war - but the Swiss' meditative quiet was so prolonged she felt the first stirrings of alarm. At last, he turned to her, his plump jowls pinking with embarrassment.

'We do hold the monies from the sale of your late husband's former estates in Haiti,' he confirmed. 'The Count owned a large part of the colony. There is now a considerable fortune - some hundred million francs.'

The Countess set her cup down in her saucer with an audible click that cutoff the banker in mid flow. She was distracted for a moment by the foam of creamy chocolate that fringed her upper lip. The banker's eyes followed each movement the tip of her tongue made as she cleansed her mouth with feline precision, licking his own lip in unconscious imitation. The Countess looked down at the cup in her hand to hide her amusement at the man's susceptibility to feminine tactics. 'Continue,' she said.

The banker touched the bundle of documents as if to remind himself where he was and what he was doing. He paused. He only wanted to please this woman, but the next piece of information was bound to upset her. 'I regret... This money has been left to the Count's son, not to you.'

'Not so,' the Countess replied calmly. 'My husband disinherited Alexandre.'

'Not entirely madame Countess. His last communication to us was incomplete in that respect.' The banker pulled the tape binding the papers loose, picked out a letter. 'We were informed that... yes... title and lands... to you and your heirs.' He scanned the document; let it drop back on the pile. 'However, cash, shares, stocks held on account, we have had no specific instructions. Without the express authority of the testator - your late husband the Count that is - the fortune can only be claimed by Alexandre Dumas.'

The Countess banged her cup and saucer down on the desk. The cup shot from its saucer, bounced once without breaking on the polished mahogany then rolled from the desktop to shatter on the floor. 'I see,' she said in the silence.

The banker tugged a handkerchief from his sleeve and wiped his palms. 'I regret it madame Countess. The banking codes. My hands are tied.'

'Enough. Be quiet.' The Countess sat motionlessly, staring down unseeing at the broken porcelain at her feet, deep in thought. Nor did the banker move. He dared not. His comfortable office had somehow become a circus cage and he, penned in with the man-eater. The Countess stirred. The banker jerked to attention as she fixed her eyes on him. 'The young man is unmarried... a serving soldier. What if he should be killed?' The banker's eyes popped. The Countess smiled; does this fool think I am going to make him murder my stepson? 'In action of course,' she finally added.

'Why...' the banker began, gulping drily, his Adam's apple working visibly among the damp creases of his cravat, 'You are Alexandre Dumas' heir as long as he is single.' His confidence returned as the intensity of the Countess' scrutiny lessened, relaxed into pleasure as his stuttered words opened up a new way forward for her ruthless ambition. 'We would pay the monies over to you in the event of his untimely demise... on active service as you say.'

†

The last French farm before the Belgian border lay in a valley - a well-made stone house set in a wide yard, with outbuildings that stretched as far as the ford across which clear water sparkled before slowing and darkening into a mud-rimmed duckpond. In its deeper stretches the river wound through water meadows of waist-high grass that spread out from the reeded shoulders of the banks as far as the higher, drier, ground, where neat orchards stepped up the steeper sides of the valley. An idyllic scene marred by black smoke coiling into the still air from burning hayricks and sight of the sword-hacked bodies of twenty French infantrymen that sprawled along the margins of the pond, their wounds feeding a spreading slick of blood across the still waters.

The victors in the unequal skirmish were a full squadron of hussars, all exiled French royalists riding with the Austrian cavalry. They had thrown the reins of their horses over the farm's picket fence then forgotten the animals. Tethered in the hot sun, the neglected mounts moved restlessly, made more ill tempered by the smell of fresh water close by, and, through the picket fence, tantalizing glimpses beyond the reeds of the cool river itself.

The short vicious engagement between the infantry and cavalry had broken over the farm at milking time. The Austrians and their French allies were supposed to respect the lives and property of the civilian population - King Louis would not thank them for despoiling his kingdom. When, as now, the fortunes of war delivered French peasants back into the power of their former masters, the opportunity for the exiled aristocrats to rehearse their old feudal pleasures one more time overpowered all prohibition. On this occasion, all common sense too, since the hussars were not in friendly Belgium but in France, in an area patrolled by the Free American Legion.

†

Shrieks of female fear and rage counterpointed the deep protesting lowing of cows left unmilked in their stalls, as some dozen of the hussars, passions inflamed to bursting by blood and victory, stood in line to ravish the farm's women, turn and turnabout.

A larger and noisier crowd surrounded on three sides a lone pair of infantry officers backed up against the flints of the farmhouse wall. They, the only survivors of the massacre, were not prisoners. The terrified men still carried swords, though intimidated by such superior odds they did not attempt to use their weapons to fight free. They still had weapons because the hussars' commander, Count de Malpas, rejected their honourable offers of surrender. Instead, he had sworn to let them all go - they had been seven then - if any one of them could defeat him in fair fight.

It had soon become clear that de Malpas' proposal was less than magnanimous - there was not even the smallest possibility that the infantry officers could win their freedom by such means. De Malpas' steel was as efficient a means of cold-blooded execution as any hangman's hemp. Their hopes of escape dwindled with their numbers as de Malpas cut them down one by one. The best of them he mocked, correctly calling out cut, guard, point, or parry, before his opponent had even thought to make the move - countering their wild despairing gyrations with an insulting economy of movement. The poorer swordsmen he simply butchered, with one smooth irresistible lunge full to the throat.

Alexandre bit his lip in frustration and shame as he observed the butchery through his spyglass. He was perched up in the spreading branches of an apple tree. The trees were in full leaf at this time of year giving good cover to the dismounted lancers who waited for orders in the long grass below him. He had sent for reinforcements immediately the forward scouts brought word of the marauding hussar squadron, and rushed on at once with the sixty-strong patrol. With only half his opponents' strength, he dared not engage the enemy directly in spite of the enormities they were committing - hence his shame. Then too, Alexandre had recognized the enemy uniforms through his spyglass. This was de Malpas' regiment - hence his frustration.

Outside the farmhouse, the second to last infantry officer kissed his companion adieu. All eyes were on him as he came to stand head bowed before de Malpas. Only the Free Americans watching from the hillside were aware of the small party of lancers that emerged dripping from the river to crouch in the reeds.

Each man trailed his lance and carried his saddle holsters slung over one shoulder, to keep the powder in the heavy horse pistols they contained dry. The advance party exchanged knowing looks with one another at the bestial roars of the enemy hussars in the yard and the heart-rending wails from the women in the cowshed. They could not see much from their hiding place in the reeds, but they were seasoned soldiers well able to guess what cruel sports the hussars were enjoying.

Not wishing to delay certain death with more fruitless struggle, the French infantry officer in front of de Malpas relaxed his grip on his sword and let it drop into the muck of the yard. He knelt beside his abandoned sword - all dignity gone, all soldierly pride lost. There might have been a feeble glimmer of hope in the kneeling officer that, witnessing this total abasement, de Malpas might pity him, might spare him from his fate. If so, he had still not plumbed the true depravity of the man standing over him.

De Malpas passed his own sword to his captain, and commanded, 'Hand me his weapon'. Sweet joy suffused the kneeling man at hearing these words. The enemy commander was taking his sword, by so doing was formally accepting his surrender, was accepting him as a prisoner of war - he was going to live.

De Malpas drew himself up to his full height, pointing the sword at the kneeling man as he drew back his hand until it brushed against his right ear. He sighted along the blade over the infantry officer's bent head, at the bony lump made on the nape by the crest of the seventh cervical vertebra. Like a southern bullfighter, he rose up onto his toes and with a delicate half step forward plunged the sword's entire length into the kneeling man's body. It chipped the top of the spine as it entered, juddered across the inner curves of the back ribs, slashed its honed edges through the unresisting contents of the pelvic bowl. The sword's point splintered the dying man's coccyx as it burst out again into the light.

The astonished onlookers watched de Malpas uncurl his fingers from the hilt and step back to let the captive's rigid body topple forward to fall in final obeisance at his feet. The surrounding hussars roared in approbation of their commander's stupendous feat of swordsmanship.

The dead man with his own sword still drilled through his trunk was dragged off and tipped into the pigpen - making the bristle-backed sows look up for a brief instant before lowering bloody snouts again into the torn remains of de Malpas' earlier victims.

The last survivor saw de Malpas beckoning him, had began to obey the peremptory summons to death, when pandemonium erupted. The hussars felt sudden warmth on their backs as if the door of an oven opened behind them, followed by the smell of fire and smoke from the horse lines. The ear-splitting blast of a nearby volley of pistol shots shook the air. Then scores of terrified horses overran the yard, sweeping round the mass of bewildered men like a wild herd; the hussars' own mounts, stampeding from the burning reeds and the yelling lancers.

Above them in the orchard, the Free American Legion was already cantering fast down the slope.

Alexandre dropped from the apple tree into his saddle, and heeled his mount forward as soon as he saw the advance party begin to cut loose the enemy horses. The lancers followed his lead now at full gallop down through the trees.

Alexandre called to Gabriel to sound the charge on the silver bugle that bounced at the boy's back - he wanted the hussars in the farm confused and disoriented, not hunting down the small group of brave lancers who had volunteered to steal into the farm and frighten off the enemy horse. He laughed to see the frantic milling about in the farmyard still to a tableau as every hussar froze in their tracks, lifting their heads to stare open-mouthed up the hill at the bugle's call.

For a second the hussars were stunned at the sight and sound of the charging cavalry. The Free American Legion - known along the frontier as a crack regiment - thundered towards them; an avalanche of the dreaded lancers in their black and silver uniforms and bobbing green cockades swept down through the orderly rows of fruit trees. Frenzy immediately replaced immobility as panicked hussars attempted to capture and remount any horse left in the farmyard.

The Free Americans lowered their lances as the leading horses splashed across the shallow ford. The ranks of horseman crossed the river crowded so tightly together, stirrup-to-stirrup, that there was no necessity to use lances or any other weapon against the first hussars they encountered. The bunched horses simply pounded over anyone caught on foot on open ground.

The overwhelming momentum of the Legion's impact herded forty or so of the hastily mounted enemy into the same corner in which de Malpas had been executing the infantry officers. With the hussars and their mounts squashed into an unmoving mass against the rough stones of the farmhouse wall, the lancers could only get at those on the outer fringe of the troop, who they rapidly dispatched leaving a core of survivors trapped, but out of reach, behind the now riderless horses.

Impatient lancers shook their feet out of their stirrups so their companions on either side could grab a leg and hoist them up to stand on the backs of their horses. Hopping nimbly from one empty saddle to the next, using the riderless horses as stepping stones, they were able to walk across the packed horses to hack down with their sabres at the hussars trapped in the middle.

With most of the enemy killed, the press in the yard eased and Free Americans spread out into the home fields to search for anyone fleeing the main onslaught. The remaining mounted hussars in the yard made a despairing stand against the farmhouse wall. Lancers on foot drove off the barrier of riderless horses protecting the hussars, and, darting in amongst the clump of survivors, thrust the points of lances up into the hussars' armpits, pole-vaulting them out of their saddles to tumble under the hooves of mounted Free Americans - who stuck them like wild pigs.

Alexandre surveyed the jumble of fallen enemy. 'Where is de Malpas, Demoncourt?'

'He's not among the dead Citizen-Colonel.'

A sergeant shouted; the two men turned to see the man pointing up the hill that rose behind the farmhouse. Three hussar officers stopped at the brow of the hill to look back before turning to make their escape. Even with the naked eye, Alexandre could see one of them was de Malpas - Alexandre watched him out of sight.

The enemy's horses were rounded up, the sergeant in charge driving most into the paddock to leave as some compensation for the farmer's losses. Miraculously the farmer himself was still alive despite a beating that left him senseless after he tried to defend his wife and daughters. The women who helped him into the house were dishevelled but grimly satisfied. When the Legion attacked, and the hussars in the barn panicked, the milkmaids had seized the moment and pitchforked two of their abusers to death.

Alexandre heard the sergeant tell the farmer to bury the French, and burn the rest. 'Bury all or burn all Sergeant,' he countermanded, 'They all came into the world the same way.'

'For that matter,' observed Demoncourt, 'We're all of us Frenchmen too.'

The farmer cleared his throat and spat. 'You're all murdering bastards. Soldiers? I'd bury the lot of you if I could.'

†

The three hussars who had escaped the Legion's devastating attack rode away towards their camp to the east. The riders did not speak, nor could they meet one another's eyes - they had sacrificed a hundred and twenty men by their stupidity and cowardice.

Once de Malpas was satisfied they had galloped sufficiently far for them to be beyond immediate danger of capture, he stopped his companions on a small rise from which he could maintain a cautious watch on their back trail. He was amused to see the anguish and shame that pinched his brother officers' pale features and rounded their shoulders.

He was glad Nature had not inconvenienced him with a conscience like theirs; they suffered already, before the ordeal of judicial punishment had even begun. A court martial for all of them, a toothless formality for him since he was under the King's protection, but these two would almost certainly face the firing squad.

Unless, that is, something could be done to improve the account of the day's events. By reversing the odds for example, to fashion a heroic defeat from this ignoble rout. Let the hussars be the ones outnumbered two to one by an irresistible foe A little embroidery here and there and they would have a stirring tale for the General of the last brave stand of the squadron at the isolated farm.

The two men cheered up somewhat as de Malpas outlined the report he proposed to make. A thought occurred to him as he spoke, a possible problem. Fortunately, they could remedy it easily, even enjoyably. 'We're going back,' he announced. 'Once the Free Americans have left, we need to silence the farmer and his women. We don't want them spreading false rumour far and wide.'

†

When they finally rode into camp the next morning, de Malpas' servant was waiting at the guard post to salute and hand up an urgent letter. De Malpas recognized the seal, ripped the letter open to scan its contents. Beaming at what he read, de Malpas shook his boots from the stirrups, threw one leg over the horse's neck, and slid two-footed to the ground. Leaving the report for General Choiseul to his junior officers, and the care of his horse and tack to his servant, he strode off to his quarters, unbuttoning his jacket as he went. The previous day's debacle was already blurring to insignificance, a troublous thing but passing. All his thoughts fastened on the future - the immediate future in which the explicit almost crude promise spelt out in his sister's letter would be deliciously and comprehensively fulfilled.

†

The bright morning light flooded into the room through the folded back shutters, warming de Malpas' back where he lolled in the huge copper bathtub two tiny hotel maids had dragged into the middle of the floor then filled with hot water - bucket by laborious bucket.

The Countess sat at the dressing table gazing into the looking glass with unseeing eyes as Aimée burnished her red-gold hair with long strokes of the brush. Those Swiss millions, she mused to herself. Her thoughts went somewhere dark - the perfect features contorted, a scarlet blotch flared high on each cheek, and hot round tears spurted from her eyes. She half stood. 'Mine!' she cried out smashing doubled fists down amongst the boxes and bottles crowded in front of her. Perfumes and powders exploded from the dressing table. 'Mine!' She glared into the looking glass, daring her infuriated image to deny her claim.

She resettled herself on the seat, rubbed her eyes dry with the backs of her hands like a child. Her maid began again to dress her hair with the same methodical strokes as before. Her brother did not even bother twisting round in his bath to look at her. Neither of these intimates feared her open anger - they knew that the Countess practised her worst cruelties when at her most serene.

'Once we are rid of Alexandre,' she began. Now her audience stiffened into sudden attentiveness - for she spoke with the arctic calm that meant harm would soon be winging its way towards some unfortunate.

'He doesn't know he's rich?' de Malpas queried over his shoulder.

'He'll never know,' the Countess promised.

De Malpas blew his nose into his flannel, swirled the square of fabric clean again in the bath water. 'Not so easy,' he said. 'Not so long as he's surrounded by the Free American Legion.' He began wringing the flannel, coiling and re-coiling the cloth until it twisted into a cable - the tight intense movements at odds with the drawling voice. 'I've been against them in the field once or twice. They are...' He shook out the dry flannel, draped it over his face. There was a silence. The women, hearing the masked fear in his voice, exchanged women's looks. 'They are,' he continued unnecessarily, 'best avoided'.

'When he's on leave then.' The Countess took what her brother said seriously. 'He has a woman?'

'Marie Labouret. Her father keeps the Coin.'

'Oh! Where you mislaid that pretty little page?'

De Malpas snorted, exasperation fluttered out at the corners of the flannel. 'Obviously I can't go. A man of military age. Questioned at every turn. If the Garde Nationale suspected who I really was...'

'Not you,' his Countess interrupted. 'Me.'

De Malpas snatched the flannel from his face at his sister's declaration and twisted round to look at her.

'I'm going,' she confirmed flatly. Her brother made a face and slipped back in the bathwater. 'Not as myself of course.' She got up and sauntered round the tub until he could see her. She wore her own red hair, not her customary powdered wig, and a good, though not fashionable, dress.

She grinned at his puzzled surprise. In flat nasal plebeian, she presented herself. 'Do I make a pleasing peasant?' She turned her feet out, copying the blatant signal she had seen the peasant women use to their men, saw in his eyes the automatic male response to the vulgar offer of sex. 'Attractive? In a coarse sort of way?'

Grinning, de Malpas lunged and caught up her hem. She resisted his attempts to pull her closer. 'But virtuous. A respectable matron.' The Countess allowed herself to be drawn by her skirts nearer to the tub. 'Fairly respectable,' she amended.

She jerked her hem from his grasp, then began gathering her skirts up provocatively. The teasing movements progressively revealed her calves, knees, lower thighs, and then on her right thigh a black garter gripping an edgeless knife with a finger-long skewer for a blade.

She pushed him back in the tub with one foot, and then knelt beside him. 'Respectable. Except when I get my hands on a big rough soldier.' She rested an elbow on his knee, swished at the soapy water with the tips of her fingers. 'Oho!' she cried in delighted discovery, 'I didn't know you found lower class women so exciting. You're not a democrat by any chance?'

Seeing her maid begin a discreet slide towards the door, the Countess commanded, 'Aimée. Stay.'

†

Marie opened the door to the Coin's best chamber. The new guest followed her in and stopped by the bed in the middle of the room.

'My husband has to go here and there,' the woman said. 'Tasting and buying the local wines.'

The woman poked at the mattress, sat on the edge of the bed, even bounced up and down like a child to test it.

I like her, Marie decided. She doesn't pretend to be anything other than what she is.

'This will do well. I don't know for how long, my husband has a contract to supply the Army. War can be good for the wine trade.' Marie pulled back the curtains. The woman came to stand beside her, looking up at the wooded hill behind the inn. 'He could be a week,' she went on. 'He could be a month.'

'These are difficult times for us all, Citizeness. I must confess you're our only guest. But however long your stay, we should be able to take good care of you.'

'You make me feel welcome. What is your name child?'

'Marie, Citizeness.'

'Marie,' the woman said, as if it were a new name to her. 'I'm going to rest now, Marie. Will you call me later?'

When Marie had left the room, the Countess allowed herself a small smile of satisfaction - she obviously made a convincing merchant's wife. Without her wig and caked makeup, her beauty patch and jewels, she was confident that even those that knew her best would not recognise her in this guise.

†

That evening the Countess did indeed find herself dining alone - the other tables, laid ready since noon in hope of passing trade, were still empty at past nine. Marie brought her meal, filled her glass.

'Bon appetit, Citizeness,' Marie said. 'I hope everything pleases.'

'I'm sure. Pour some wine for yourself, Marie. Keep me company whilst I eat - if your father can spare you?'

'Thank you.' Marie was willing to chat, so she sat without protest. 'We're not too busy. The war. We're near the border with Belgium here. The fighting's cost us our regular patrons. Most people keep to their homes.'

The Countess drank deeply, and appreciatively. 'Mmm. M'sieu Labouret keeps a good cellar. My husband goes here, there, everywhere, tasting the local vintage, and if it pleases, buying it.'

'With a war on? He must be a brave man,' Marie ventured.

'Brave? Fontenelle? Not at all. Not in the mornings anyhow. The more wine he samples during the day though, the fiercer he gets. By evening, he's ready to take on Austrians with one fist, Prussians with the other.'

'You're teasing me. I'm sure Citizen Fontenelle's a wonderful husband.

'Wonderful. Husband. Do these words belong together? In the same sentence?'

'You are teasing me. I am sure, when I marry, my husband will be wonderful.'

'You do seem sure of that. Is there a name yet for this lucky man?'

'Alexandre. Alexandre Dumas. He is a colonel in the cavalry. We shall be married, soon, and I shall have lots of babies - all like him.'

'Lots of darling little Alexandres. Well! Well! There's an ambition. But take care now,' the Countess said, holding up an admonitory finger, 'Children can be the death of their parents!'

'You're right!' Marie laughed. 'Do you have a child of your own?'

'Of my own? No. I mean, no children. Fontenelle. The wine... You know drunks. He can find his way home all right, but he can't get his key in the door.' She sighed with regret. 'Dumas? Now I know that name. Did my husband buy wine from his father's estate? I think so.'

'You know Alexandre's family?

'Yes. I can't think why I should remember.' She pursed her lips in thought. 'Something. No matter. But he belongs to one of the great families of France. You are to marry him! Become his countess! These days being a countess is not easy, believe me.'

'Oh no! Not a countess. I'll be just the same as I am now. Alexandre is... is not going to be...'

The Countess clapped her hand over her mouth. 'Ah! I remember! I'm so sorry Marie. I had forgotten about that scan... business. Forgive me I beg you. I spoke without thought.'

'Did you say... scandal?'

'You don't know do you? Oh dear.'

'Please tell me what it is.'

'Well I don't know. It's gossip. Hearsay. If he loves you, trust him. Believe what your Alexandre says. Surely he would not lie to the woman he loves?'

'I do trust him. Of course I do.'

'Well then. Good. Thank goodness. No real harm done.'

Marie took a large gulp of wine and sat silently. After a moment, the Countess continued her meal, watching her victim from the corner of her eye. With satisfaction, she saw a tear well in Marie's eye, roll down her cheek, and plop into the wine glass.

'Tell me. Everything.'

The Countess sighed reluctance. 'The Count was a widower,' she began, 'an old man. He married a beautiful woman. His son saw her, wanted her, desperately. She loved his father. She rejected him. Alexandre...' The Countess interrupted herself. 'This is just gossip! Don't make me repeat this dreadful story.'

'Go on. I want to hear it all. Even if it's not true. Go on.'

The Countess looked deep into her victim's eyes, watched the black of the dilating pupils almost fill Marie's irises as she said, 'Alexandre. He took her anyway.'

'Took her anyway? Raped her you mean?' Marie rose to her feet in agitation, caught her head in her hands, and dug her fingers into her hair. 'Raped her?'

'Dear Marie! It's just idle talk. We were not there, were we? How can we judge?' The Countess stood too and went to embrace Marie. 'Alexandre will tell you what really happened. You must ask your young man. Give him a chance to defend his actions.'

Marie calmed in the Countess' arms, allowed herself to be comforted. 'Thank you,' she said. 'You are right of course. The Alexandre I know is honourable... could never do such a thing. We will talk when he comes. Everything shall be explained.'

'That's sensible.' The Countess gave Marie a last hug and released her. 'Will he come soon?'

'Tomorrow.'

'Tomorrow? How lucky. I see I've upset you with this old story. It was thoughtless of me. Please forgive me.'

'Do not distress yourself on my behalf Citizeness Fontenelle. It was I that made you speak of it. I sensed there was something in his past life he'd rather not speak of. This must be it. Alexandre must have felt too embarrassed... couldn't bring himself to repeat such a disgusting falsehood. I'd have understood!' she declared. 'He'll be relieved to find I know what has been said. He doesn't like secrets.' Remembering her duty as hostess, Marie gave the older woman a contrite smile. 'I've spoilt your meal. I'm so sorry. Please excuse me.'

†

The next morning, Marie, swollen-eyed from lack of sleep, carried a breakfast tray covered with a napkin along the panelled corridor that connected the guests' quarters to the public areas of the inn. She stopped and checked she was alone, changed her grip so she could support the tray on her left forearm, to free her right hand.

Just as she reached out to press the section of carved frieze that released the catch on the concealed door to the cellar, she felt a change in the air as someone entered the corridor behind her. Smoothly she altered the direction of her hand movement - looping a straying strand of hair behind her ear instead, to hide her first intent.

'Good morning Marie,' the Countess said, almost at her back. Marie turned to face her; surprised her guest was up so early. The Countess peered at her with concern.

'Oh dear!' She touched Marie's arm solicitously, 'Did you not sleep well?'

'I think I might have caught a cold.' She managed a sniff. 'Although I can smell your lovely perfume.'

The Countess moved her hand from Marie's arm and lifted a corner of the napkin that covered the tray. 'You like it? You don't think it too heavy for morning?'

'No. It's delicate.'

'I'll leave you some when I go. I mean to give you something to remember me by.' The Countess folded back the napkin a little, to examine the tray's contents. She raised a quizzical eyebrow at what she saw. 'Silver? Porcelain? A posy of flowers? And it's only breakfast.'

'It's for my father,' Marie explained quickly.

'Lucky papa!' the Countess said, staring now into Marie's eyes.

Marie looked down trying to conceal her alarm at the woman's interest.

'I thought... hoped... there was another guest.' The Countess clarified, 'For my amusement.'

Marie was relieved to find her guest's interest motivated by no more than simple boredom. 'When I bring your breakfast,' she assured her, 'I shall sit with you Citizeness - though I may not be the best of company'.

'I should like that,' the Countess responded. 'There's no rush. She stood gazing at Marie. 'Citizen Labouret first then.'

Marie looked puzzled.

'Your father's breakfast?' the woman prompted.

'Oh!' said Marie, recalling her excuse. 'Yes!'

The Countess followed Marie along the corridor as far as the door of the dining room, and went in. Marie gave her a moment then doubled back to the door and saw the woman was seating herself - luckily, the place laid at the table put her with her back to Marie - and stole quietly by.

The Countess sat at her table attentive to every faint suggestive sound from the corridor. Once it was quiet, she rose and came back into the corridor, returning to the place she had first seen Marie. She put her hand up to her hair with the same gesture the girl had used. Her fingers almost brushed a frieze of autumn fruit carved in relief. The Countess peered at it closely.

In amongst the apples were two pears. She pushed one - it seemed to move a little. So did the other. When she pressed both at the same time, an almost inaudible snick was her reward; but the panel bordered by the frieze remained in place. She turned her attention to the opposite side of the panel - here were two more pears. She pressed again and the whole panel swung open. The Countess stepped in.

When she reached the foot of the stair, the Countess paused. She could hear voices at the back of the cellar - one was Marie's, the other a man's voice. She crept towards the candlelight, taking care to keep the rack of wine that concealed her approach between her and them.

She could hardly believe her eyes, and her luck, when she spied Saint-George lying on his cot. She knew he had been badly wounded, had heard he had gone into exile, but there had been no word of him since. She lurked in the dark, listening.

Marie stirred the bowl of bread-sops and milk encouragingly. She smiled at her patient keeping the distress she felt to herself as she noted further signs of deterioration. Saint-George's eyes were bright with fever, sunken in their sockets; the skin about them purpled almost black.

'If I could, I would eat just to please you, child. You are the best of nurses. But I can't seem to eat.'

'Perhaps later.' Marie set the slops aside.

'Alexandre's not come?'

'He's coming.' She busied herself with the tray, aware of his regard.

'What's wrong?'

She had intended not to burden Saint-George with her problems, but found herself blurting 'You and he are friends.

Could you still be friends if one of you did something... something evil?'

'Has Alexandre done something evil?

'No! I don't know. Has he ever said anything to you?'

Saint-George felt for her hand. 'Alexandre is an honest, decent, man,' he said with all the force his weakened body could muster. 'Nothing that he has told me, or that I have heard from others, makes me think otherwise.'

'I knew it!'

'You doubted Alexandre?

'No. Not really. I love him too much.'

'I am sure he is worthy of that love.' His feeble grip slackened completely. 'My apologies Marie I'm feeling...'

'Here am I... Whilst you... What an idiot I am! Yes. Yes. Rest now.'

Saint-George had already closed his eyes. She thought he slept but when she leaned forward and kissed his forehead, she heard a whispered, 'Thank you. Wake me when he comes.' Marie sat a little longer then picked up the tray and made her way from the cellar.

On the narrow stair, she halted. What's that? Something out of place. She went back down a few steps. A smell. Stronger here. A woman's perfume. Not hers, but instantly recognized, for she had first smelled it less than half-an-hour before. She ascended again, and rounding the last turn of the stair, found her suspicions confirmed. The concealed door was ajar now - there was a knack to closing it from outside.

Hurrying to the dining room, Marie confronted the Countess. 'Citizeness Fontenelle. You came here as a guest. May I ask what you were doing in our cellar?'

'Why Marie. Whatever do you mean?'

'You were in my father's cellar without leave.'

'I was not. I swear!'

'I smelled your perfume.'

'Ah. I confess I did put my head in for a moment. Curiosity, no more, Marie. The door was open. I saw the wine racks and thought to myself... my husband might want to buy this wine. I wonder if Citizen Labouret would sell?'

'I cannot believe you Citizeness. To my certain knowledge the door was closed.'

Drawn by the raised voices, Labouret came in. 'Marie, why are you shouting at our guest?'

'Father. This woman was in your cellar.'

Labouret rounded on the Countess. 'The Government? Have you been sent to spy on me?'

'How dare you! I am accustomed to going where I please without asking permission from persons such as you.'

'Persons? Such as we?' Marie cried. 'What cheek!'

'I will not have my actions criticized by a common tavern slut and her half-wit father!'

'Enough!' bellowed Labouret. 'Out. Leave my premises this instant.' He herded her towards the door. 'Out! Out! Wait in the yard for your coach. Your servant will bring out your luggage. Now go.'

'As for you,' the Countess snarled at Marie as she left, 'You and your rapist are well matched. Everything I told you about that monster was the truth.' The Countess swept out of the door.

'Your lies cannot harm me,' Marie called after her.

The Countess paused for a Parthian shot, 'Ask yourself,' she purred, 'Why should I lie?'

She went out leaving Marie looking doubtful again and Labouret mystified.

†

In the yard, the coachman strapped the last of the Countess' luggage on the back of the coach watched by Marie who was determined not to let the woman out of her sight until she was gone. The Countess sat in stony disregard of Marie's intent gaze, though inwardly she vibrated with anger and frustration. Her plans had misfired. She had enjoyed demoralizing the girl so much she lost sight of her main purpose - Alexandre's assassination. Still, she consoled herself, now she knew Saint-George's hiding place, surely she could find some way to finish him? Then the Countess saw a sight that made her smile openly with pleasure - Alexandre riding into the inn's yard.

With a hasty greeting to Luc the stableboy, who ran out to take his horse, Alexandre rushed to embrace Marie. Labouret came out to look on indulgently at the lovers' reunion.

Seeing everyone in the yard had forgotten her presence, the Countess raised the lid of the cushioned bench opposite her and drew out one the heavy pistols kept under the seat. Carefully she checked its priming. Holding the weapon down out of sight, she leant out of the window on the far side of the coach and quietly called her coachman to her.

'Leave all that. Prepare to leave suddenly. When you hear a pistol shot, whip up the horses.'

The Countess returned to her seat on the nearside of the coach. She was confident that Alexandre would not recognize her - wearing her own hair as she was, with her face unpowdered. He was standing with his back to her in any case. She could hear the servant climbing up to the driving bench as she checked the priming again.

She cocked the pistol and lifted it to rest the end of the barrel on the ledge of the open window to steady her aim. Just as she began to squeeze the trigger, two riders moved into the empty space between her and her target.

Gabriel and Demoncourt hadn't tried to keep up with the eager Alexandre as he galloped to meet Marie. Now with their arrival in the yard, they unwittingly screened him from his would-be killer. Even when they dismounted, their animals continued to hide Alexandre from her view.

Feverishly the Countess attempted to get a clear shot but once Labouret began to move everyone into the inn, she realized her chance had gone. The Countess uncocked the pistol and flung it into the cushions of the other seat. Half hanging out of the window she screamed up at her coachman to go. The Countess' cry, the coachman's loud ged-ups and the crack of his whip, made everyone turn to look.

'That dreadful woman!' said Marie.

'Who was she?' asked Alexandre.

'I wonder if I truly know.' Marie leaned closer to say quietly, 'I caught her prying... down there.'

'Is he safe?' whispered Alexandre, taking her meaning.

'Yes of course he is.' Marie said indignantly. She went on in more normal tones. 'That was Citizeness Fontenelle. Did you think her attractive?' She watched his reaction, not sure herself if she was teasing or testing him.

'What? Her? Your mad guest?'

If he had said yes or no that would have been an end to it. To her ears, he sounded evasive or at least defensive. She drew back a little, the better to study him. 'You do like pretty women don't you?'

'What? I don't understand?'

Marie gave him another searching look. She felt tears of disappointment welling under her eyes - couldn't he just say yes or no? She turned sharply on her heel so he would not see her distress and ran into the inn.

Perplexed, Alexandre hurried after her. 'Marie?' She didn't seem to hear him, just went more swiftly to the stairs. 'Marie?' he tried again. Alexandre stopped at the foot of the stairs and watched her run up to the first landing. When she darted a quick look back, he realized what was going on. With a whoop of delight, he gave chase.

Hearing his noisy pursuit Marie cried, 'No! Alexandre! Leave me!'

'Here I come. Here comes the big bad wolf pretty woman.' Growling like a rutting beast, he raced after her through the corridors to her room. She gained the safety of her chamber and slammed the door shut. He easily pushed the door open against her frantic efforts to keep it closed. Laughing at her struggles and protestations, Alexandre bundled her up and threw her onto the bed.

Marie screamed in his face, 'Don't you touch me!' Alexandre went rigid with shock. She scrambled to the end of the bed, crouching on the pillow - as far from him she could get in the small room.

Horrified at the fear he saw in her face - fear of him - Alexandre backed away to the door. 'Marie?'

'I mean it Alexandre. I would not have you touch me.'

'Not touch you? But I thought... Marie. I don't understand. When you ran, I thought... it meant... I see I was in error. Stupid. Insensitive. Forgive me please.'

She uncurled a little, took a deep breath, and rubbed her face vigorously with the flats of her hands as if to wake herself from a bad dream. 'It's not you. It's me.' She moved to the edge of the bed. 'Being silly I think.' She looked up at him, 'For a moment I thought you... It felt so real! There's so much I don't know about you. Perhaps you are the sort of man who could...?' Her voice trailed off as she saw his face change.

'Man who could? Could what?'

'Rape.' Her hands flew to her mouth. Too late. The word was out. 'No! Alexandre.' She came to him. He just stood there. He did not take hold of her. 'I did not mean to say that.' She tried to hold him. 'I'm so confused.'

He shook free of her embrace, stared over her head at some distant scene, some distant time. 'Of all things,' he murmured at last, 'This! Again. It is more than I can bear.' Now he directed a look of such anguish and betrayal at her she felt a rush of tears once more. With no further word, Alexandre turned and left.

Marie did not follow him. 'Again' he had said. She twisted his ring from her finger and held it in the centre of her palm. For a long time she sat on the edge of her bed staring at it.

There was a knock on the door. Alexandre! He had come back. She leapt to her feet, snatched the door open. It was Gabriel.

'He said to get his things,' the boy offered by way of explanation for his presence. He came into the room, closing the door behind him. 'What's happening Marie?'

'You do love Alexandre, Gabriel?'

'I love you both. Why has he gone? I cannot bear to see you two parted.'

'You know what happened with his stepmother?'

'You know?'

'What did you see?'

'Alexandre was falsely accused.'

'What did you see?'

'Only the Countess' maid, shouting.'

'What of Alexandre?'

'He passed me on the stair.'

'He said nothing?'

'Nothing. Just rushed by.'

'He was running?'

'Mistress Marie. He could not do such a thing. Alexandre's innocent. You must believe me.'

She did not doubt his sincerity. Marie had hoped there would be some word, some observation, from Gabriel that would ease her mind. Unfortunately, the little he had directly witnessed seemed to her to confirm Alexandre's guilt.

†

Saint-George was restless when Marie came to him. Even though he was so pale, he shone with sweat. Gently she dried his face and chest.

'Has Alexandre come?' he asked.

'I'm sorry. I know you were hoping to see him. He's gone.'

'Trouble?'

'No. Not as you mean. It's to do with us. We quarrelled. He went.'

'I've lain here for long now under your kindly care. I know you love him as I love my love. My Marie who's in such danger.'

'I am sure the Queen is safe,' she hastened to reassure him.

'Sweet child. They have executed Louis. Do you think they will let his queen, or his heir, long survive him? Even Philippe-Égalité has been condemned to die.'

'You must not tire yourself.'

'My dear,' he continued, speaking in a low breathy rush, 'Marie-Antoinette and I, each in our own way, is sentenced to death. Yes death child. She and I shall be together again soon - in that better world.' He caught at her hand, his grip surprisingly strong, 'But you and Alexandre must learn to live, to love, in this one.'

'Don't talk like this. The Queen will be freed! You will get well. You tire yourself with these anxieties. Try to sleep.' She reached for the wine of opium, stopped when Saint-George shook his head in adamant refusal. 'At least rest.'

She smoothed his sheets, snuffed out all but one of the candles, waved away a moth that fluttered at the remaining flame. As she rose and turned to leave, he called her back.

'Thank you,' he said.

Marie smiled, though the finality in his voice caught at her breath.

'Love is all, sweet child...' Saint-George watched her go before he finished his thought '... to lose love is to lose all.'

With a grunt of effort and pain, he threw back the sheets. He rested for a while, waiting for a little more strength to return - he wouldn't need much for what he planned.

Now two moths flicked in and out of the lone candle flame - their magnified wing shadows wheeled across the whitewashed arches of the vault so the massive stonework seemed to come and go as light followed darkness.

'Time to go.'

He reached out to take hold of the hilt of his sheathed sword. Rested briefly again. Suddenly he raised the sword high and, with a sharp cry of agony, swung it down alongside his leg so forcibly the scabbard flew off to lodge between the bottles in the racked wine at the foot of his pallet. He lay breathing heavily, trying to master the pain that flooded into every part of his body from his unhealed wounds.

Saint-George lifted the naked sword once more to sight along the blade. His Final Adversary stared back at him along its steel-sharp edge. 'Death? I surrender to you at last.'

He smiled in self-mockery - but now the moment was here, he felt alive as never before. The pains had gone, he breathed steadily, and his blood pulsed strongly in his veins. He lowered the sword, bringing it to rest on his chest, the hilt couched under his chin, the razor edge uppermost.

†

In distant Paris, muffled drums began to beat the long death roll. The watching crowds stopped moving, stopped talking, stopped breathing.

With slow grace, Saint-George stroked one bared wrist along the sword's cutting edge, then the other.

'My love. I go before. To greet you at the threshold.'

He brought his hands together in prayer, pressing the bloody blade between his palms, his life pulsing from the severed arteries with every beat of his heart.

In the Place de la Révolution, the drum roll quickened, strengthened to a crescendo, and then ceased. The hush in the square was interrupted by the greased slither and thud of the angled blade falling in the guillotine's frame, then shattered completely as the head of the Queen of France bounced into the basket beneath, releasing a deafening roar of approval from the massed spectators that went on and on.

The fluttering moths collided in the flame of the last candle and fell - wings singed to stumps - into the puddle of hot wax at the candle's base. The black shadows waiting in the corners of the cellar for these last two little deaths raced in to the guttering flame and extinguished it.

PART FOUR

De Malpas

ONE FOR ALL

The Rue de la Pontoise was crowded with rowdy river folk who had left their boats moored on the moon-rippled Seine to climb up the dark mossy water-stair that debouched eventually into the street's north side. At the top of the steep steps, new arrivals merged into the slowly moving celebration of off-duty soldiers, shopkeepers, petty officials and all the city's night people out to savour, or dispense, the cheap but potent pleasures of the poor. The street's numerous brothels were full of drunks, its many taverns full of whores.

A marching band playing a wild and discordant mix of wind, string, and percussion instruments thrust itself into the street at the head of a singing, shouting, capering, carnival parade that boosted noise and movement to almost intolerable levels of clamour and frenzy. Many of the new revellers had masks, some fancy dress, some hardly any dress at all. Everyone in a state of hypermanic delirium - emotionally blasted by the drink, the constant drumming, and the bloody execution earlier in the day of their universally detested Queen, Marie-Antoinette.

'Marie Antoin-e-yette lost her head head head. Put it ina bask-e-yet. She's dead dead dead,' they sang.

'The Bitch is dead! The Bitch is dead! Vive La Nation! Vive La Republique!' went the chorus.

Further down the street, Alexandre and Demoncourt - their uniforms somewhat disordered, their arms entwined over each other's shoulders - made their way through the crowds with the painstaking ineptitude of the exceedingly drunk.

Alexandre sported a cat's mask with whiskers as wide as his shoulders, whilst Demoncourt's rooster mask had a huge, obscenely swollen pink comb.

A surge in the street's human tide half-lifted them from their feet and washed them up in the sudden quiet of a narrow alleyway.

'What am I?' Alexandre slurred to his friend. 'No. No. Not what. Who am I? Eh?' he demanded, 'Tell me that. Who I am?'

'Who? Who you? My friend. You my friend Arex...xandre. Zandra!' Demoncourt howled in delighted discovery. 'Look lovely tonight Zandra.' He threw both arms around Alexandre's neck. 'Let me give oos a big wet...'

Alexandre disengaged himself with some trouble.

'No, no, lissen. Lissen! What's my name?' said Alexandre. As Demoncourt started to answer, he put a hand over his friend's mouth to prevent him.

'No,' Alexandre explained, 'Question's rhetortical. Rhecortickle. Me. Just me talking. Start again. Who am I?' Alexandre Dumas, he mouthed silently to himself, then aloud, with despair, 'Still'.

'Never mind,' Demoncourt consoled. 'Never mind you poor old sod. You can be me for a bit. Be me. Be happy me.' He caught at Alexandre's arm as his friend lurched back out into the main street, 'I said', he said with drunken insistence, 'I said you can be me. Who will I be? Eh? Who me? I'll be you. This is you this is.'

Demoncourt mimicked Alexandre's morose expression so faithfully he made him smile then laugh. He pulled off his mask, replaced it with Alexandre's cat mask, and began caterwauling like a randy tom on the tiles. Alexandre put on the rooster mask and joined in the chorus with cock-a-doodle-does.

'Drink!' Alexandre suddenly decided. 'I want more drink!'

The main press of the carnival crowd moved around and past them. From nowhere, a masked woman insinuated herself between them and seizing Alexandre's attention began a supple gypsy dance to the music of the band. An appreciative hand-clapping circle formed round her. Demoncourt joined in enthusiastically, obviously interested in the beautiful dancer with the flying red hair though she took little notice of him, flashing hot-eyed looks at Alexandre instead.

A second gypsy woman joined the redhead and began dancing with Demoncourt.

As the music and frolics became wilder and more demented., violin bows sawed, trombones slid urgently in and out, drumsticks pounded with increasing force and tempo.

†

In private rooms, all plum plush velvet and gold trimmings, a modest orgy was developing against the hubbub of continued revelry from the street outside. A single candle balanced on a stand moulded into the plaster frame of the mantelpiece mirror threw its redoubled light onto the small party around the table. Alexandre sat slumped back in a chaise longue his rooster mask pushed up. The still masked redhead lolled between his outstretched legs. Opposite them, Demoncourt looked up at the naked Romany girl on the table as her body arched and quivered its way through the impassioned stamp and click of an Andalusian folk dance.

The redhead hooked an arm around Alexandre's neck and pulled herself across his body to kiss him. Sure of the effects of the close embrace, of the heated weight of her body on his, she rose and went to the open doorway of the bedchamber. She stood for a moment facing away into the unlit room beyond as, watched by the two men, the bare dancer forgotten, she loosened the fastenings of her dress. She let it slide down around her legs. Without turning, the woman stepped out of the discarded garment, pulled her mask off, left it dangling on the door handle.

Alexandre swung his feet to the floor and stood, grinning randily towards Demoncourt. He pulled his rooster mask down over his face and flapped his elbows like wings, scraping the floor with one foot.

In the bedchamber, the open window let in moonlight and the noise of continuing nocturnal merriment from the street below. On the darkness of the bed lay the pale shape of the woman. In the lighted doorway stood the dark shape of the man in the rooster mask. He threw back his head and crowed cock-a-doodle-do!

†

The street had been silent for a time. Now calls and laughter briefly disturbed the quiet as a last group of revellers passed beneath the window. As the noise moved away down the street, the breathy sound of male and female in the middle passages of lovemaking reasserted itself in the bedchamber.

Pale legs clenched the man's thighs. A pale forefinger searched for and found the bottommost rib on the dark plane of his back. As the man's breathing deepened, the pale fingers tripped upwards - stepping lightly from rib to rib. The left hand reached its intended destination under the left shoulder blade, index balanced on the fifth rib, middle finger on the sixth.

The woman's right hand rose from the tangled sheet. The slender bodkin invisible in the dark. She slid the dagger's tip between the fore and middle fingers - below her hand the man's heart pounded against her palm. She waited for the last noisy exhalation and at its peak pulled the dagger in to the hilt - giving hurt and bliss in equal measure. With both hands, the woman worked the little knife from side to side in the bloodless wound.

The assassin lay pressed beneath the sudden heaviness of her victim for some time listening intently. At last - a deep male snore sounded in the next room. Reassured once the snoring developed a steady cadence, the Countess began to edge her way out from under the dead man.

†

The morning greetings of tradesmen getting their premises ready for the day woke the snorer on the chaise longue. He kicked the plush throw covering his legs onto the floor, groaned, sat up, and groaned again. Carefully he got to his feet, gingerly scraped open a shutter. Pain-giving sunshine spilled into the disordered room.

'Demoncourt?' Alexander winced at the rasp of his own voice. He searched for his buskins, pulled them on. Took a gulp of water from the jug on the table.

'Demoncourt? When I said you can have her I didn't mean...' He had to stop, to press his hand tenderly against his head - it did not help. He continued more quietly. 'Give it a rest man. A whole night in the saddle? Even a cavalryman needs a break.'

Hearing no response Alexandre felt his way round the bottle-strewn table to listen at the bedroom door. Nothing. He pushed it wide.

†

The French occupied the eastern side of the wide valley. On the further slope, the lines of the Austro-Prussian invaders stretched rank upon rank into the far distance - the totality of their overwhelming numbers mercifully obscured behind curtains of falling rain. Floods and troop movements had made a quagmire of the lush water meadows in the valley bottom.

The opposing armies contrived a slow strangely bloodless cavalry action in the middle of this swamp. There was no head-on clash of men and horses. Instead of conflict, an incessant circling that avoided real battle. Indeed, a small group detached from the rest had given up any pretence of fighting and supposed enemies engaged, instead, in what looked like animated chitchat.

On a grassy hillock, the Commander-in-Chief of the French army General Kellerman and his senior field staff sat fuming on their horses as they watched the strange performance of the mounted wing. General Kellerman's aide-de-camp turned to speak to his companion, pulling the uncomfortably wet collar of his coat away from his cheek.

'What's going on Dumas?' he enquired, 'What does Dumouriez think he's doing?'

Alexandre didn't respond. The aide-de-camp looked past him to Gabriel who just looked back blankly, as mystified as he.

Below them the engagement slowed further, dwindled to an inconclusive end. The opposing forces separated politely and rode back to their lines. There were no empty saddles, no gaps in the ranks.

'That wasn't a fight at all,' said Alexandre, roused at last from his brooding. 'They're playacting. It's a Spanish circus.'

'Don't think our General cares much for circuses,' said the aide. 'Especially when our side's got all the clowns.' He watched the General's galloper dash off towards the returning cavalry. 'Look's as if he's sending for Dumouriez now.'

†

Dumouriez walked his horse up the gentle slope to where the field commanders waited. His two senior dragoon officers flanked him - the three men riding together without sense of urgency or sign of anxiety as if returning from some ceremonial parade or a day's hunting. Their proud bearing, fine uniforms, choice blood-horses and costly accoutrements made many of those who watched feel shabby, provincial, inconsequential - exactly the intended effect. General Kellerman was not so easily impressed.

'Dumouriez! I asked you to kill the enemy not kiss their arses.'

'My dear fellow,' said Dumouriez. 'You are a general of infantry merely. You may be sitting on...' He looked at the General's mount disparagingly, '...some sort of beast, but what can you know of cavalry?'

Dumouriez turned in his saddle to study the face of his companion on his left then to study the one on his right, satisfying himself that both his fellow officers appreciated how neatly he had skewered their so-called superior's pretensions.

'Say you so? My military experience is at least sufficient to recognize you and your officers as cowards and traitors. Provost-Marshal. Arrest these men,' said the General.

Once the escort had taken Dumouriez's party away, the General called for Colonel Dumas. 'Congratulations,' he said to Alexandre, 'I'm making you commander of horse'.

'My honour Citizen-General.'

'Don't say `thank you' do you? Wise. Those damned jockeys are the most arrogant bastards in the army. Get them to fight, Alexandre.'

'That may be difficult General,' the aide-de-camp said pointing to the battlefield.

Below them all the French cavalry, except the Free American Legion, streamed out across no man's land, trotting unhurriedly towards the Austro-Prussian lines, indifferent to the boos and jeers of the loyal French infantry.

As Alexandre and his companions watched the mass desertion, the General's galloper returned to report that the prisoners had disappeared too, and that a search for them was in hand.

'No matter,' the General said, 'I believe I can see the scoundrels from here. And, unless I'm much mistaken, my Provost-Marshal is deserting with them'.

Out on the plain the treacherous Dumouriez and his fellow deserters reined their mounts in, making a small island in the tide of deserting hussars and dragoons that surged around them. Finally, only they remained on the churned-up plain. A horseman, carrying a furled banner, rode out to them from the enemy forces.

Through his spyglass, Alexandre recognised the unmistakable figure of de Malpas. He watched as the man snatched the Republican tricolour from Dumouriez' standard bearer and flung it to the ground. De Malpas unfurled the new flag, lifting the gold and blue fleur-de-lys of Royal France into the air. As the renegades left the field, they walked their horses over the discarded tricolour, trampling it into the mud. At this last insult, the loyal French booing became a great roar of fury - which Dumouriez acknowledged with an ironic wave.

'I pray they're as worthless fighting against us as they have proved fighting for us,' said the aide-de-camp.

'It matters not at all. Until the ground hardens after the rain, cavalry are of little use. And even then this battle will be decided from that hill over there,' said Alexandre, nodding at the hill that rose precipitously behind the Austrian lines.

All along the cart track cut up the side of the hill to service the windmill on its top, stood the heavy cannons of the enemy. The sudden appearance of white puffs of gun-smoke along the line of the track was the first sign that the distant battery had fired its opening salvo.

'Their heavy artillery gunners appear to be well-trained,' said the aide-de-camp, admiring the coordinated firing of the huge guns.

An anxious stir passed through the waiting French infantry, accompanied by scattered cries of individual alarm and dread. Officers shouted commands to be quiet, to hold steady. Only the battle-hardened Free American lancers sat with fatalistic fortitude on their horses.

'Here it comes,' said the aide-de-camp.

With a whistle and a ragged booming crash, the incoming bombardment arrived. All the shot fell short, plopping impotently into the mire well in front of the French lines. After a moment of stunned disbelief at their reprieve, the inexperienced French troops broke into hoots and catcalls, mocking the Austrians' poor aim. Some man among them started up with the Marseillaise. It spread through the army until every man present sang it. A joyous defiance that was short lived. It instantly transformed into grief and terror as, with an eardrum-bursting, bowel-loosening thump, the second ordnance barrage fell smack on target.

The heavy shot bounced through the ordered ranks of soldiers, summarily dividing the quick from the dead as the killing iron balls carved corridors of bloody death and injury through the massed troops.

It was the shock of the sudden and complete destruction of their comrades, coupled with disbelief at their own continued existence, which kept the survivors in position - rather than military discipline or courage.

'May not the men lie down?' said Alexandre.

'Oh!' said the aide-de-camp and immediately turned to the General to pass Alexandre's suggestion on.

Once the General had sent gallopers off with the new orders, Alexandre moved his horse nearer to speak directly to the General. 'I am not needed here Sir. I prefer to be with the Legion when it's under fire.'

'Safer up here Alexandre,' said the General. When Alexandre made no reply, the General said, 'In fact the Legion can stand down. I don't want to expose my last mounted force unnecessarily. The infantry can hold this position until dusk'. Alexandre saluted and rode off to rejoin his men.

The Legion left the battlefield and retired to the French encampment behind the lines. The main camp teemed with female civilians. They carried food and firewood. They cooked and washed. They stretchered the wounded. Their industrious bustle slowed the progress of the Free American Legion towards its quarters.

'Where have they all come from?' said Alexandre.

'All about,' said the Lieutenant riding at his side. 'Most of the men in the infantry regiments come from towns and villages round here. Their mothers, sisters, sweethearts, come to help.'

'Hoping to catch a sight of their loved ones,' said Alexandre. Something in his voice made the lieutenant glance at him.

Two serving women he knew from Labouret's inn passed in the crowd. Seeing Alexandre, they waved and grinned saucily. Alexandre looked at them in surprise. Their presence made him wonder if there was anyone else from the Coin here. He began to smile then remembered he had nothing to smile about. In spite of himself, his eyes continued to roam across the milling crowds, searching vainly for a glimpse of one face.

The column of lancers reached the surgeons' camp. The canvas sides of the field theatre, rolled up, revealed a scene of sordid horror. Lanterns, swinging from ropes, cast broken lights and shadows across the blood and struggle within. Outside, a small boy with catapult and stick kept stray dogs away from a handcart of amputated limbs.

Alexandre beckoned to Gabriel to join him. 'Wait here. I'm going to see our casualty.'

Only one enemy shot had reached the Legion, where it had killed a horse. Camille, the trooper sitting on the horse at the time, had fallen badly. Alexandre went into the nursing tent.

The wounded lay in rows on straw pallets - some had a relative with them to feed and care for them, others relied on nuns from the nearby convent. A nun pointed Alexandre towards the lone lancer. A nurse was dressing the injured man's arm.

'Sir,' said Camille on seeing his commander approach. The nurse, busy with bandaging, did not look up as Alexandre hunkered down at the side of the pallet.

'Not too badly hurt?' asked Alexandre, examining the lancer's arm as the nurse continued to dress it. On the nurse's finger, he saw his mother's ring.

'Will it heal well Citizeness?' he said.

Marie lifted her face. They stared at one another with the same look - half fearful, half hungry. Embarrassed at the naked show of feeling. Camille tactfully found something of great interest to scrutinize at the far end of the tent.

'I beg you, forgive me Alexandre! You will not hold my cruel words against me?'

'I am incapable of so doing,' he said, taking her hand. She pressed it to her heart.

'Camille, close your eyes,' she instructed, leaning towards Alexandre - they kissed.

Camille gave them plenty of time before he cracked one eye open. He found himself alone. 'I'll just carry on with this by myself then shall I?' he said to the air, and with mock resignation, finished winding the bandage around his arm.

Outside the tent, Marie let go of Alexandre and ran to greet Gabriel, who grinned down happily from his horse.

'Gabriel, I'll ride with you. Lift me up Alexandre.'

He lifted Marie up to ride side-saddle behind Gabriel. She twisted on her perch, her eyes shining with excitement, to watch Alexandre as he mounted. She smacked her horse's rump, startling it into a gallop. Alexandre had to heel his own mount vigorously to keep up.

†

Bugles sounded the reveille in the encampment below the farm requisitioned by the army as Alexandre's billet. He rolled from the bed and went to push the window shutters wide. The sky was blue, the early morning sun already warming the stones of the farmhouse wall. Marie pushed herself under his arm to look out too.

'A beautiful day,' he said.

Marie smiled agreement, then realizing the military implications, said, 'Does that mean..?'

'If the ground dries. This afternoon perhaps.' On the horizon, a line of white smoke suddenly streaked the side of Windmill

Hill. The muted boom of the first salvo of the new day carried to them. 'They're starting early.'

'How sad. That hill has such happy memories. We used to climb it when we were children. The miller's wife gave us dough buns full of honey with sweet milk still warm from the goats.'

They watched Gabriel lead two saddled horses out of the stables into the yard below.

'Long walk and a hard climb for little legs,' said Alexandre.

'Not really. A spring behind the windmill feeds a stream that runs down a gully. It's steep, but there are plenty of boulders in the stream to climb up. There are deep cold pools full of trout and crayfish.'

'One day. We'll go there.'

Gabriel tied the horses' lead reins to a fence rail. He looked up to salute Alexandre and smile to Marie.

†

The Free American Legion waited in battle formation on a rise overlooking the plain. Alexandre wondered if this would be the last time he would speak to them before action. Not that he feared for the men - they were tough and looked out for each other in a fight. It was more that he knew that de Malpas was with the Austrians, and that if they met, the war would take second place to their personal feud. He thought he could match de Malpas' combat skills now, but the other man remained vastly more experienced and wholly unscrupulous, capable of any deceit. Alexandre was honest enough to know that he might not survive a close encounter with his archenemy.

He raised his voice to address the Legion. 'Free Americans. We face enemies arrayed in great strength before us. Austrians, Prussians, the aristocrats of Old France. Those who fight for honour against such odds the world rightly names 'heroes'. Such are you. Heroes of the Revolution. Heroes that France shall never forget. A new day dawns. On this day, Citizen-Soldiers, we are free. There's nothing set above us but this fair sky. No aristocrat. No king. No emperor. We fight so freedom may last longer than just a single day. Vive La Republique!'

'La Republique!' roared the Legion.

'Vive La France!'

'La France!' came back the call.

'One for all!'

'All for one!'

†

The Austrian artillery boomed continuously on Windmill Hill. In the valley, the French infantry regiments plodded behind their tricolours through the increasingly thick fog of gun smoke. The Austrian barrage abruptly ceased. In the sudden quiet, the only noise, the small rhythmic exertions of the marching French.

Enemy trumpets blared. As the tenor notes faded, a low subsonic rumble began to build. The noise and vibration came up through the boot soles of the marching men, nauseating them and making them break into cold sweat. Somewhere in the pall of smoke that hung in the air, massed cavalry were charging invisibly towards them at full tilt.

When the wide ranks of de Malpas' hussars burst into view out of the fog, the whole French advance swayed in alarm, faltered, came to a ragged halt.

On the rise, Gabriel shouted 'They're going to run.'

'No time to wait for orders,' said Alexandre, 'Gabriel blow your horn!'

The French foot hastily bunched together making corridors in their ranks to let the yelling Free Americans gallop through. De Malpas' hussars, expecting an easy ride over raw infantry, found their charge met by a thousand seasoned lancers instead. The main body of hussars wheeled away from the head-on assault, their sabres no match for lances.

The French foot soldiers, encouraged by the success of their cavalry, eagerly followed the Free Americans to dispatch fallen hussars with their bayonets.

Alexandre accompanied by Gabriel - and the score of lancers self-elected as his bodyguard - fought his way towards de Malpas who continually taunted and challenged him to come and fight. Each time Alexandre's small contingent battled near enough to engage him direct, de Malpas retired before them.

'He's drawing us in,' Alexandre finally realized. 'Fall back! Fall back!' The lancers begin moving away, back towards their own lines.

Seeing he was about to lose his prey, de Malpas for the first time pushed to the front of his hussars. He dragged a heavy horse pistol from his saddle holster as he shouted, 'Dumas!' Alexandre turned to face him. De Malpas shot him at point blank range in the head. The force of the shot bowled Alexandre backwards off his horse. He crashed lifelessly to the ground. De

Malpas yelped with delight. Seeing Gabriel's shocked look, de Malpas gave him his serpent grimace.

Large numbers of Austrian dragoons arrived to bolster de Malpas' hussars. The tide of battle turned in the enemy's favour and bore the fighting Free Americans away.

Gabriel managed one last despairing glance back at Alexandre's corpse; only to see it kicked and trampled under the horses of the advancing Austrian dragoons before it was lost to view.

The clamour of men fighting faded as the core of the fighting moved away and the combatants disappeared from sight in the dust and smoke.

Into the hush of the aftermath of battle, came the sound of someone whistling - whistling one of Saint-George's favourite airs. Then Saint-George himself, incongruously dressed in court clothes, strolled out of the drifting gun smoke. He rapped the sole of Alexandre's boot with the end of his cane.

Alexandre gave a great gasp and sat up. Resurrection! Amazed he stared, eyes bulging, up at Saint-George. He knew his friend could not be here - Alexandre had helped to bury him. But here he was.

Alexandre could not think about that, his head hurt too much. He leaned to one side and vomited. That helped. Now he could focus better on Saint-George - who was still there, dressed for a ball at Versailles, smiling down at him.

'Get up dear boy. You can't be snoozing now. France needs all her sons to be on their feet and smiting the enemy hip and thigh.'

Alexandre got a finger under his chinstrap and pulled off his lance-cap so he could rub where the pain was fiercest - in the centre of his forehead. Something bright glinting in the upturned lance-cap in his lap caught his attention. He picked out Marie's lucky coin, followed by the heavy lead ball from de Malpas' horse pistol. The coin was saucer-shaped. He rested the lead shot in the dent - it fit exactly.

'The beauteous Marie,' said Saint-George, 'So thoughtful.'

'Saint-George. You are dead.'

'I'm keeping the promise I made to you when first we met. Come now. Time to be up.'

Painfully Alexandre struggled to his feet. 'What can I do? We have been left to die.'

Trumpets sounded, near and far around them, all urgent.

'The Austrian recall,' said Saint-George.

Galloping hussars loomed out of the billowing smoke before them, crashed by on either side without a glance.

'Maybe I'm dead too, so it doesn't matter,' said Alexandre.

Saint-George made no reply - he just smiled and began to dance. As Alexandre watched his friend, he caught a movement out of the corner of his eye. He turned to see a lone rider approaching - it was Gabriel.

'Alexandre, you're alive.'

As the elated Gabriel dismounted, Alexandre looked towards Saint-George - there was no sign of him.

He put out his hand to touch Gabriel, to make sure he was truly there. Mistaking this gesture, Gabriel seized his hand and shook it hard enough to convince Alexandre that they were both alive.

'I thought you were...' said Gabriel, 'I came looking for your cor...' He did not need to finish the word for here was no corpse, but Alexandre himself alive and safe.

Alexandre gingerly put his lance-cap back on, taking care to avoid the sore spot on his forehead. With Gabriel's help, he pulled himself up into the saddle. Gabriel spied Alexandre's sword sunk to its hilt in the mud, and handed it up. They shared a smile, remembering this had happened before.

The Free Americans were the first to notice Alexandre as he and Gabriel rode back into the French lines. The Legion greeted the return of their commander alive in the customary way - with raised lances and a mighty 'HURR'. The entire French infantry joined in the second 'HURR'. Alexandre drew his sword and brandished it in acknowledgement. The third and final 'HURR' was deafening. Alexandre's raised sword caught the light of the setting sun and blazed like a fiery brand.

†

Above the climbing men loomed the windmill, dark against the moon-bright sky. Its sails occasionally moved in the light winds, the loud random creaks freezing the climbing column in fear of discovery. Every man had a lance hanging by its loop at his back. Some had machetes swinging from their belts. Many had wrapped scarves around their heads - those that went bare-chested and barefoot too, looked more like pirates than soldiers.

Below them, moon shadows chased across the pasture where a rearguard of lancers guarded the horses. Marie looked up to wave a final goodbye to Alexandre - though the men labouring up the narrow gully were scarcely visible to her now and she had no idea which of the dark figures might be Alexandre. She had pleaded with him to let her be their guide - she knew the best route up the tumbled boulders and the internal layout of the windmill as well, but he would not listen.

Marie had to be satisfied with her role as guide, bringing them by a roundabout route through a labyrinth of forgotten paths overgrown with brambles to the foot of Windmill Hill. Then to point out the mouth of the gully scored by the torrent that ran down the side of the hill.

Acknowledging the impatience and anxiety of the two lancers detailed off to be her escort - they were very close to the Austrian positions here - she turned her horse back to the farmhouse.

The Free Americans assembled at the top of the gully, crouching down among the gorse bushes. Once the last man joined them, Alexandre and Gabriel went forward to reconnoitre the windmill.

They found a vantage point behind a chicken house in the miller's yard. No livestock had survived the Austrian occupation, so there were no chickens left to be disturbed and give alarm.

Alexandre felt nauseous, he rubbed his forehead, though nothing could relieve the piercing pain that came and went without warning. When he was able to look towards the windmill again, he saw Saint-George, sitting on an old millstone nearby, turn and hold a finger to his lips.

'Can you see anyone there Gabriel?' whispered Alexandre. Gabriel shook his head.

Saint-George waved a hand in the direction of the windmill. 'It's full of Austrians - all asleep,' he said to Alexandre.

Alexandre glanced at Gabriel, who plainly heard nothing.

'They think they are safe so far from the front. No vedettes, no sentries, can you believe!'

'All asleep. No sentries,' Alexandre repeated Saint-George's words to himself. Hearing them, Gabriel signalled the men forward before Alexandre could stop him. The lancers streamed past. Half a dozen lay down their lances, unsheathed their machetes, and ran to crouch silently, three to a side by the door to the windmill.

Alexandre hurried forward, signing them to wait. He had seen the beam of a sack hoist jutting out from the side of the windmill above their heads. The loading bay was too high to jump up to - twice the height of a man - so he put his back to the wall underneath the hoist, cupped his hands to make a stirrup, and threw three lancers up into the dark opening.

A count of thirty to give time for the lancers inside to get into position, then a lance was jabbed through a window to smash the lantern hanging inside. Lancers flowed into the dark interior of the windmill. The sounds of struggle were soon over. There was no outcry from within. The lancers reappeared, sauntering out into the moonlight, wiping the wet blades of their machetes on pieces of sacking.

Beyond the windmill, the heavy cannons stood cold and massive in the moonlight. A few Austrian cannoneers sat hunched over the dying embers of a cooking fire. The rest lay mostly out of sight bivouacked against the stacks of cartridge-bags, sharing the shelter of the canvas covers rigged to keep the dewfall off the gunpowder.

A cloud scudded across the face of the moon. Before eyes had a chance to adjust to the pitch blackness, the moonlight returned - revealing a long line of Free Americans standing in the undergrowth at the side of the cart track. They stepped forward silent footed - lances prodding, stabbing, and skewering any cannoneer who did not immediately surrender. Those that chose to fight found a sword much too puny a weapon to use against lances.

Supervised by the lancers, the surviving cannoneers stacked the cartridge-bags beneath the cannons and laid fuses. Once the fuses were well alight, the lancers let the cannoneers flee down the cart track, whilst they themselves dashed back to the windmill to put its bulk between them and the imminent explosion.

The warning cries of the fleeing cannoneers went unheard as long thunderous roll of explosions burst the huge cannons apart, scattering broken wheels, barrels, and mountings down the steep escarpment onto the heads of the Austrian troops in the valley below.

On the other side of the valley, at the farmhouse billet, Marie ceased her pacing as the concussive booms shook the air. She twisted Alexandre's ring on her finger, praying he was safe.

In an inn a few miles behind enemy lines, the noises in the night woke the Countess. She threw open the window shutters and wondered at the flashes of the distant detonations lighting up the undersides of the clouds.

†

The next day for a change there was no early morning barrage from Windmill Hill. That one difference so demoralized the Austrians, and so encouraged the French, that the whole course of the battle changed too.

The French infantry brigades advanced on the Austrians with renewed assurance. The French horse artillery was able to deploy without being under fire. When the Austrian cavalry began their first charge, a lethal hail of grapeshot from the French horse artillery cut them down in swathes. The massive French foot columns hammered their way deep into the demoralized Austrian infantry.

Giving the French artillery a wide berth by circling around them, de Malpas' hussars furiously sabered their way into the French flank. Absorbed in their butchery of the foot soldiers, the hussars were unprepared for the fearful shock of the Free American Legion smashing into them in a solid mass.

The hussars fell back to regroup. The Austrian foot soldiers, already reeling under the revitalized French infantry offensive, thought themselves abandoned by their cavalry, and started to fall back too. Seeing the entire enemy force retiring before them, the French pushed harder.

The triumphant sounds of the Marseillaise soared up over the din of battle as a hundred thousand Frenchmen realized victory was near. The Austrian soldiers began to stream away from the frontline as, harried by the Free Americans, the disorganized Austrian retreat crumbled into full-blooded rout.

Alexandre studied the enemy flight through his spyglass. The Austrians were plainly beaten. There was no order or discipline in their withdrawal - they dropped their backpacks, dropped their weapons, and ran for their lives.

He decided to let the French foot pursue them - to keep the enemy harassed and running, so they could not reform into a coherent fighting force. He did not want the Legion spread out over miles of country - it was still France's only mounted corps.

Gabriel waited at his colonel's side for Alexandre to finish his inspection. He was half aware that a short distance beyond

Alexandre, a troop of French infantry was disarming a small group of hussars they had captured.

A single enemy rider burst free from the circle of bayonets. The movement attracted Gabriel's attention. He immediately recognized the rider spurring his horse towards them - it was de Malpas. Gabriel yelled a warning to Alexandre, pointing behind him.

Alexandre twisted in his saddle to face the danger, just managing to get the shaft of his lance raised high enough to deflect de Malpas' sabre thrust. The hussar's horse, galloping at full tilt, crashed into Alexandre's, tossing both antagonists to the ground.

Alexandre was back on his feet first. He had not let go of his lance - he leaned on it as he waited for de Malpas to rise.

'Confound you! You're damned hard to kill, Dumas.' As de Malpas spoke, he searched the ground for his lost sword, looking perplexed when he finally spotted it under Alexandre's foot.

'Tell me de Malpas - it's a great puzzle - why do you and your sister hate me so?' said Alexandre.

Instead of answering, de Malpas pointed wordlessly at his sabre. Alexandre stepped back from the sword and de Malpas came forward and without taking his eyes off Alexandre, stooped to pick it up. He returned to his original position before replying.

'We hate you... because.' He pulled off his hussar's busby, tossed it to one side, took a couple of warmup swings with the sabre.

'Was it for money?'

De Malpas shrugged.

'For property then?'

'Because. Because. Because,' de Malpas said - with increasing violence so he shouted the last word with such vehemence he surprised himself into silence.

His outburst was a revelation. Alexandre could see from the man's face, that if de Malpas had not known the source of his hatred before, he knew it now, and the knowledge had shaken him to the core. Looking at his old enemy, Alexandre realized he knew the reason too - just as surely as if de Malpas had told him. Both men knew a door had opened, exposing what had been hidden, and forgotten.

'My father loved me. That is what you cannot forgive,' said Alexandre.

With an incoherent roar, de Malpas rushed at Alexandre, swinging his sabre down on Alexandre's head. Alexandre blocked the blow, catching the sabre's edge in the cloth tied behind his lance head. They stood, straining face to face, sword and lance locked over their heads.

Abruptly, de Malpas disengaged, stepped back. The physical effort had given him time to regain control of his emotions. With his usual cold manner restored, he looked up at Gabriel - who had drawn his sword and was ready to use it. De Malpas shook his head in disbelief at the sight of his former page threatening him. 'No interference?' he said.

Alexandre nodded agreement. Gabriel reluctantly put up his sword, pulled his horse back a length.

'And like for like Dumas?' said de Malpas, holding his sabre out.

Alexandre nodded again, reversed his lance, and rammed it down into the ground. The effort brought on a spasm of pain in his head so intense it briefly blinded him.

An instant's inattention, and his opponent weaponless, was all the opportunity that de Malpas needed - up went his sabre as he stamped forward and brought the sword down as hard as he could on the crown of Alexandre's head.

For the first time Alexandre really understood what Saint-George meant when he said that everything comes from nothing. He did not think about drawing his sword; it found its way into his hand. He did not think about raising the blade horizontally over his head, but without thought or effort, that is where it was waiting when de Malpas brought down his sabre in that first lethal attack. Alexandre angled his blade to make de Malpas' blow shear off harmlessly to one side.

From that moment, whatever his opponent tried, whether hacking down at Alexandre's head and shoulders - first on one side, then on the other - or cut and thrust to the body, Alexandre's sword was ready in just the right place to block each attempt. Finally, exhausted by the impenetrable defence, de Malpas fell back and lowered his sword, mouth hanging open, panting hoarsely, all the fight gone out of him.

Alexandre heard a languid handclap and Saint-George's voice behind murmur 'Very pretty swordplay Alexandre'.

When he got his breath back, de Malpas said 'You're nothing like as good as Saint-George was.' He passed his sword to his left hand, holding it by the blade. 'But,' he went on, 'you're too good for me.'

He held the sword out hilt first, for Alexandre to take, and started to make the customary statement of surrender but almost immediately stopped because the din of a string of captured horses galloping past led by a Free American made his words inaudible.

With a small shrug of apology, de Malpas turned to watch the horses, waiting for them to go by before completing his speech. As the last horse in the string passed, de Malpas spun back on his heel and hurled his sabre full into Alexandre's face.

It was not an effective attack, Alexandre just batted it away, but attack was not its purpose - it was a diversion. With a yelp of triumph, de Malpas reached behind him, snatched Alexandre's discarded lance out of the ground, and waved the blade under Alexandre's nose.

'So you've learnt a few flashy sword tricks,' said de Malpas. 'Well let's try something different. Am I wrong, or was Saint-George the only swordsman who could beat a man with a lance?'

'You are not wrong. Unfortunately, that's one `flashy trick' my friend never showed me.'

At Alexandre's words, Gabriel pulled his lance from its holster, nudged his horse nearer, and held out the lance for Alexandre to take.

'You agreed, no interference,' de Malpas said to Alexandre.

'And like for like,' Gabriel said to de Malpas. 'You've got a lance. That changes everything'.

'I've given my word. I can't take it back,' said Alexandre.

'He's broken his word, Alexandre.'

'It doesn't make a difference, Gabriel. I gave my word knowing I was not giving it to a man of honour. I can't take your lance.'

De Malpas jabbed at Alexandre, forcing him to take a step away. He did it again, then again. He had the upper hand now, there was no need to rush, and he could enjoy himself. His attention focussed on the cloth wrapped round the shaft of the lance where it met the blade. 'What's the point of the rags?'

'To soak up the blood.' Alexandre could hear Saint-George answering with him.

De Malpas grinned at the reply, licked his lips slowly - deliberately exhibiting his forked tongue. He jabbed the lance at Alexandre, this time meaning to wound. He pressed the attack forcing Alexandre to retreat with each thrust. Nearly every jab cut into him. The blood did not show on the black cloth but he could feel the uniform getting sodden from dozens of wounds.

Alexandre had no real defence, his sword was too light to parry the lance and too short to mount a counterattack. De Malpas attacked in flurries of rapid stabs, keeping the lance moving too fast for him to catch hold. He tried to regain the state of mental calm he had achieved earlier, which had made him invincible. Now the unrelenting onslaught, in which he was continually chivvied, prodded, and stabbed, made it impossible for him to settle and find that place of serene detachment.

Alexandre could feel his strength running out with the blood from his many wounds. How long would de Malpas toy with him? He saw Gabriel draw his sword, a look of determination on his face. Alexandre did not have the strength to shout 'no', tried instead to signal stop with his hand, but could only manage a weak flutter of his fingers.

Seeing Gabriel's move, de Malpas stopped his assault, drew back. 'You have been told not to intervene,' de Malpas said to Gabriel.

Gabriel looked to Alexandre, begging his permission to join in. Alexandre shook his head. De Malpas laughed, walked over to Gabriel, and wagged his forked tongue at him in his old way. Gabriel was not intimidated; the days of fearing this man were past. Gabriel stared down at de Malpas, letting his contempt show. Letting de Malpas see that, whatever the outcome of this contest, he would not leave here alive. De Malpas tried to outstare Gabriel. In the end, it was he who dropped his gaze.

With a snarl of anger, de Malpas wheeled away from Gabriel, ran the few steps that separated him from Alexandre and plunged the lance full into Alexandre's thigh. The blade cut straight through - the tip came out the other side. 'Dance!' his tormentor mocked, 'This is your last dance.'

Alexandre knew he was going to die, knew it, and accepted it. It was an honourable death, his conscience was clear. He could rest in peace. With that understanding and acceptance, a great calm spread through him. From the calm that had eluded him until now, came strength.

De Malpas leaned on the shaft to push the lance in further - but the bunched rags would not let him. Alexandre reached down, caught hold of the lance shaft with his free hand and let himself fall backwards - pulling the lance tip out of his leg - at the same time lifting the lance upwards.

Instinctively, de Malpas gripped the lance more tightly - confident he could use his body weight to jerk the weapon from Alexandre's hand - only to find he was flying up into the air with the lance. De Malpas hurtled over Alexandre's head, still clutching the lance desperately, as Alexandre continued his fall backwards.

Alexandre sat up laying the lance on the ground beside him. He noted distantly that the lance blade had come out of his thigh cleanly, leaving surprisingly little blood.

Unable to stand for a moment, he hauled himself round on his hands to confirm de Malpas' fate. His enemy was dead, legs and arms sprawled, mouth gaping. The dead man's torso was arched up, propped clear of the mud by the full blade's length of Alexandre's sword buried to its hilt in his chest. His father's sword, avenging its dead owner.

Gabriel leapt from his horse and hurried over to bind Alexandre's leg with a scarf. He brought Alexandre's horse over and helped him into the saddle.

Alexandre surveyed the carnage that surrounded them on all sides. 'Why them?' He stared down at his arch enemy's corpse. 'Why him? Why not me?'

Not attempting an answer, Gabriel put his foot on de Malpas' chest and dragged Alexandre's sword out.

Alexandre took it from him, looked down at de Malpas again. 'Even he shouldn't have an unmarked grave.'

'I doubt he would do as much for you Alexandre.'

†

She had gone to all but one of the churches in the locality - and still not found what she searched for. When she came to the last, more a chapel than a church, she stood outside hardly daring to enter. It was dark now, the dew fall made the gravestones gleam palely in the light from the small lantern she carried. The grass, unscythed all year, was waist high and clung wetly as she pushed her way through, soaking the hem of her cloak, chilling her feet.

Inside, the little church was full of choking smoke curling up from a cooking fire made next to the altar. Two women sat as close to the flames as they could without scorching the rags they wore. A little girl with them stood to see who had come in.

Three candles on the altar lit the desecrated chapel. The candles could not light the faces of the saints in the stained glass windows - every one was smashed, nor the heads of Jesus and his saints - each broken from its effigy. There were no pews, no pulpit, not one crucifix. It was just like every other church she had seen today.

At the foot of one wall, a row of uniformed bodies lay shoulder to shoulder on the bare flagstones in a last pathetic parade. All had lost their boots and some parts of their clothing to scavengers - likely the refugees who warmed themselves at the fire. The Countess ignored the family as, one by one, she examined each body.

The little girl, curious to see what the hooded figure could want with dead soldiers, came on bare feet to stare at the Countess. One look from the hooded figure sent her scampering back to the safety of fire and family.

The Countess continued her inspection, moving more quickly now as she neared the end of the row. She gasped aloud as she recognized the last body.

'Oh dear brother! Sweet brother, you are dead.' She fell to her knees, lifted his bare feet, kissed them, and pressed them between her hands and thighs. 'Cold. You are so cold brother.' The Countess leant forward on one hand to peer into his face, touched her palm to his cheek. 'Husband.' Openly sobbing, she stretched herself out upon his body. 'Friend.'

†

Labouret, Marie, and Alexandre sat at table in the private rooms at the back of the Coin Inn. No-one had much appetite; Alexandre least of all, his meal was untouched. He looked apologetically at Marie, pushed his plate away.

Alexandre rubbed his forehead. The bruising had almost gone, but from time to time he still suffered headaches. Seeing his pain, Marie got up, kissed the top of his head.

'Get some fresh air. Take a stroll up the track,' she said.

†

The Countess stood by the old shrine, where the track levelled off before winding into the trees. Studying the back of the inn, she started with surprise to see Alexandre come out of the inn and pull the door close behind him. She watched him stand outside for a moment, rubbing a bruise on his forehead that was so dark it was noticeable, even at a distance.

Alexandre looked up the track; saw Saint-George standing next to the old shrine. Would these visitations never end? He set off up the track.

Saint-George smiled in greeting as Alexandre came near. 'You trust me Alexandre,' he said. Then he said it again, but this time, as Saint-George repeated the words, Alexandre realized it was not his old friend speaking - he was hearing a woman's voice saying again, 'You trust me Alexandre?'

He pressed the heels of his hands into his eyes, hard, until he was seeing swirling colours. Was he asleep? Was he mad? When he looked again, he saw it was the Countess who stood before him.

'You trust me Alexandre? Me? Are your wits addled? You come up the track like a little lost lamb. Do you not know I mean to kill you, fool?'

She raised an arm. She held a small pistol in her hand, concealed until then behind the fullness of her riding skirts.

'Why do you hate me?' asked Alexandre.

'If I told you why, would you die happy?' She straightened her arm. Her finger whitened as she pressed on the trigger.

'I asked that of your brother yesterday. He refused to say.'

She half lowered the pistol. 'My brother? It was you? You murdered him?'

Alexandre gazed steadily at her.

'The fortune your father left to you, his darling boy, were reason sufficient to finish you. But now...' she said as she raised the pistol again, '...vengeance is better'.

Marie thrust herself between the antagonists, her rush up the path when she saw who was with Alexandre unnoticed. He took her by the shoulders, was about to lift her bodily away from danger, when he heard Saint-George's voice. 'Alexandre. Be still!'

'Ah! The tavern slut,' said the Countess. 'You're used to her stink?' she asked Alexandre as she smiled a smile full of malice at Marie.

'Is it you Citizeness Fontenelle?' asked Marie.

Alexandre gaped - his mind began to race. The Countess smiled, reading the direction his thoughts were taking him by the changing expressions on his face. 'In Paris?' she prompted.

'Demoncourt's killer.'

'Your fault your friend died. Such tender passion. Maybe we..? I almost spared you that night. Except, it was not you lying with me was it? Not you. And so my brother is dead.'

'Why did you come Marie?' said Alexandre.

'Just as well I did!'

'What possible difference can a slut make?' said the Countess.

'Your toy pistol has but a single ball,' said Marie.

'You mean to sacrifice yourself? For him? Die in his stead? How noble. How stupid.' The Countess lifted her other hand bringing a second pistol, identical to the first, into view. She aimed the barrel at Marie's stomach.

'Alexandre! Trust Marie!' Saint-George's voice urged in his ear.

'And what of the unborn child you carry?' The Countess acknowledged Alexandre's surprise with a snort of amusement. 'You did not know Alexandre? How droll.' She began to squeeze the triggers of both pistols.

Marie, shielding her belly protectively, uselessly, with her hands, stepped back in horror, forcing Alexandre back with her. Reflexively the Countess followed their movement, stepping forward too - onto the capping stone of the old well.

With a grate of heavy masonry, the thick sandstone slab tilted slightly under her feet. The Countess almost lost her footing as she suddenly dropped several inches. This was only a temporary reprieve for almost immediately the capping stone tilted to the vertical and dropped again, sliding down into the well shaft.

Even as the Countess plunged out of sight, Alexandre dived forward and caught the rim of the descending stone with one hand. Its great weight almost yanked him in after her - he only managed to save himself by throwing his other hand out to catch the far edge of the well.

Spread-eagled across the mouth of the well - with a single hand on one side, feet on the other - he felt the enormous burden of the capping stone dragging down on his arm beneath him. He judged he could hold on for half a minute, not much more.

Marie wrapped her hands around the wrist of the arm that supported him, determined to snatch him back out of the well if she had the strength, or fall to her death with him if she did not

They both peered down into the dark of the well shaft. It was difficult to see past the clumped ivy encrusting the top of the stone. They listened, but heard nothing other than their own laboured breathing.

'She's gone,' said Marie. 'Let go of the stone Alex.'

Alexandre was on the point of complying, when he felt the stone twist a few degrees in his hand.

'Still there,' he said.

The stone turned again, more forcefully this time, and the Countess' head swung into view. She hung below, swinging on a forearm hooked through the stone's ivy. She stared up at them, her huge eyes and ashen face freakish in the dark of the well.

'We can't save her. Let go, or you'll fall in too,' said Marie.

'I won't let go,' replied Alexandre.

'He's too stupid to let go.' The Countess' mockery had no trace of fear in it, though she must have known that these were her last moments of life. 'He'd rather die than hurt a woman.

Anyway, I don't want him dead. Not now Alexandre,' she said, talking directly to him. 'I want you alive and suffering as I have suffered. You,' she emphasized contemptuously, 'can't hurt a woman'. Her free hand came into sight as she spoke; she still had a pistol. 'You can't hurt a woman. I can.'

All in one movement, she raised the pistol above her head, sighted the muzzle at Marie.

Alexandre let go without hesitation the instant he saw her lift the weapon. Even as the Countess fired, she fell from sight.

The shot aimed at Marie went wild - ricocheting off the rim of the well - as the capping stone plummeted down the well shaft with the Countess hanging underneath its mass. There was a long screech of stone scrapping on stone as the massive slab plunged to the bottom of the well - pushing the screaming Countess down beneath it.

There was a great splash which cut off all noise abruptly. Everything became still, and quiet.

Marie squeezed Alexandre's wrist. 'Are you alright?'

'Yes. You?'

'How are you going to get back?'

Alexandre took stock of his predicament, 'I'm not sure,' he confessed.

He was secure for the moment where he was, balancing on his hands and feet. The difficulty was that he was stretched to almost his full extent. His hands were on the opposite side of the well from his feet and his body only just bridged the well mouth.

The arm he used to hold the massive weight of the capping stone started to tremble, and an empty feeling in his wounded leg warned that it too would not hold up for long. There was little time to think - he had to act.

'Come round to my side,' he said to Marie. 'Give me room - don't get too near the edge.'

He did not know what he was going to do - leaving it up to his body's instincts to find a way to back to solid ground. His arms and legs suddenly snapped themselves straight of their own accord, throwing him up and to one side. He fell on his side against the stones rimming the well.

For an instant, he was at the point of balance and thought himself safe, then he began to roll back into the well with nothing to clutch at but empty air.

Just as he thought he was bound to join the Countess at the bottom of the shaft, he felt Marie's fingers dig into shoulder and hip, hard as grappling irons. She rolled him back towards her with the strength of desperation away from the well's edge.

As he was spun over onto his back, Alexandre's view into the dark deeps of what might have been his grave was replaced, first by a flash of the bluest blue sky he had ever seen, and finally by the face of the woman he loved.

Alexandre lay quietly with his head in Marie's lap, as content to look up at her as she was to look down at him.

'So. Still with us,' she teased.

He reached to gently rub her stomach. 'I didn't want to miss what happens next.'

She pressed her hand over his, and smiled with her whole being.

'The headache?'

'Gone.'

Alexandre did not need to look around for Saint-George. He knew his old friend was gone as the headache had gone, gone to rejoin his own Marie.

EPILOGUE

Chateau de Monte Cristo, 1846

ONE FOR ALL

Dumas, a large, handsome, bushy-haired man, sits in a study - lit only by firelight and a single candelabra on a massive writing desk. Opposite him - almost lost in a huge winged chair - perches the little Publisher, his face rapt with attention.

'My mother told me tales of my father's life,' said Dumas. 'I would go to bed at night, my head filled with acts of bravery and daring-do. I would dream dreams of my father, and me, and of Saint-George, together, back to back, fighting off a hundred, a thousand foes.'

Dumas suddenly lurched out of his chair, slammed his glass down on the mantelpiece. He strode to the desk, snatched up a long writing quill and brandished it over his head like a sword.

'Shouting above the roar of cannon and rattle of drums the battle-cry of the Free American Legion.' He tossed the quill back on the desk. ' No dammit! No! We've got to do this right.'

Dumas strode to a dark corner of the study where he scrabbled around noisily in an umbrella stand.

The Publisher slipped out of his armchair and walked towards Dumas the better to see what was going on. He stepped back quickly in alarm as Dumas grabbed at a hilt half-hidden among the walking stick handles and brought a yard of bright steel singing up into the air.

'My father's sword,' Dumas cried as he slashed the air with the heavy sabre.

The Publisher stepped back quite a bit more, hastily retiring to the safe refuge of his armchair.

'One for all and all for one!' shouted Dumas. 'Yes. That's the way of it. That's a story to be told.'

Oblivious to the presence of his guest, Dumas went to his desk, slammed the sword across it, sat, regained his quill, plunged it into the inkwell, shook off the excess ink and began to write rapidly.

To the frantic scratch of quill on paper, the Publisher slid out of his armchair and crept out the room, carefully drawing the doors closed behind him.

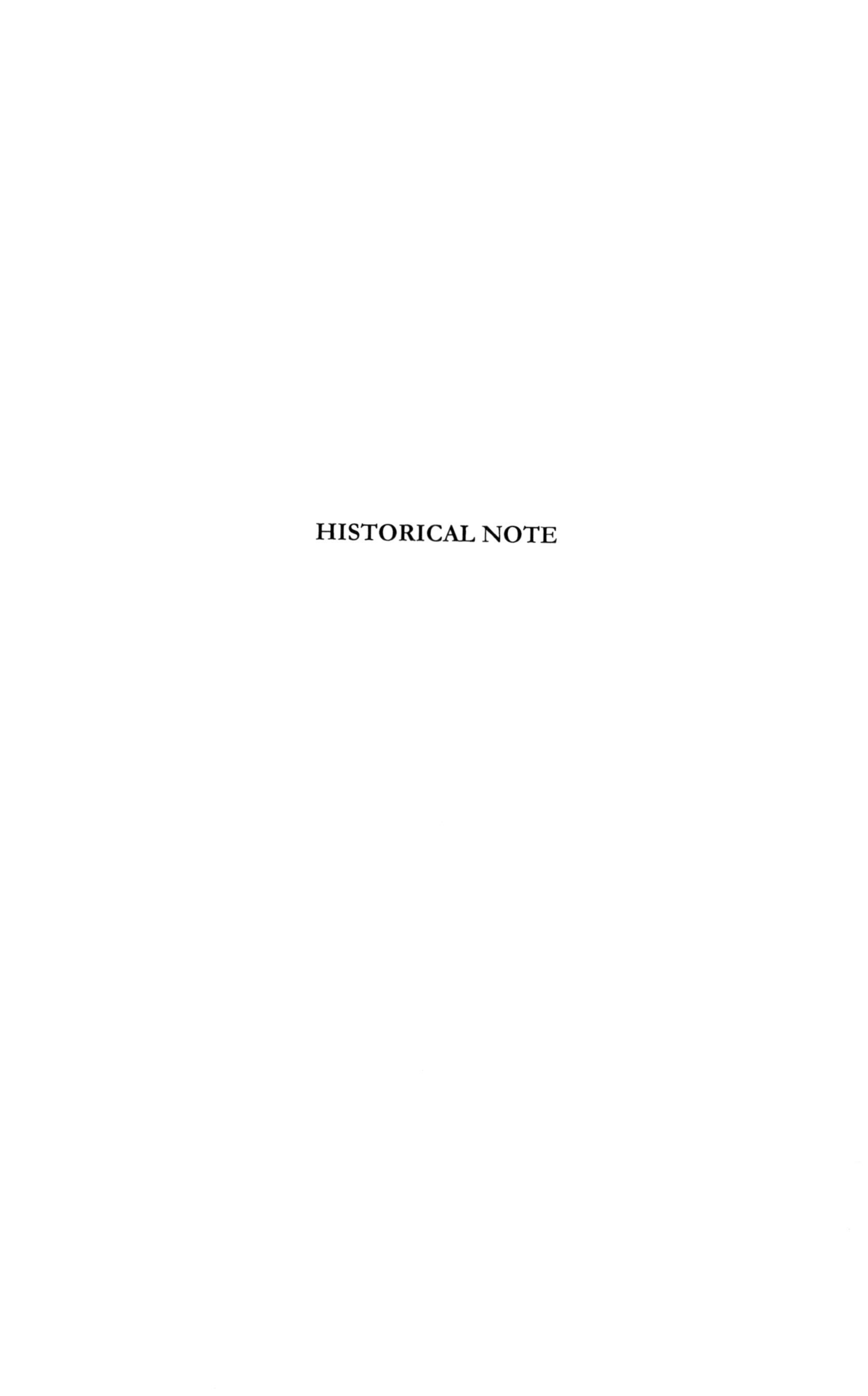

HISTORICAL NOTE

General Alexandre Dumas

Alexandre Dumas was descended from a noble family: his father, the Marquis Antoine-Alexandre Davy de la Pailleterie, Chevalier de Saint-Louis, was a direct descendant of Norman royalty, and a one-time colonel and Commissaire-General of artillery in the French Army. Antoine-Alexandre left France in the 1760s for the West Indies where he bought a large plantation outside Jérémie on the eastern edge of Santo Domingo (now Haiti).

He married Marie-Louis-Céssette Dumas, a Black freed slave who had the education and energy to take charge of all the details of the Marquis' properties.. Such marriages were unusual in the French colony but not unknown. Their fourth child, born on March 27, 1762, was Thomas-Alexandre. Alexandre was given the Marquis' family name and was raised in the West Indies until 1780, eight years after the death of his mother.

The Marquis finding it difficult to continue without Marie-Louis-Céssette, and possibly also hoping to return to the glittering social life he had enjoyed at Versailles in his youth, rid himself of his West Indian properties and returned to the ancestral chateau in Normandy, taking eighteen year old Alexandre with him. However it was Alexandre, tall and powerfully built, with strikingly handsome features, who threw himself into the Parisian social whirl. His constant companions were the sons of other aristocrats like La Fayette, Dillon, and Lauzun. He was first among the pupils of La Boissiére, the most noted fencing master of his time [the same man who twenty-five years earlier had instructed Saint-George].

When the Marquis remarried suddenly in 1786 and became reluctant to continue to fund Alexandre's hectic social life, a coolness developed between father and son. Alexandre disliked his stepmother and decided 'to enter the service' as a private, in the first regiment that would take him. His father was outraged, 'I do not mean that you shall drag my name through the lowest ranks of the army', so Alexandre enlisted using his mother's maiden name. Following the French Revolution, the Marquis lost his estates, but Alexandre so distinguished himself in the revolutionary army that in only twenty months he had risen through the ranks to become a general.

Alexandre was a man of commanding presence, great courage and colossal physical strength. His son says of him in his memoirs. 'During exhibitions of strength with which the soldiers amused themselves... (he) would sit on his horse under a beam... (and) raise the horse, gripped between his thighs, from off the ground. He could lift four army muskets by putting a finger in each barrel, crush a helmet with his hands, lift a massive gate off its hinges...'

On one occasion, having seen a soldier commit some breach of discipline, Dumas rode up to him, grasped him by the collar, and without even bothering to put the man across his saddlebow galloped off with him to the nearest police post. Once, in Austria, when some infantrymen were unable to scale a palisade, the general simply picked them up and threw them over it one by one, thus putting the terrified Austrians to rout. He was a veritable one-man army, and unquestionably the model for Porthos in The Three Musketeers.

His single-handed defence of a bridge in the Tyrolese campaign - when he was wounded in the arm and leg, had a bullet shatter his steel helmet, his cloak riddled by seven more shots, and his horse killed under him – so delighted Napoleon they became fast friends, making a pact they would be godfathers to each other's sons.

Dumas accompanied Napoleon in the expedition to Egypt. The cavalry was divided into four brigades (commanded by Leclerc, Murat, Mireur and Davout), under overall command of Dumas. When the French reached Egypt in July 1798, Dumas went ashore without waiting for his cavalry, borrowed a musket, and set off into the interior with the advance guard. He took part in the battle of the Pyramids. When the insurrection of Cairo took place, according to some it was Dumas who led the counterattack at the head of the French that restored French control.

In 1799, Alexandre said openly what the rest of the general staff only whispered - that the campaign was foolish and its direction incompetent. Furious when informed, Napoleon accused Alexandre of sedition. 'Your five feet ten inches,' Napoleon threatened Alexandre towering over him, 'could not save you from being shot by a firing squad now if I ordered it!' Alexandre resigned, never again to serve in the French army.

On the way home to France, storms forced his ship into Taranto and into the prison of Ferdinand, King of Naples and the Two Sicilies, then at war with France. In a neighbouring cell, the geologist Dolomieu, another prisoner of war, applied himself, using soot, a stick and the margins of Bibles, to the composition of The Philosophy of Mineralogy – circumstances re-enacted by Edmond Dantès and the abbé Faria in The Count of Monte Cristo. Alexandre was kept starved and incommunicado for two years. Extended attempts were made to poison him with arsenic, and by the time of his release, he was partially paralysed, almost blind in one eye, deaf in one ear, his exceptional physique broken. General Alexandre Dumas died in 1806.

However, what goes around, comes around. If Napoleon had his finest ever cavalry general, Alexandre Dumas, still with him at the battle of Waterloo, instead of the inept Marshal Ney, he might have defeated Wellington, and never been exiled to Saint Helena, and never died of arsenic poisoning himself.

Alexandre Dumas, the world famous author

Dumas was only four when his father died and left his mother, Marie-Louise Elizabeth Labouret, in near poverty. His mother's stories of his father's legendary deeds fed Dumas' appetite for adventure and heroes. Though poor, they still had Alexandre's distinguished reputation and aristocratic family connections. After the restoration of the Bourbon Dynasty to the French throne, twenty-year-old Dumas moved to

Paris where he obtained employment at the Palais Royal in the office of the powerful duc d'Orléans.

Dumas's life sometimes seemed as action-packed as his six-hundred novels; he participated in three revolutions, courted countless women and duelled when his honour was insulted. The lavish Chateau de Monte Cristo that he built outside Paris, always open to starving artists, the families of his mistresses, and even strangers, has been restored and opened to the public.

Buried in the place where he was born, Dumas remained in the cemetery at Villers-Cotterêts until November 30, 2002. Tthe French President, Jacques Chirac, had his body exhumed and in a televised ceremony, his new coffin, draped in a blue-velvet cloth and flanked by four men costumed as the Musketeers: Athos, Porthos, Aramis and D'Artagnan, was transported in a solemn procession to the Panthéon of Paris, the great mausoleum where French luminaries are interred.

In his speech, President Chirac said: 'With you, we were D'Artagnan, Monte Cristo or Balsamo, riding along the roads of France, touring battlefields, visiting palaces and castles—with you, we dream.' In an interview following the ceremony, President Chirac acknowledged the racism that had existed, saying that a wrong had now been righted with Dumas enshrined alongside fellow authors Victor Hugo and Voltaire. (The Enlightenment philosopher Voltaire argued that Africans and their descendants were genetically inferior to White Europeans – one in the eye for him then).

The honour recognized that although France has produced many great writers, none have been as widely read as Alexandre Dumas. His stories have been translated into almost a hundred languages, and have inspired more than 200 motion pictures.

Chevalier de Saint-George

In 1740, Georges de Bologne de Saint-George owned a plantation on the French West Indies colony of Guadeloupe. His son Joseph (the future Chevalier de Saint-George) was born in 1745 to Nanon, a Senegalese slave.

They came to France in 1755 where Georges became Gentleman of the King's Chamber to Louis XV. Joseph joined an elite boarding school for the sons of the aristocracy run by the fencing master, La Boessiére, to learn mathematics, history, foreign languages, music, drawing, dance, and fencing. Joseph trained with La Boessiére's son, another fencing master, who later wrote that Saint-George was the most extraordinary man of arms ever seen. When Saint-George was 19 his father offered him a fine English horse and a fashionable 2-wheel cart if he could defeat Picard, a skilled fencing master at Rouen. Saint-George won the match and was soon riding in style on the streets of Paris.

By the time he left the academy he was a famous fencer (he invented the fencing mask in association with La Boessiére) universally known as Le Chevalier de Saint-George.

He excelled at everything; trained by swimming across the Seine with only one arm; was an expert skater; rarely missed with the pistol; was one of the best runners in Europe; was a master horseman, and for a time, an elite musketeer.

In addition to his athletic skills, Saint-George was also an excellent musician, a virtuoso of harpsichord and violin, and one of the earliest French composers of string quartets, symphony concertantes, and quartet concertantes. He conducted the Concert des Amateurs, reckoned the best orchestra for symphonies in Paris and perhaps in Europe; performed music with Queen Marie-Antoinette at Versailles; commissioned Haydn to write the Paris symphonies for his new orchestra, the Concert Spirituel; and influenced Mozart - the music for Les Petits Riens copies a theme of his.

Saint-George's music is still performed today and is readily available from Amazon and elsewhere.

Free American Legion

In September 1, 1791 a delegation of men of colour, led by Julien Raimond of Saint-Domingue, asked revolutionary France's National Assembly to allow them to fight in defence of the Revolution and its egalitarian ideals. The next day, the Assembly approved a corps of Black and Mixed-Race volunteers, composed of 800 infantry and 200 cavalry personnel - the légion franche de cavalerie des Américains. Saint-George was appointed to be its Colonel and his friend and protégé Alexandre Dumas, its Lieutenant-Colonel.

When the Austrian army invaded Northern France, the Free American Legion was among the first in combat and repulsed the Austrians. Later the authorities began removing men of colour from the Legion and eventually renamed it the 13e Régiment de chasseurs.

Queen Marie-Antoinette

Marie-Antoinette went to watch Saint-George's one-armed swimming exploits across the icy river Seine. She was tutored by Saint-George in the violin and sponsored his nomination for Director of the Paris Opera. The Queen's painter, Vigée Lebrun, made one of the most charismatic portraits of Saint-George. Historians have found mention of Saint-George in the Queen's diary as 'my favourite American'.

Printed in the United Kingdom
by Lightning Source UK Ltd.
128652UK00001BB/257/A

9 781847 990297